UNMASKED

Unmasked: A Benevolence & Blood Spin-Off Novel by Lauren M. Leasure

Published by Kindle Direct Publishing

Copyright © 2022 Lauren M. Leasure

Editing by ReJoyce Literary Editing Co.
rejoyceliteraryediting.com

Cover by Ivy at Beautiful Book Covers

Paperback ISBN: 979-8-9872349-4-5

THE BENEVOLENCE & BLOOD SERIES

UNMASKED

LAUREN M. LEASURE

To all those who told me Miles was their "baby" — this one's for you

Stay in Touch

www.instagram.com/laurenmleasure
www.facebook.com/laurenmleasure

Receive special offers, giveaways, discounts, bonus content, and updates by signing up for my newsletter at www.laurenmleasure.com

Content Warning
This book includes content that may be sensitive for some readers, including

- Violence and death
- Blood and gore
- Loss of family members
- Explicit sexual content
- Mental health and suicide
- Sexual violence
- Drugs and addiction
- Profanity and potentially offensive language

ROUGHWATER ISLAND

SILENT BAY

CABILLIA

PORT OF
XOMMA

PORT OF
CABILLIA

AERA

XOMMA

THE IRON MTS

TAITHA

SOUTH RIDGE

DRY GULCH

LAKE
DEADKEEP

FROSTHOLD MTS

DEEPWATER
LAKES

THE PLAINS

MAPLENOOK

CARCALUN

SAUVEIL

REDW

ONYX PASS

ONYX MAN MTS

LIA

BLINDBARROW

WIDORAS

ESERENE

MILLMOUTH

ANICOLE

THE CONTINENT OF
ASTRAN

EDDENA

NESAN

ARAQINA

WIDOW'S SEA

TADRANA

KRURIA

OVEDEL

GALYRA

THE CONTINENT OF
LOSINA

The Benevolent Saints

Katia, Keeper of the Benevolent Saints
Tolar, Saint of Wealth
Onera, Saint of Miracles
Aanh, Saint of the Home
Soren, Saint of Heaven

The Blood Saints

Rhedros, Keeper of the Blood Saints
Faldyr, Saint of War
Liara, Saint of Hell
Idros, Saint of Storms
Noros, Saint of Pain
Cyen, Saint of Death

Pronunciation Guide

Names

Miles – MY-uls
Kauvras – KOVE-ris
Cielle Andyr – see-ELL ann-DEER
Nieve – NEEV
Cenric – SEN-rick
Isalyne – EE-sa-leen
Bowen – BOH-in
Camus Vorkalth – KAY-mis VOOR-kolth
Olion Summercut – OH-lee-awn SUH-mer-cut
Domicilium – dom-eh-SILL-ee-um

Places

Taitha – TAY-tha
Cabillia – cuh-BILL-ee-uh
Eserene – ES-er-een
Aera – AYR-uh
Widoras – wid-DOR-is
Nesan – nuh-SAN
Eddena – eh-DEEN-uh
Astran – AST-ran

Disclaimer

Unmasked takes place five years before the arrival of the Daughter of Katia. This story is best read after *The Bones of Benevolence* but before *The War of Wings*. This is not a necessary read in the series, though it does give important background information regarding multiple characters.

Please be advised this story may contains spoilers for *The Sin of Saints* and *The Bones of Benevolence*.

Happy reading!

Prologue

"*Fuck.*" Johan's hands shook as he tore them through his silver-streaked, chestnut hair, the strands scraggly and rain-soaked. The fisherman was no stranger to death on the seas, but even still, trembling breaths followed each frantic word. "What d' we do?"

"We stay calm," the man answered.

"*How?* How could 'e survive that? And why're the waves so big?" The panic was like another person in the boat, adding a weight heavy enough to sink it into the depths completely. The cliffs hung overhead, dark and looming as the tiny craft bobbed in the waves of the hidden inlet.

Johan's face was beet red as he stared at the boy. His small form was facedown and limp, neck oozing blood that collected with the rainwater at the bottom of the small wooden rowboat. There was no question a scar would remain — if the wound that mangled his throat managed to heal at all. An arrow protruded from his back, which still rose and fell with steady breaths.

"Look at me," the other man urged. "*Johan,* look at me." Johan obeyed, wild eyes landing on his counterpart in a crime neither of them had wanted to commit. "As soon as the waves die down, we're going to row back to shore."

Lightning ripped the sky apart, the thunder that followed so loud the men felt their bones quiver. "In all my years fishin' these waters, I've ne'er seen a storm the likes o' this one." Johan swiped the rain from his eyes, taking a shaky breath as he looked to the rolling clouds above. "Idros is angry. There's no tellin' when this'll die down."

"It's going to, and soon. When it does, we're going to row back to shore, okay? Your sailboat is still at the docks, yes?"

Johan nodded, brows furrowed as he listened. "Yes."

"I want you to wrap the boy in one of your spare sails and hide him on the deck of your sailboat."

Reality closed in and Johan began to grow dizzy as his breaths somehow became even more rapid, even more shallow.

"I need to get back to Castemont to tell him his plan was a success and that I'll bury the boy in the Backwoods. The boy's brother is up there on the cliff right now, but he's going to lose consciousness soon."

Johan's eyes narrowed momentarily. "How d' you know?"

The man ignored Johan's question, instead pressing forward with his instructions. "When he wakes up, odds are he'll come running to look for a boat so he can go out and search. He'll find Castemont walking in the street, and Castemont will send him to you. And you'll be..."

"At the dock," Johan answered at the man's silent urging. "With my sailboat."

"Yes. Now I'm going to take your sailboat—"

"But—"

"I know. The boy will be wrapped in the canvas on the deck. With the impact of the fall, he's going to be out for a while. I'm going to take his brother out on your sailboat to look for him. We won't find him, of course." The man stared up at the cliffs before looking back at Johan, his eyes squinting against the rain that pelted their skin. "I need you to listen very carefully." Johan nodded and swallowed hard. "When we come back with your sailboat, you're going to leave Eserene. I don't care where you go, but make sure it's far."

"I don't have—"

"I left a pouch of coins on your sailboat. That's more than enough to finance the trip and then some."

"B-but–" Johan's head shook wildly. "I cannae just *leave* Eserene. What about my life here?"

"If Castemont finds out we didn't kill the boy, you will no longer have a life here. You'll no longer have a life at all. You'd best find a place far from here, beyond this horizon and maybe the next. Do you understand?"

Johan opened his mouth to speak but quickly closed it and nodded. All at once, the rain began to lighten and the boat's movements grew less violent as the waves that tossed them started to calm. Johan's eyes narrowed with confusion at the sudden change in weather, his head turning wildly as he surveyed the sky and surf before looking back to the man in front of him.

"You're going to take the boy to an orphanage," the man continued. "Try to find one where the caregivers are kind. You tell the boy there was a fire and his parents didn't make it out alive. If he asks, tell him he hit his head or a beam fell on him and that's why he has no memory. You were a friend of his parents but you can't take care of him because your job as a fisherman takes you away from home too often."

"What if 'e asks questions?"

The man's eyes moved from Johan to the boy, still unconscious at the bottom of the boat. "He won't."

Johan's hands were shaking now, the look on his face evident of the distress that whirled within him. "What's his name?"

The man's lips thinned, as if he were holding back the answer. "Better if you don't know. Give him a new one." He looked to the sky again, surveying the lightening sky. "Let's move."

"I dinnae feel good about this," Johan murmured.

"I don't either, and I'm so sorry I involved you in this, but I need you to trust me. Can you *please* trust me?"

Johan swallowed hard as the rain turned to a fine mist then dissipated altogether. "I trust you, Tyrak."

◆ ◆ ◆

The boy was still unconscious as Johan sailed out of Pellucid Harbor. The fisherman had arranged a makeshift pallet out of torn canvas and fishing nets in the cabin of his sailboat. He'd quickly lost track of how many times he'd peered inside to make sure the boy's chest still moved. He'd packed cloth to the arrow wound on his back and wrapped his neck as well. Both wounds still bled enough to darken the makeshift bandages, though the flow seemed to be slowing.

"I'm going to take ye somewhere safe," Johan murmured to the sleeping boy, "somewhere miles and miles from here." He blinked, staring hard at the boy's sleeping form. "Miles." Johan nodded to himself. "Good name." Johan shuffled across the deck as the wind picked up and Eserene grew smaller behind them. "Somewhere Castemont will nae find you, Miles." He gnawed at a fingernail, eyes wide and brows turned up. "You're goin' to live a long life, yes. You will nae rest in a watery grave because of someone playin' Saint. You'll grow old and be laid to rest in the earth the way the Saints intended." Johan looked out at the setting sun over the sea, his mind grappling with the task ahead. "Miles Landgrave."

Three Years Later

"Your thumb always stays tucked in when you throw a punch."

I scratched my head, because what Bowen was saying really didn't seem right. We'd fought many times — usually to practice, but sometimes for real. I'd never tucked my thumb in once. But I rarely won against him when it came to fistfighting, so maybe I should listen to him. "Are you sure I won't break my thumb?"

"I'm sure. I wouldn't steer you wrong. Ready?"

I bit the inside of my cheek as I stared down at my hands, folding my fingers over my thumbs and clenching them into fists. "Ready."

Bowen jutted his arms out to hold the pillow in front of his chest. Determination was etched into his every feature. "Go."

I cocked my fist back, putting as much speed behind it as I possibly could and winging it forward. It collided with the exact point Bowen had been holding the pillow, his hands protected as something in mine popped. I tried to keep quiet but I couldn't help but cry out in pain as I hit the ground and cradled my hand to my chest.

Bowen looked down on me, his face unamused. "Looks like you broke your thumb."

I really didn't want to cry. Not in front of Bowen, especially. Hot tears were in my eyes, though.

He scoffed, bending down to get a look at my face as I tried to hide it. "Are you crying?"

"No," I choked out.

"Poor little Landgrave, crying 'cause he hurt his thumb."

Anger heated the back of my neck as my lips pursed. A string of taunts left Bowen's mouth.

"Boys!" Miss Ria barked through the mossy courtyard behind the orphanage. "The dinner bell rang five minutes ago. Get inside now! What–" I didn't need to look up to know her eyes had landed on me. "Miles, what happened?"

If I spoke, I was going to cry. Silence was my best option right now.

"He hit me, Miss Ria," Bowen answered. I looked up to see him wringing his hands together innocently. "And now his thumb is hurt."

Miss Ria raised a bushy eyebrow at me, her wrinkled face twisted in disappointment. "Is this true, Miles?"

It was either tell the truth and risk crying in front of Bowen, or stay silent. My thumb throbbed so hard I could feel it in my wrist and my vision still swam. *Don't cry in front of Bowen.*

"It's high time you stop acting like feral boys and begin acting like men. You're both fifteen years old." I saw Miss Ria's anger slip for just a moment. She wasn't really sure if I was actually fifteen. No one was. It was just a guess, and my age ticked up one on the eve of each new year. But I didn't have time to dwell on it now. Embarrassment flooded me, and all I wanted to do was run as far from Bowen as possible. "Now get inside," Miss Ria continued. "I don't want to hear one complaint from you, Miles. You hit him, you deal with the consequences."

With that, Miss Ria disappeared through the doorway. I swallowed hard and pushed myself to my feet, avoiding any movement that could hurt my thumb. It had begun to swell, the base of it puffy where it connected to my palm.

I looked up at Bowen, his form a few inches taller than me. "Why did you tell me I wouldn't break my thumb when you knew I would, Bowen?"

Bowen threw his arm over my shoulder, the movement sending a shockwave of pain up my arm and back down again. His hand came up to ruffle my hair as he sneered. "Just trying to toughen you up for the Cabillian military."

"My thumb is broken. You lied to me."

"That's what brothers do."

I stayed silent, but wondered to myself if that's what *real* brothers did, or if it was just Bowen.

FIVE YEARS BEFORE THE ARRIVAL OF
THE DAUGHTER OF KATIA

Chapter 1

Miles

"Fuck me!" I almost rolled my eyes at her words.

It was fun, I guess. A stress reliever if anything. But really, it was something I did because there were some days when loneliness closed in on me so tightly I had to remind myself to breathe. I'd never *really* enjoyed it. I'd pin her hands down, she'd squeal and moan, roll her eyes back in a feigned attempt at pleasure, and then say something like, "Wow, that was great."

Then I'd pay her.

I wasn't one to choose favorites, but I could choose a least favorite. This morning, the only woman available was Assandra, who'd filled that role since the first evening I spent with her. She was devastatingly beautiful in the way that would make a man hand over everything he had, then thank her for taking it. But the few instances I'd spent time with her, I could tell her head was somewhere far away. The fact she always seemed to be withdrawn never sat right with me.

Today, Assandra seemed...animated. Not somewhere far away. She was *here*. But it was painfully obvious her own enjoyment was not at the front of her mind. I gripped her hips as she rode me, her head thrown back in mock ecstasy as she palmed a breast in one hand. "Yes!" she cried out. There was absolutely no way that what I was doing — or wasn't doing — was worthy of this reaction.

Discomfort tightened my chest and I couldn't keep my face from twisting. "You don't have to pretend, you know."

She froze, her head dropping forward to look down at me. I was still seated completely inside her as she pinned me with wide hazel eyes. Deep red hair cascaded perfectly over her shoulder, not a single knot in the length that hung to her waist.

Part of the training I'd received so far was learning how to read my opponent in battle. Assandra wasn't my opponent, so to speak, but for the life of me, I couldn't decipher the look on her face. Was she angry? Confused? Relieved?

"*What?*" she spat, narrowing her eyes.

Okay, angry. I shifted uncomfortably beneath her, trying to find words that wouldn't further stoke her anger. Her very *rightful* anger. I was an idiot for saying anything at all. "I'm just saying," I started gently, "you don't have to pretend you're enjoying this."

She didn't move, looking over my face as if it were a page from a book and she didn't know how to read. Suddenly, her typical expression returned — resigned indifference. All traces of her forged excitement were gone.

When she finally spoke, her voice was flat, not even a hint of emotion behind it. "I am enjoying this."

"Really?" I asked incredulously. She pushed off of me, finding her feet on the floor, brows furrowed. "You're really going to tell me you were enjoying that?"

Her body was completely bare, and Saints, she really was stunning. With graceful, feather-soft hands on her perfectly curved hips, her eyes roved down my body and stopped halfway. "You're going to tell me you weren't?" Her lower jaw jutted to one side, one thin, perfectly shaped brow raising in amusement. "I see a few rock-hard inches telling me you *were* enjoying it."

A few? Damn. "It's more than a few," I said quickly as I sat up and threw my legs over the side of the bed, reaching for my leathers. "And of course I'm turned on. I'm fucking a beautiful woman."

She burst into laughter, a lilting chime of a sound. I tried not to read too far into the timing of that laughter as I slid my pants up my legs and fastened the ties. She still stood naked as the day she was born, watching me as she regained her composure. I'd never seen her so full of life.

"What's so funny?" I finally managed to ask as her laughter died down.

A thumb raised to one eye to wipe away an errant tear. "Seems all you soldiers are using the same measuring stick, and I'm beginning to question its reliability." She plucked a pale pink robe from a hook near the door and pulled it over her shoulders, a contented sigh leaving her lips. "Thanks for the laugh."

I smirked. "Would you like to get paid or not?"

She cocked her head and ran her tongue across her teeth antagonistically. "Do you think Hjalmar is going to let you leave without paying?"

She was right, and we both knew it. The brothel's guard didn't take bullshit from anyone. Big motherfucker. His appearance alone was enough to make the most decorated, most battleworn soldier pay double.

"Only idiots fuck with Hjalmar. I'm not that stupid," I remarked, smoothing my hands down my leathers and double checking that my sword was secure at my hip. I dug through my pocket and dropped a few silver pieces on her vanity. She pushed the coins around, counting them one by one to make sure everything was there.

"Yet you're stupid enough to tell a whore not to do her job."

I shifted my weight on my feet. That word. *Whore.* "Don't call yourself that."

She scoffed. "Why not? That's what I am."

"It's just so..."

"What? Derogatory?" she cut in. I nodded, and she flicked her hair over her shoulder. "It's only derogatory if I give its speaker the power to make it so. I've never once done that, and I don't intend to start. Yes, I am a whore. This is a whorehouse. The power is mine." She was completely unbothered as she picked at a fingernail before raising a brow. "Why are you looking at me like that?"

I straightened and forced my face to take on a neutral expression, unaware I'd been looking at her in any particular way. "Our visits are usually a bit more...formal." I tried to say it as politely as possible. "You've never spoken to me this much."

"Apologies," she mumbled, turning back to the vanity.

"Apologies? For what?"

Assandra swallowed hard, meeting my eyes in the mirror. Her gaze stayed trained on mine for a long moment, as if she were assessing me. I could sense an air of apprehension as she rolled her bottom lip between her teeth. "My bed has been empty more often than not lately. Turns out men want their whores to be *personable*. So I'm trying that out for a bit."

I blinked. I hadn't been expecting that. "So you put on a big show to try to seem personable?"

"Well surely I can't just be myself," she answered as if I should've known that already. "I have a feeling most of my customers would have a problem with that. So, I've been trying to play the part a bit more."

I measured my words, afraid she was going to take them the wrong way. "Men who have to pay to fuck shouldn't have opinions about who they're fucking."

She let out another laugh, her shoulders relaxing slightly. "Well, Miles," she started, running a brush through hair that didn't seem to need it, "sometimes your survival depends on the opinions of others. I only have myself. No family. I do what I have to do."

The words hit me harder than I'd been expecting. I didn't have it in me to tell her I understood exactly what she was saying. I understood a little too well, in fact.

Though the light of the room was just as dim as when I arrived, I felt like I was seeing Assandra differently all the sudden. "I like you, Assandra."

She let out a deep breath and I saw some invisible barrier fall away from her face. "It's not Assandra," she said, jaw squared. "It's Isalyne. Isa."

"I knew it," I quipped. She cocked a brow. "A...*whore* named Assandra? Too convenient."

"You got me." She flashed a coy smile, one that I could tell was not an attempt at being personable. That was her real smile, and it was breathtaking. "And you were right, I wasn't enjoying it. Not because your few inches weren't pleasant enough."

"I'm pretty sure it's eight."

"Mhm," she cut in with a wicked smile. "I, like you, prefer the company of women."

Shock made my face slacken. "Oh? You prefer women yet you *service* men?"

Isa shrugged, her face the picture of indifference. "Like I said. Survival. It's a job. I don't have to like it. I just have to do it."

Shuffling boots sounded from the hall, hardly muffled by the thin wooden door. "Let's *go*, Landgrave!"

"Saints, Leo," I heard a woman laugh, "he's not going to finish if he hears your voice."

A heavy fist pounded against the door. "If we're late for training and I miss Domicilium because of you, I'm going to beat your ass."

"*Let him finish*," the woman's voice responded seductively. "I can think of something we can do to pass the time."

Isa dipped her finger into a small pot of what looked to be salve. Her eyes flicked to the door as she ran it over her lips. "Sounds like your friend's waiting for you."

"Yeah, yeah." I checked the mirror one last time to make sure my appearance was up to standards.

"Any plans for the evening?" she asked absentmindedly.

I'd almost forgotten today was Domicilium. Either that, or I'd purposely pushed it from my mind. I was going to celebrate the same way I did every year. With Bowen. The closest thing I had to family. We'd buy a cut of meat from the butcher and get piss drunk. We'd done the same thing on this day every year since we were fifteen, hiding from the childminders at the orphanage as they tried to force us into a stuffy dinner with a table full of snotty children.

If I thought about the whole thing hard enough, it could really get depressing, so I checked to make sure my mental walls were in place to protect myself. In my brain, facts were like bricks, and I could use them to build walls. The cold reality of what they meant couldn't hurt me if I used them to protect myself. I supposed it was a similar conclusion to the one Isa came to about her profession. I wouldn't give these facts the power to hurt me.

Fact: Domicilium was a day to honor Aanh, Saint of the Home, and though I couldn't participate in truth, I clung to my honor in place of a home. Fact: I had no home, but that meant the only space I was responsible for keeping clean was my bunk in the barracks. Fact: I had no family, but I had Bowen, and that was enough.

"We'll see," I answered simply, betraying none of the pitiful truth I was thinking about. Her face didn't convey that she was expecting me to ask after her plans, but I was genuinely interested since she had no family, either. "And you?"

She turned to me in her chair, her satin robe hanging open in a very distracting way. "I'll be here. Charging double for anyone who feels like celebrating in a whorehouse." The way she said it was emotionless, but I could tell there was a kind of sadness behind her comment that few could ever comprehend. I glanced around the room, to the closet door that was halfway open and bursting with clothing, to the dozen pairs of shoes stacked neatly on a shelf next to the vanity.

Isa lived here.

I nodded, offering as much of a smile as I could manage. "Well, I hope you enjoy your evening, Isa."

A harsh finger shot up in my direction and pinned me in place. "When you leave this room, it's Assandra."

My chin dipped in understanding. "I hope you enjoy your evening, Assandra."

She watched me as I walked for the door. "Come again," she called. I turned back to see a teasing smile on her lips. "Maybe you actually will next time."

Damn. "Very funny."

Bowen was practically steaming with anger when I slipped out of Isa's room, a woman hanging from his arm. "Took you long enough," he grumbled. He peeled the woman's hand from his bicep like he was disgusted by her touch. She didn't seem to mind, though, and she planted a kiss on his cheek before strutting down the hallway and around the corner. "Why do you always have to say goodbye to your whores?"

I side-eyed him as we started for the stairs. "Saying goodbye is a common courtesy."

"They're *whores.*" His mouth curved around the word in a way that made my shoulders tense. "They don't need common courtesy, much less do they deserve it."

It took a conscious effort to hide the disdain I had for his statement. Any sign of weakness would set him on me like a hawk to a mouse. "Who pissed in your porridge this morning?"

"Shut the fuck up, Landgrave," he spat. "Now let's fucking move. I won't be scrubbing floors tonight because of you."

I rolled my eyes. Always so pleasant, Bowen.

The annoyance coming from him was palpable as we descended the stairs and started for the front door. "We're paid up," Bowen grumbled to Hjalmar as he pushed through the doorway, but the guard stepped in front of him. Bowen was tall, but Hjalmar's massive frame dwarfed him completely. Either Bowen didn't see it or...he just didn't care. "Is there a problem, friend?" he asked antagonistically, and tension rose in my body once again.

Hjalmar was silent, ruddy brown eyes scanning over our faces. I'd never seen the man smile. The lines on either side of his mouth told me that frown was as good as permanent.

"They're good to go." I spun to see Isa at the top of the stairs, nodding to the guard. Hjalmar let out a low growl as Bowen pushed past him.

The dusty cobblestone street was crowded with the residents of Taitha as they prepared for the feast of Domicilium. We joined the buzzing mass of people as we headed for the training yard. I craned my neck to be sure we were far enough away from the Blushing Dove that the guard wouldn't hear men when I spoke. "You've got some balls talking to Hjalmar like that, Bowen."

"Hjalmar?" Bowen's face was marked with feigned confusion. He knew exactly who I was talking about.

"The guard. You know, the one who could stomp your teeth in with his little toe."

Leo Bowen moved through life like it owed him something, playing whatever part he needed to get what he wanted. It had bothered me to no end since we were kids, the way he seemed to think the world would bend for him if he told it to. It didn't help his ego that he commanded attention everywhere he went, with sandy blond hair, steely blue eyes, and a smile even I found myself envious of.

But it was never enough to secure him a home, and just like me, he'd always been passed over in favor of the babies and younger children. He aged out of the orphanage three months before I did.

So I learned to live with Bowen and his ego, because the two of us had been the only ones close in age. We'd been brothers since we were twelve.

Bowen cracked his knuckles, a childhood habit of his that signaled he was doubting himself, and the ego trip was coming to compensate. "Motherfucker will let me pass without a second glance after today." He straightened slightly, stretching his neck and giving a smile to a pretty young woman as we passed her. "Might even feel the need to salute me since I'll be a commander."

"You really think you'll go from unranked soldier to commander?"

"Vorkalth did."

"Vorkalth's mother was the sister of King Divos," I retorted. "Of course he became commander the second he wanted to. He's just lucky he wasn't beheaded the second King Kauvras killed Divos and took the throne. And that's only because he fell to his knees and swore fealty."

"Doesn't matter. I'm still going to get promoted to commander today."

My eyes caught the clock tower that watched over the street. The minute hand was inching dangerously close to scrubbing floors. Bowen easily matched my pace as it quickened. My attendance record had been perfect throughout training, and I had no intention of sullying it now. Bowen's attendance record held one red tick mark due to an illness that mysteriously hit him the morning after I watched him chug an entire bottle of whiskey in a dirty pub then swing on a man twice his size.

"You'll have no chance of making commander if we're late," I remarked.

38

"You think *you're* going to get promoted, Landgrave?" he laughed, deflecting the doubt back to me.

I pursed my lips and shrugged as I jogged. "Maybe. Lieutenant Landgrave doesn't sound too bad, does it?"

"Commander Bowen sounds better."

We rounded the last corner, hustling through the gates of the training yard and between the barracks to our spots in formation. I tried not to think of who — *of what* — was on the other side of the walls. To our left was a standard barrack. A few hundred bunks all crowded into one dark, dingy building to house a number of soldiers. To our right was a building that had been converted from soldier accommodations for...Vacants.

I cringed, unable to keep my lips from pursing at the thought of the thousands of leechthorn-addled, bloodthirsty animals that had once been normal people in towns and villages across Astran. There were so many of them now that another building was being cleared of soldiers to make room. Our barrack had already been shifted and rearranged twice to squeeze in the displaced soldiers.

As I settled in place and stood at attention, I took a deep breath, ridding myself of the uncomfortable, strange twinge of guilt. I pulled as much air into my lungs as I could and let myself smile as I exhaled.

Today was the day I'd be promoted to lieutenant.

Chapter 2

Miles

"Attention!" Commander Camus Vorkalth shouted. Every man straightened. His voice was bellowing, but it somehow seemed too high for his body. Almost whiny. The octave made it hard to want to follow orders sometimes, especially when he yelled with so much force that spittle landed on my cheek.

Vorkalth walked leisurely to the front of formation, his face slackened with something like amusement. "As you're all aware, we're a year and a half into your three year training protocol, which means it's Selection Day. The best of you will be chosen for rank promotions."

I had to keep myself from wincing at the way his voice raked down my back. A year and a half into training and I'd never gotten used to it. I'd heard that voice more than my fair share, because he despised the orphan boys. Bowen and I were the only two from the orphanage on Merchant Street, but Taitha's other homes for orphans had produced maybe a dozen and a half more. And Vorkalth made his disdain for us clear from the very first day.

"You will become leaders within Cabillia's military," he continued. "With this comes better pay, better accommodations, and of course, the honor of receiving your mask a year and a half before your comrades." Vorkalth's face turned down into a twisted sneer, and I couldn't tell from this distance, but I felt like he was looking directly at me. "The rest of you worms will stay here at the bottom to train until you're worthy of the mask. Understood?"

The entire formation answered in unison. "Yes, Sir!"

We were fifteen when Bowen started talking about how excited he was to get his mask. He couldn't wait to don the face of an animal and help expand Kauvras' army of Vacants. But the idea of it always made me uncomfortable. Claustrophobic. We wore the masks to protect us from the leechthorn fumes, but sometimes I thought maybe they were to keep us from the truth of what we were doing.

I never let that thought dig its claws in too deep, though. I couldn't.

Bowen was two dozen rows ahead of me, but I could see his face in my mind as if he were staring straight into my eyes. It was the same expression he'd worn since we were kids, the same smug look that came around just before one of his argument-ending low blows, but toned down enough to pass as neutrality. I knew it was anything but.

A piece of parchment was handed to Vorkalth. My palms were immediately damp with sweat as I clenched and relaxed my fists. Part of me was confident I would be promoted; I consistently finished in the top five in every physical fitness trial, and when it came to handling a sword I was one of the best in my year. I didn't have many people I'd call *friends* — really just Bowen — but my comrades did respect me.

The other part of me, however, was sitting back in the orphanage, watching another couple walk past me without a second glance.

No. Facts. Bricks. I was strong. I was fast. I was respected.

"The following men have been chosen for promotion," Vorkalth announced. I took a steadying breath as he began his list. "Finnerty! Sherris! Hegan!" He worked his way down, calling out the names of men who were officially moving up in the ranks. Some deserved it. Some didn't. "Wulfram! Halseth!" His eyes moved dangerously close to the bottom of the parchment. *Come on.*

Vorkalth's face twisted in a sneer when he arrived at the final name. "And Bowen!"

My stomach bottomed out. Not because my name wasn't called, but because my name wasn't called and Bowen's was.

"You've all been promoted to lieutenant," he called. A small win, if anything, that Bowen hadn't made *commander.* I didn't want to delight in his disappointment, but it took the sting out a bit. "And since Selection Day coincides with Domicilium, our new lieutenants have been invited to dine with King Kauvras tonight. Please join me, gentlemen," Vorkalth shouted through the crowd. "The rest of you worms, ten laps *now!*"

Happy fucking Domicilium.

◆ ◆ ◆

Bowen was nowhere to be seen after training. Most likely, he'd been whisked away to be briefed on his new position and its responsibilities. He was probably sitting at the table with King Kauvras now, rubbing elbows with Cabillia's royalty while he ate a meal worth more than an entire year's pay.

One of the generals held a gathering for the soldiers without families, but I couldn't bring myself to attend. I had no interest in sitting at a table of vague acquaintances, making polite conversation with a group of men just as lonely and pathetic as I was.

Domicilium had a way of reminding people of what they lacked.

The barrack kitchen was empty, and I tried to appreciate the quiet that was so rare to find in such a space. Bowen was always the one to cook on Domicilium, but the butcher had given me a quick rundown as he wrapped a cut of meat in paper. I'd roasted rabbits and squirrels over campfires on training missions. Could this really be all that different?

The iron pan that I pulled from its hook on the kitchen wall was deceptively heavy. With my flint and steel, I lit the coals beneath the stove and waited for the pan to heat. This seemed right. Right?

"Onera, help me," I murmured, summoning the Saint of Miracles as I slapped the steak down in the pan. It hissed louder than I thought it would, smoke quickly rising from the meat. I flipped it after a minute, revealing charred black skin. I couldn't keep the grimace from my face, because even though I'd only had steak a handful of times in my life, this didn't look like any steak I'd ever seen before.

But it was steak. How bad could I possibly fuck it up?

I carefully speared it with a fork and shimmied it out of the pan onto a plate. The sound of ale filling a mug was a welcome reprieve to the silence as I tapped one of the barrels that sat in the corner of the kitchen. I let the foamy piss-water hit my lips and didn't stop until the mug was empty. Steam rose from the blackened flesh of the meat, and the quiet settled over me again.

Fact: I was alone. Painfully alone.

◆ ◆ ◆

"What if I have an actual customer tonight, Miles?"

Isa stood in the doorway of her bedroom, staring at me like I was a madman. "I'll pay double," I offered, "just like any other customer."

The decision I'd made was rash. Completely unplanned. Probably a bad idea. No, *definitely* a bad idea. But the solitude had become too much to bear tonight, and so I found myself at the Blushing Dove. The halls were quiet and still, a stark contrast to the moans and barefoot, half-dressed women that usually populated the upper levels of the brothel. Even Hjalmar was gone, the door left unguarded.

"I brought dinner." I lifted the plate I'd haphazardly wrapped in wax paper. "You'll be paid and fed."

Isa lifted a brow as she stared at the plate in my hand, skepticism in every feature. "It's Domicilium."

"And neither of us have family."

"Don't you have friends?"

I swallowed back my embarrassment, because no, I really didn't. "I have steak."

She let out a sigh and stepped out of the doorway begrudgingly, ushering me into her room. "I insulted your cock this morning, and you still want to fuck me?"

I jolted, blinking hard as I realized what she was saying. "Isa, I'm not here to fuck you. I just thought we could...spend the evening together. As friends."

She was staring at me as if I told her I could fly and had invited her to join me on the roof to watch me hurl myself over the edge. I lowered myself to sit on her bed and placed the wrapped plate in front of me.

Isa scoffed, staring down at me. "You want to spend the evening together?"

"Why not?"

She furrowed her brows, staring intently at me. "You're not here to fuck me?"

"Not only did you insult my cock," I started, "but I should also point out that you told me you don't even like them at all." I unwrapped the plate and pulled out the two forks and knives I'd tucked in my rucksack.

Her eyes fell on the steak and flew comically wide. "What did you do to the poor thing?"

"I...cooked it."

"*You* cooked it? Or a fucking driva cooked it?" She lifted the meat with her fork slightly, trying to peer at its underside. "This thing is torched."

I shrugged. "I put it on the pan."

"Was the pan on the sun?"

"It was on a stove."

"Was the stove on the sun?"

The steak didn't look that bad. Really, it didn't. But I couldn't help but wonder if this was the kind of banter that was being tossed back and forth in dining rooms tonight. A silly, misappropriated thought I suppressed. "It's just well done. Go ahead, try it."

She sucked her teeth for a moment before looking up to me again. "You try it." She nodded her head toward the plate. "Cut a piece."

"Worried I'd poison you?"

"I'm worried you won't be able to cut through it."

She was being dramatic. I held the steak in place with my fork as I began to cut through — or at least, I tried to cut through. The thing was a Saints damned stone.

Air puffed my cheeks. I sure as hell didn't want to admit defeat, but I didn't have to admit defeat when the evidence was sitting right there, clear as day and hard as a rock. "I may have slightly overcooked it."

Her head fell back suddenly, her body shaking with howling laughter. Apparently, this woman liked to laugh at me. "Come on," she finally said, her face still lit up by a smile as she rose. "We have some food in the kitchen. Some ale, too, if we're lucky."

Chapter 3
Miles

"What made you want to become a soldier?" Isa asked as she popped a cube of cheese into her mouth. The table was wobbly on the packed dirt floor of the brothel's kitchen, and the light from the hearth illuminated the grime on the windows. It wasn't a particularly pleasant room, but the ale was surprisingly good.

I sniffed, blinking at the question. No one had ever asked me that. Hell, I'd never even asked myself the question. "I grew up in the orphanage on Merchant Avenue. When boys age out of the orphanage, they become soldiers."

Her lips pursed. "I'm sorry."

"Sorry?" My tone was easy. She nodded slightly. "There's nothing to be sorry for."

"But is that what you wanted to be when you grew up?" she pressed. There was a softness in her voice I recognized as pity, and that made me wildly uncomfortable. I didn't want her pity. Didn't need it. I held no resentment toward my upbringing.

"I don't really know," I answered in a voice that conveyed no sadness. I took a long drink of ale and let out a contented sigh when I placed the mug back on the table. "There isn't much about my childhood that I remember."

"Tell me about it."

I cocked a brow, letting out a small laugh. "I know I paid double, but are you going to charge me extra to listen to me piss and moan about my childhood?"

"Oh, hush." She waved her hand in front of her face with a scoff. "Tell me."

I took a deep breath through my nose. "I, uh..." I shook my head. "There was a fire when I was twelve. My mother and father both died and one of their friends brought me to Merchant Street. A man. But I don't remember his name." I stared at the bubbles sitting on the surface of my ale. "The only home I ever knew was the orphanage."

She bit the inside of her cheek. There it was — that look of pity in her eyes, and I couldn't keep from squirming. "Do you miss them?"

My discomfort gave way to surprise. "The other children at the orphanage?"

"Your parents."

My mind went blank for a moment. My parents. Even as a child, I never once let myself wander down that darkened path in my brain. As far as I knew, it was overgrown and impossible to wade through, so there was no use trying. I had one single memory of who I assumed was my mother — a flash of long, black hair and the smell of bread baking. Someone else was there, too. Probably my father. That was the extent of the memory, though, and I'd never tried to push for more. I kept that to myself, almost like I'd lose the image if I spoke it aloud.

"I don't remember my parents," I answered simply. She didn't press, but I felt the need to continue for some reason. "It had taken me a while to get my bearings after the fire. There was nothing, and then there was the sound of horse hooves on dirt. I was in a horse-drawn cart." I could see that moment clearly in my head, though the time between then and the orphanage was blurry. "And there was a lot of pain."

Isa leaned forward, arms crossed on the table, face plastered with concern. "You were hurt, then? Burned?"

I pointed to the scar on my throat. "I got this in the fire one way or another. I think that's the reason my voice is a bit raspy. And there's a nice scar on my back, too. Some kind of puncture wound."

"But no burns?"

A question I'd thought of but never really spent much time considering. "Luckily."

"Do you have a way to find the man who brought you to the orphanage?"

The lack of information I had about my past really didn't bother me, so why did it seem to bother Isa? I checked in on my mental walls, adding a few bricks as I did. Fact: I had no memory of my parents, but it meant I had no one to mourn. Fact: I didn't remember anything about the man who brought me to the orphanage and that meant there was no rabbithole for me to go down, anxiously searching for answers.

I wasn't sure why Isa was asking me these questions, but I answered her anyway. "My last memory of the man was when he was speaking with the caregivers at the orphanage telling them about my wounds. And then, that was it, I was another child at the orphanage. I just knew, even at a young age, that the life I'd lived before the orphanage was gone. Any energy I put into trying to remember would be wasted. I have no memory before my twelfth year."

Her expression was unreadable. "And you have no idea what this is from?" She leaned forward, pointing to my throat. The scar was strange, yes. It wasn't a slice or cut. It wasn't a puncture, either. It was...almost both? And neither. A creased, knotted patch of skin that gave me no clues.

"It came from the fire," I responded. She blinked at my answer, her mouth hanging open. "Does it matter?"

"Of course it matters." She sat straight up. "That's an important part of who you are. See this?" She extended one leg and pointed to a small divot of a scar on her shin. "I was just a girl. Middle of the night, pitch black. Got up for a drink of water and walked into the frame of my bed. Cut my leg open and left a scar."

"And that scar is a part of who you are?"

"Yes. It's the reason I'm afraid of the dark."

"I just..." I shrugged again. Why did she care so much? "I never really thought much of it. I always knew I'd be a soldier. I sure as hell didn't need to look pretty while doing it."

Isa straightened in her chair, steepling her fingers and resting her wrists at the edge of the table. "Before my mother passed, she always told my siblings and me that your true identity lies in your childhood-self, specifically in the first ten years of your life. The things you really want, the things you hold important... All of it can be traced back to your first ten years."

I didn't really want to broach the subject, but I felt the pull to do so. "Your family?"

She flexed her fingers, nodding. "Red delirium took them all." I winced, because the red delirium was not a fate I'd wish on my worst enemy. Drowning in one's own blood while suffering from delusions... No, thank you. "My father was never around. But my mother, my two sisters, and four brothers... It took them quickly. The only mercy." Isa and I were both alone, but the sigh she let out was filled with a sorrow I'd never understand, because she actually remembered her family. She had people to grieve, a past life to mourn. "I still wonder why it spared me. I was fifteen. Been here at the Blushing Dove since then."

"I'm sorry, Isa."

She gave a weak smile and hummed a quiet thanks.

Desperate to change the subject, I blurted the first thing I could think of. "What did you want to be when you were ten?"

The smile that graced her face now was genuine, and I could tell she welcomed the distraction. "I've always liked animals. Something about them." Isa sat back, her tone unbothered and her energy along with it. "Always thought maybe I'd end up on a farm. A farmer's wife, perhaps. With a barn full of chickens and goats. Maybe a few cows." A light suddenly went out in her eyes I hadn't noticed was burning. Her amber irises turned dull as she looked back to me. "But working with horny drunks and unruly soldiers probably isn't that different from working with animals. Life has a funny way of working out, doesn't it?"

I couldn't help but laugh. "That it does." I sat back, too, matching the way she lounged in her chair. "Ten-year-old me probably wanted to be a soldier."

That dullness remained in her eyes. "You don't know that, though." The words were pensive, said with a furrowed brow and tight lips. Almost like she hadn't meant to say them out loud.

I let the silence settle, the normal sounds of the street outside now absent. Those sounds were confined to houses tonight as families laughed and prayed and celebrated Domicilium. I could feel my brain beginning to fixate on the intimate gatherings, then on my parents and the life I'd had before the fire.

No.

"No one else around the Blushing Dove tonight?" I asked, cutting off my spiraling thoughts as I looked past Isa to the door of the kitchen.

She shifted in her seat. "Not tonight."

"Everyone have family around?"

"You could say that."

I stared at Isa, at the way she suddenly looked uncomfortable in her chair. She took a long drink of ale, gently placing the cup down on the table, still avoiding my gaze. I didn't want to pry, but something about her answer propped the door open just enough that I couldn't help but peer inside. After a long moment, she inhaled. "The girls here are kind of like a family. Every family has a black sheep," she offered, the words clipped. I could tell she wanted to say more, so I remained silent, hoping it would nudge that door open just a little wider. "They're all at Miria's house on the west side of the city. Our madam."

My gaze narrowed on her. "They're all at Miria's, and you're here."

"I don't usually get an invite to gatherings outside the brothel," she said quietly, then quickly stood up. "More ale?"

"Your family doesn't invite you to their gatherings?" Suspicion made the hairs on the back of my neck stand on end. She didn't answer, instead busying herself with the pitcher of ale on the countertop. "Why not?"

She let out a soft sigh. "I'm different than they are."

My palm flattened on the table. "Because you like women?"

Her laugh was dry. "No. Half the girls here prefer women. That has nothing to do with it." She took my still half-full mug from the table, topped it off, then placed it back in front of me. Suddenly, she was very interested in cleaning one spot on the countertop.

Isa was nice. She was witty, intelligent, and seemed pleasant enough from what I could tell. She was downright beautiful. Sure, she might not have been the most personable with her customers, but I'd be hard pressed to find a brothel customer who preferred their whores personable over beautiful. What the hell could make her an outcast here? Was it really because she didn't interact enough with her customers? I didn't want to add salt to that wound, though, so I approached it another way. "Is it because they're jealous that all the patrons choose you?"

She laughed again. "Very funny."

"What is it?"

She turned to me, leaning against the counter, fidgeting as she passed a rag back and forth between her hands. She worried her bottom lip as her eyes darted around the room. "I've talked myself into a hole here, haven't I?" The laugh she let out was nervous before she chewed on her thumb nail. "I tend to do that. I'm sure my big mouth will lead me straight to the gallows one day."

I watched her carefully but gleaned nothing from the way she moved. "That bad, huh?"

"Not in my eyes. But maybe in yours."

Every muscle in my body locked where I sat in the ramshackle chair. There was only one thing she could be referring to. She had to have been drinking heavily before I got here, because there is no way she would tell me something like this if she were sober. Why the hell would she admit this to *me*? I suddenly became very aware of the sword at my hip and the oath I'd sworn.

She didn't believe in Kauvras' conquest. Isa was a dissenter.

"You don't support King Kauvras' mission?" I asked carefully.

She straightened, arms at her sides, jaw squared and chin high. She didn't give an answer. She didn't need to.

Disbelief and conflict melted together in my gut. I had a duty to kill her here and now, or, at the very least, turn her in for treason.

"Isa, why would you tell me that?" I felt the need to look over my shoulder just to make sure no one had overheard.

"I'm tired of pretending that what he's doing is fine. You're the first soldier I've met who doesn't support him either."

I shot to my feet, unsheathing my sword and extending the blade in her direction. Isa didn't even flinch. She looked past my blade, directly at me, like she knew something about me I didn't. I couldn't keep my hand from trembling slightly as my grip on my sword grew sweaty. "How dare you suggest that."

"It's the truth."

I swallowed hard, trying to prepare myself to carry out my sworn duty. "Are you aware that you'll be sentenced to death for saying that?"

"Don't pretend you're the only soldier without family in Taitha. You could be with the others, celebrating Domicilium and praising your glorious King Kauvras. You can't tell me some officer isn't putting on a feast for the ones without a home to celebrate? Why did you decide to come to the Blushing Dove instead? To see *me*?" She saw right fucking through me. She was whip smart, and I hated it in this moment. My blade inched closer to her throat, but I remained silent. Isa shifted her weight, crossing her arms flippantly, as if she didn't have a broadsword pointed straight at her. If anything, she seemed *bored*. "No. You don't have any friends because you don't *want* to be friends with your fellow soldiers. Because you don't support Kauvras' mission either."

I breathed heavily through my nose as I stared at her, trying to steel my nerves. "That's not true."

"You're here because you can't stand to be around the others, nor can you stand to be alone with your own thoughts for a single night."

"That's not true," I repeated. It was the only thing I could manage.

"Haven't admitted it to yourself yet?" she taunted. *This* was the woman who'd been hiding behind the resigned eyes and forced moans? Fucking Saints.

My teeth gnashed together. "I swore my life in support of his mission."

"If you support him," she started, straightening again, "kill me right now. It's your duty to *King Kauvras*." The words were a sneer. "Kill me right now."

I'd trained for this. I'd *trained* to kill people who dissented from King Kauvras' mission. It'd been hammered into my head every single day since the moment I swore the oath. I figured that if — *when* — the time came to kill a dissenter, it'd be easy. So ingrained in my being that I wouldn't even need to think about it.

And here I was, faltering.

Isa didn't even blink as she watched me try to keep myself from unraveling. "In order to work in this industry," she started, her arms waving to gesture around her, "you have to be able to read people. That's how you survive. Physically, mentally, and emotionally."

I also had to read people, and I'd apparently done a horrible job. "I'm a soldier of King Kauvras," I snapped. "His mission is my duty."

"It's your job. You don't have to like it to do it," she said, echoing the same words she'd spoken earlier.

"I have to turn you in," I said evenly, my sword still extended in her direction. I couldn't kill her, but I could turn her in and let someone else do it. Like a fucking coward.

She shrugged. "You could turn me in. But I'd tell them right then and there that you're a dissenter, too."

"And you think they'd believe you?"

"Maybe not." She absentmindedly ran a hand through her hair and twirled a strand around a finger. "But I'd be willing to bet they'd kill you just to be safe. Maybe just pump you with leechthorn. Either way, the loss of an unranked soldier is no skin off your king's nose."

I let out a silent breath, still staring at her. "*That's* why the other girls don't invite you to gatherings? Because they believe in King Kauvras' mission and you don't?" She nodded easily. "Why haven't they turned you in for dissenting?"

She laughed. "They're catty bitches, not monsters."

"I'm the monster, right?" I spat through gritted teeth.

"No, you're not a monster. Not until that mask goes over your face." My jaw ticked as I tried to think of a response. No one had ever questioned my allegiance. Why would anyone have cause to? My entire life revolved around my duties — around my honor. Any discomfort I felt with it all was kept carefully to myself and stuffed into a deep pocket of my mind. Almost like the unsettled feeling was a hazard of the job. It had never even occurred to me that it was discomfort with...everything I'd built my life around.

I'd never questioned my allegiance. Until now.

"I understand," she said suddenly. "You do what you have to do to survive. We all do."

My blade fell to my side, every muscle in my body still tensed as I stared at Isa. At the woman who fucked men all day even though she hated it, just to keep her belly full and a roof over her head. The woman who, like me, was just trying to survive.

"I won't turn you in." My words were short, but there was an air of exhaustion behind them I hadn't meant to let through. "But in return, you don't breathe a single word about this."

"Yes, sir," she said antagonistically, pushing herself off the counter with a mug of ale in her hand. "I'll even do you a favor. I'll teach you how to cook a steak."

I finally relaxed, letting my shoulders drop. "Fine."

She gave me a shit-eating grin, slinging an arm over my shoulder. "This is the beginning of a beautiful friendship."

◆ ◆ ◆

The evening air had taken on a chill by the time I left the Blushing Dove. It seemed that every chimney in the city puffed smoke into the sky. Every home's windows glowed with light from hearths and candles. I could even pick out silhouettes within a few of them. Muffled chatter and laughter could be heard filtering into the street. It all seemed to haunt me.

I couldn't shake the feeling that part of my armor had just been stripped away. I was exposed. Isa had spoken something into the world that I hadn't even admitted to myself. I didn't even know it was there to admit. My honor was the most important thing in my life. I couldn't betray that.

I wasn't a dissenter. I wasn't. *I wasn't.*

King Kauvras wanted to ascend to Sainthood. *That* was his mission. And we just went along with it.

I shook my head, trying to rid my brain of the thoughts. Treason was punishable by death, but treasonous thoughts were punishable by an internal war I didn't feel like fighting, especially against myself.

Fact: The Cabillian military was three meals a day and a roof over my head. Fact: The Cabillian military was a guaranteed job. Fact: The Cabillian military was survival.

I nodded in greeting to the guards, double checking that my mental walls were solid as I pushed through the doors of the barracks. There was Bowen, standing at his bunk with a small chest open beside him.

All conflict melted away from my face as I pasted on a smile and shot a hand out in front of me. "Congratulations, brother."

He met my handshake, his face beaming. "I told you I'd be promoted."

"Not to commander though," I jeered, punching his shoulder. His smile faltered for a moment, so quick I almost didn't see it. "Lieutenant is impressive, though. You deserve it." A lie.

"I'm moving into my private room tonight." His tone was boastful, and he made no attempt at humility. He never did though, even as he packed his measly selection of belongings into his trunk. "No more fucking in the brothels."

"That's right. Now you can afford to have them come to you."

"Not what I meant and you know it." He shot me a warning glare. "Girls love an officer. I'll have no problem finding someone to warm my bed whenever I wish now. But don't worry, I'll still accompany you to the Blushing Dove."

I gave a close-lipped smile. For some reason, the thought of Bowen being anywhere close to Isa sparked a new kind of anxiety in my chest. "Don't be too hard on me out there, Lieutenant."

"I won't be seeing you for a bit," he said, his jaw squaring with a smirk. "I leave tomorrow with my new squad for the Port of Cabillia."

I stared at him blankly for a second until understanding hit me like a brick to the face.

He reached down to a burlap sack at his feet that I hadn't noticed, pulling back the fabric to reveal a polished gold mask sculpted in the shape of a lion's head. My blood went icy, my heartbeat picking up for some reason as he lifted it and placed it over his head. "How's it look?"

I blinked, raising my brows, trying to think of the words for what I was feeling. I was strangely proud to see my friend — my brother — reach the goal he'd had for so long. But the pride was broken with jagged edges dripping in poison, noxious gas floating from it, making me sick to my fucking stomach.

He spread his hands in front of him, as if prompting me to answer. "Pretty fuckin' badass, right?"

"Pretty fuckin' badass," I confirmed, leaning forward to clap him on the shoulder.

He threw his arm around my neck, trying to fold me in a headlock, something he hadn't been able to do since I had finally grown taller than him at seventeen. I bent forward, letting him take the small victory, if only to shield my face from him for a moment. "A year and a half and you'll have yours. Maybe *then* you'll be promoted to lieutenant. Probably not, though." He let out a deep laugh as he pretended to land a punch in my stomach.

And though his punch stopped short, it landed harder in my gut than if his fist had actually made contact.

Kindly deliver to the Port of Coldwater

Dearest Mother and Father,

 Nothing of note to report here. Everyone in Taitha has been
kind for the most part. We were all surprised at the relative peace
in the city. We have a lovely estate on the edge of town and have
hired a large staff to help run it. No need to worry about us from
across the Widow's Sea. We have quite a few appointments
scheduled and are feeling very hopeful. Something good is just
around the corner, I know it.

 We miss you terribly.

Yours,

Cielle

Chapter 4

Cielle

Eyes were on me. I could feel them. It wasn't uncomfortable, just noticeable enough. Eyes were always on me back home, but here in Taitha, it felt different. Here in Taitha, *I* was different. It was instinct that had me turning to search through the market crowd, meeting the gazes of multiple people. None of them seemed to be the one I *felt*.

"You get everything you need?" I asked Nieve, shaking off the feeling as I peered into the basket hanging from the crook of her elbow.

"Think so."

"Do you mind if we stop by Timble's shop?"

The sigh that left my cousin's lips was so loud and dramatic, a few people actually turned to look at her. "I do mind, actually. You want to look at that busted old harp *again*? Fucking Saints, just buy it and be done with it already. I know you have enough coin."

She wasn't wrong. It was true that our family had been blessed by Tolar, Saint of Wealth. There was more than enough money in the pocket of my cloak this very second. In fact, I could buy a brand new harp with what I had in my cloak. There was just something about that one. It had lived a life of its own, evident by the dents and scratches that marred the polished wood.

There was no way I was going to let Nieve in on that thought, though. Not only would she not understand nor make any attempt to, she'd pick the perfect time to use it against me during an inevitable future argument.

I managed a somewhat nonchalant shrug of my shoulders. "I just want to see if it's still there."

"No. We need to get back to Cenric before he sends another childminder out the door in tears."

I cleared my throat, packing the idea of a harp away in my mind the same way I'd been doing with the idea for years. My attention pivoted to a very real problem: Cenric. "That's what, three childminders since we've arrived in Taitha?"

"Four," Nieve answered flatly. "He's a fucking terror, Cielle."

I rolled my eyes. "Here comes Nasty Nieve."

"Shut the fuck up."

I fought to keep a smile from my face. Riling her up was *so* easy and always entertaining. Just a few small digs and out came Nasty Nieve, the nickname her father had affectionately given her as a child. A bit fucked up, if I thought about it enough. But oh, so accurate.

We wove our way through the patrons in the market, my little brother's smiling face clear in my mind. "Cenric really isn't that bad."

Nieve's green eyes were visibly cold as she shot me a look. "Maybe not to you. But that's only because you were twice as bad when we were kids."

The laugh that bubbled up in my chest couldn't be contained. "If I remember correctly," I started, "*I* never terrorized any of my childminders by chasing them around the house with a snake."

"No. You terrorized *me* by chasing me around with a lizard. A lizard named after the fucking Saint of War."

I stuck a single finger in her direction. "Faldyr*a*," I corrected, drawing out the *ah* sound at the end. "Once I found out *he* was a *she*. And let's be honest, you probably deserved it."

Nieve, to my shock, didn't take the bait I'd laid out for her, and instead stayed silent. She really *was* trying to work on that mood of hers, just like she'd promised her parents.

The ground rumbled as a horse-drawn cart drove behind us, and I couldn't help but tense my shoulders at its proximity. I would never get used to how crowded the market was in Taitha. Coldwater's markets were much more open, with more fresh air and less stink of pig shit. There were always dozens of fishermen selling their morning catch — fish, oysters, and lobster. My mouth watered at the thought. I hadn't had a bite of seafood since we arrived here, and even if I could manage to find it, I'm not sure I'd trust it.

For the most part, Taitha seemed to be peaceful. At least, it seemed to be peaceful on the outside. Signs of decay were around if I looked hard enough, evidence of the madman who ruled the country from the castle at the center of the city. Half the soldiers who walked through the streets wore masks sculpted to look like the heads of various animals. Unsettling at first, but we'd quickly grown used to it.

The other thing was the bodies. Father had warned us of this, but it was still a shock to witness as we entered the city and saw the bodies of traitors hanging from the outer walls of the castle. I shielded my little brother's eyes against the sight as we shuffled past, my own morbid curiosity not affording me the luxury of looking away from the dozens of people in varying states of decay.

We had our ways of discouraging dissent and treason in the Surging Isles of Tadrana — a ship would take the criminal out to sea, far from shore and they'd be dropped in the ocean. Usually, Cyen captured them by drowning, and the Saint of Death would close his fingers around his prey when they'd grown too tired to keep afloat. Sometimes it was Idros, Saint of Storms, who nudged them into Cyen's grasp with a violent squall. And sometimes, it was the sharks.

Even *that* was much less barbaric than Taitha's method, if you asked me.

It's not that Taitha was unpleasant, it was just... I could never live permanently in a city that wasn't near the water. The Rhedrosian Mountains loomed in the distance, the Iron Rise towering far above its counterparts. Rhedros' portal to and from Hell watched over the fields of leechthorn like a reaper. The violet blooms were so deceptively beautiful, contrasted against the thin wisps of smoke that constantly climbed from the Iron Rise.

It sent a shiver down my spine.

My thoughts had distracted me so much that I was suddenly stopping short of a figure — a tall man dressed in Cabillian military leathers, just *standing* in the middle of the crowd.

Nieve tensed beside me, as if she were gearing up to make one of her signature Nasty Nieve comments. I put a hand on her arm, shaking my head. Nieve's parents — my Uncle Aleksy and Aunt Nathalie — only permitted her to join me and Cenric in Taitha if she used the time to *work on her manners*. That, and she was going to be Cenric's tutor while he was away from his formal lessons. Even though Nieve was rude and entitled, she was the smartest person I'd ever met. Sometimes, I thought that was the reason she was so mean, because everyone else around her was so damn stupid.

Unfortunately, I thought the world had a better chance of seeing the Daughter of Katia than of Nieve miraculously discovering some manners.

I stepped around the man. "Pardon me, soldier." I didn't even spare him a look as I passed him then leaned in to whisper in Nieve's ear. "Leechthorn's got him so fucked in the head that he doesn't know which way he's going."

"Hey," I heard from behind me. *Shit.* Had he heard me? Surely the man couldn't have heard me insult him, right? Did leechthorn give them super hearing or something? I turned back to him, Nieve along with me.

I never quite knew what people meant when they said someone had a piercing gaze. I no longer had to wonder. His dark stare had in fact pierced through me and nailed some part of me in place. Even from this distance, I could see his eyes were depthless. A night sky so vast it was without end entirely. Perhaps the very origin of the night sky itself.

His face was blank, but it was evident he was concentrating, studying me like he was trying to commit every part of me to memory. His tall figure stood higher than the crowd that buzzed around him, his leathers as dark as the hair tied into a knot at the back of his head. He seemed to absorb all the sunlight that hit him. My gaze traveled to his hands to see them clenched into fists before flexing, the honey-brown skin marred by tiny scars and calluses.

But he was just...staring.

Leechthorn fumes. Definitely too much time breathing in leechthorn fumes.

Saints. Pull your shit together, I thought to myself. *You're gawking like an idiot.* I pushed a brow up, feigning something between amusement and disinterest. Something that said, *You aren't the most gorgeous man I've ever seen in my life.*

"Yes, soldier?" I managed to ask. That was good. That was fine.

"Just..." His shoulders tensed momentarily then dropped, as if he'd had something he'd wanted to say but lost it just as it reached his lips. I didn't miss the small muscle that twitched in his jaw. "Hello."

"Oh for the love of–" Nieve grumbled almost silently under her breath.

All that for a simple *hello?* Was his brain completely melted by leechthorn? I thought of asking him that. I knew the same words were on the tip of Nieve's tongue. The beautiful ones always seemed to have empty heads. At least, that's the sentiment I'd been fighting my entire life.

"Hello," I answered. The word landed on his skin and soaked in like rain. He studied me as I studied him, and I had to fight the urge to close the distance and reach out to touch him. I was curious, and to be completely honest, not at all disliking the view. But the view was fleeting as Nieve quickly pulled me away.

"Come *on*," she whispered, teeth gritted.

My eyes stayed on the soldier's for one extra second, his expression unchanged as we reentered the crowd and I fell into stride beside Nieve. "That was odd."

Her face was red with rage when she looked at me, linking our arms and squeezing so tightly I winced. "Are you fucking insane? Do you know how dangerous Cabillian soldiers are?" She peered over her shoulder. "He's probably following us home so he can force leechthorn on us. Do you remember *nothing* your father said before we left Coldwater?"

We turned down the street away from the market, away from the terrifyingly violent soldier. "Don't you think my *father* has motivation to degrade another nation's army? What he says about Cabillian soldiers is a stupid rumor and you know it."

Despite the fact I didn't necessarily mind Taitha, the Surging Isles' view of Cabillia as a whole was one of a land filled with brutes, rapists, and all manner of violence. Unfortunately for us, some of the world's best healers and metalsmiths happened to be here in Taitha, so it was the next stop on our list.

Normally it was my mother and a number of our household staff that accompanied Cenric on his trips to find treatment, but I managed to convince my parents to let me and Nieve take him alone this time. As much as I loved Coldwater, something told me I needed to do this. I was sick of being coddled by my parents. It was important to me that I proved to myself I could be independent, even if it was only for a short time. This would probably be my only chance to do so. My parents were hesitant to let us go unaccompanied, but Nieve struck up a deal with her father, and I struck one up with mine.

I was not looking forward to delivering on my part of the deal.

Foreign visitors were allowed into the city as long as they swore verbal support of Kauvras' mission. Did I support it? Absolutely not. But Cenric was getting worse, so I did what needed to be done. It also didn't hurt that I conveniently *forgot* to tell the city guards who my parents were.

Nieve nodded in the direction of another uniformed soldier walking toward us. "You're telling me you don't think *that* motherfucker is violent?" While the soldier had a mask resembling a wolf's head covering his face, Nieve did not, and she made no attempt to conceal any antipathy from her features. He passed us without even a look. "He was huge. He could crush you like a fucking grape."

I scoffed at her. "What a shitty thing to say, Nieve. You know nothing about that man. Everyone has been kind to us."

"They're kind to us because you look like the Saint of Beauty."

"There is no—"

"Yeah, yeah, there is no Saint of Beauty," she spat. "If there was one, she'd look like you and you know it. Or maybe you are as dumb as you look."

It made me uncomfortable to acknowledge that yes, I was...physically attractive. So, I didn't acknowledge it. "Everyone has been kind to us," I repeated.

"Go ahead and get to know that soldier, then. The one back at the market who stared like he was plotting some heinous crime against you. I'm sure he's very kind." She gave me a condescending look as she nodded dramatically.

"Maybe I will get to know him."

Our cottage came into view as soon as we turned onto Rosemary Lane, and Nieve made a garbled noise of annoyance at my answer. "You're just lucky I haven't written a letter to your parents and told them about our living arrangements."

"This is good for us, Nieve. You especially." She grumbled something under her breath, and it didn't take a stretch of the imagination to know she was firmly planted in Nasty Nieve territory. "And *you're* lucky I haven't written a letter to *your* parents telling them that despite their request for you to work on your manners, you're still an insufferable, raging bitch."

Nieve's mouth flew open but quickly slammed shut. I gave her a saccharine smile. I'd won this round.

The home we were renting in Taitha was quaint — a cottage no larger than the servants' quarters of our summer home in Eddena. It was cozy, perfect for a stay of only a few months, with a dreamy garden in the front and a kitchen perfect for me to continue to work on my cooking skills. The hallways were wide and the bedrooms were large, and two of the five bedrooms were on the first floor. Plus, it was close to most of Cenric's appointments.

I may have...fudged a few details in the first letter I'd written to my parents. No, we didn't have an estate on the edge of town, nor did we have a large staff. We had no staff, actually, because I was craving something I'd never had before: independence.

"Seashell! Seashell!"

I smiled at the sound of Cenric calling my name — my nickname. I could just make out his face peeking from behind the railing on our front porch as we pushed through the garden gate. "Seashell! Ester is still here!"

The childminder rose from the bench where she sat beside Cenric, meeting us as we ascended the wooden board we'd laid over the porch steps. The seemingly even-keeled and buttoned-up woman we'd left that morning was nowhere to be found. "You're lucky I've stayed this long," Ester growled, strands of wiry, gray hair pulled loose from her low bun and an impressive array of unidentifiable stains on her shirt. "You didn't tell me he had a jar full of crickets."

My eyes moved from the childminder to Cenric and I raised a brow. He ran a hand through his white-blond curls, feigning innocence as I stared. "I didn't *know* he had a jar full of crickets."

"Well, now you have a house full of crickets," Ester answered, her face twisted in disgust. I reached into the pocket of my cloak and placed a few coins in the woman's hand.

"Just the ones the lizard didn't catch," Cenric added. Oh boy. I blinked, waiting for an explanation that I knew was going to give me a headache. "I let the lizard go to catch the crickets." His tone implied I should've been able to figure that out on my own.

I reached into my cloak and added a few more coins to the pile in Ester's hand, offering a sorry smile and shrug. "Apologies."

"Please don't bother calling on me again," Ester snapped as she stormed down the makeshift ramp and out through the gate.

"Wouldn't want to with that shitty attitude," Nieve called after her. "And fix your hair. You look like a fucking mess."

Ester had left so quickly, I wasn't even sure she'd heard Nieve's words. I widened my eyes at my cousin. "Really, Nieve?"

Her eyes rolled. "Sorry, Cenric. I meant *bad* attitude."

"That's a silver for me," he quipped, outstretching his hand. "Thank you, Nasty Nieve."

"Hey," I said sternly, catching Cenric's attention before he could instigate an argument. "Can you relax with the reptiles, bud? Please?"

His smile was mischievous as he shrugged innocently. "Crickets aren't reptiles."

"Don't be a smartass," Nieve spat. Cenric opened his palm without even looking away from me, his face completely straight as he closed his fingers around another silver piece.

A deep sigh escaped my nose as I stared at my little brother. "Cenric."

His hands fell to his lap in a show of defeat. "The crickets were an honest mistake." I raised a skeptical brow at him. "Honest! I dropped the jar and the lid popped off."

"Where did you get a jar of crickets?" I asked.

"I brought them from home."

I blinked slowly. I didn't have the energy to ask any more questions as to where they came from. "*Why* did you have a jar of crickets? I thought you'd moved on to mealworms for the reptiles." I fought the shudder that crawled up my spine. I didn't like mealworms any more than I liked crickets, but at least they were easier to keep in place.

"Twiggy likes crickets," he answered matter-of-factly.

I looked to Nieve. *Twiggy?* She shrugged, just as confused as I was, though Nieve was visibly exasperated while I still clung to the threads of my patience.

"Twiggy," Cenric offered. "The lizard."

Cenric had always loved animals. Reptiles and rodents were his favorite. He'd been favoring the former lately, much to the dismay of most of the people around him. I didn't particularly mind them for the most part, but I couldn't keep track of what was in each of the dozens of enclosures in his room. The only reason I *wanted* to keep track was so when they inevitably escaped their enclosures, I knew whether it was a non-venomous problem or a *get-the-fuck-out-of-the-house-now* problem.

Stress tightened in my chest, a new sensation I'd discovered since leaving Coldwater. "And what kind of lizard is Twiggy?" I hoped to myself it was one I already knew of and not one I'd need to stay up all night reading about.

"A common tree lizard. Native to the southern forest region of Astran." He clasped his hands together excitedly. "Not far from here, actually."

66

Okay, I knew that one. Not venomous. Not too large. But... "I thought your common tree lizard was named Maple?"

"Maple needed a husband so she could have babies."

"Oh, absolutely fucking not," Nieve said as she waved her hands in front of her. She emptied one pocket of its coins and all but threw them at Cenric as she walked down the makeshift ramp. "I'll be staying in an inn tonight. Send for me when you find *Twiggy* and his family."

"Stop at the next healer's apothecary and make an appointment for Cenric, will you?" I called after her. "You have the list of healers, right?"

Her finger flew up in a crude gesture. That was a *yes* in Nasty Nieve language. She was not a fan of Cenric's affinity for all things furry, slimy, and scaly. She'd begged my parents not to allow Cenric to bring his animals on this trip. When Nieve's father overheard, he arranged the transport of the animals himself and claimed that the discomfort would help improve Nieve's mood.

I can confirm it did the opposite.

Cenric was unbothered by our cousin's outburst, his attention on gathering the small fortune he'd just had thrown into his lap. "You know what I have enough coin for now?" he asked with a smile as he shoved the last silver piece in his pocket.

"*No.*"

"Please, Seashell?" he asked, his eyes growing large and almost watery. "I just want another mouse. Maybe two. Then I won't buy any more until we get back to Coldwater. Seashell, *please.*"

I sighed. "Help me find Twiggy and *maybe* I'll take you down to the pet shop, *just* to look."

"Deal!" he said, his hands reaching down to fumble with the wheels of his chair, guiding them over the wooden porch and through the front door.

I watched him for a moment as he maneuvered through the drawing room at the front of the house, clicking his tongue as if Twiggy would come running. His wheelchair bumped against the wainscoting on the walls, snagging against the delicate dust cover on the side table.

Cenric was perfectly healthy aside from his legs. His ankles had been gnarled and twisted when he was born, and throughout his seven years, no one had ever been able to give him an exact diagnosis. He'd seen every healer in the Surging Isles and all of them told us they'd never seen anything like it. A few suggested that maybe as he grew, his legs might straighten out. They hadn't. In fact, they looked worse. Much, much worse, and now both legs were mangled from the knee down. Recently, he started experiencing such terrible pain, it kept him in bed for days.

So came the trips to other cities and countries. He and my mother had traveled to Araqina, Kruria, and Galyra in recent years only to be met with more of the same: healers that couldn't help.

The wheelchair hardly slowed him down, but seeing him in pain ripped a hole straight in the fabric of my soul. The pain came and went and he had more good days than bad. But the number of bad days was increasing steadily. I knew in my gut that didn't bode well for the future. He always tried to hide the look of disappointment on his face when his cousins left to go play on the shore and he had to stay behind. I had a feeling that to him, watching his cousins play without him was worse than any physical pain.

"Twiggy!" he called as he pushed himself out of the drawing room and down the hall. "Twiggy, come here!"

I had no idea how stressful it would be taking on the bulk of his care. Nieve helped me shoulder it all, albeit begrudgingly, and I was grateful for the help in scheduling his appointments. I'd been tempted to refer to his appointments as *disappointments*, because that's all the healers could seem to offer Cenric. I never said it aloud, of course.

After each disappointment though, there was always a tiny bit of hope that we were right around the corner from something life-changing.

Chapter 5
Miles

If I told Bowen what I was thinking about, he'd probably punch me in the face and tell me to man the fuck up. It wouldn't be the first time. He'd done it many times now. For various reasons. But never a reason like this, which was why I was knocking on Isa's bedroom door instead of seeking out my brother.

"Coming!" she sang from inside. I heard light footsteps and the sound of shuffling fabric. Nothing, though, was louder than the grunts and groans that echoed through the upper levels of the Blushing Dove.

A woman rounded the corner, her robe hanging completely open and her jet black hair doing nothing to hide what was beneath it. The smile she gave me was feline as she stalked toward me, soft hands running up my back. She leaned up to nip at my ear, practically purring. "Don't waste your time with Assandra."

I knew exactly what the woman meant, but I'd be damned before I gave her any sort of satisfaction. I straightened, trying as politely as I could to step away from her, but she followed easily. A fucking leech. "I won't waste a minute with her, thank you."

She ran a finger over my neck. "I can give you what you really want."

"I'd like to see Assandra." What the hell was taking her so long?

The door swung open, revealing a very scantily-clad Isa. Her eyes landed on me first, and I thought I saw relief flash through them before she looked to the woman behind me. Her face pulled up in a tight smile. "Hello, Sireshi."

Sireshi's face twisted into a sneer she made no attempt to cover. "Assandra."

Isa's hand closed around my arm and she pulled me inside, immediately donning a robe and tying it over the tiny bits of lace she wore. "Sorry about that."

"*I'm* sorry about that." I looked back to the closed door. "What the hell is her problem?"

Isa's lips rolled together. "You know what her problem is."

Oh. Yeah. Sireshi was a supporter of Kauvras. The breath I let out sounded a bit defeated. "She's trying to take your business?"

"Not trying. She *is* taking my business. Sireshi and the others." She lowered herself to the chair at her vanity, gesturing for me to sit down on the bed. "Can I be frank with you, Miles?"

"I have a feeling you're going to be no matter my answer." Considering I'd already learned a life threatening secret of hers against my will.

Her expression was strained, brows pulled up over amber eyes. "I want to get out of this place so fucking badly."

I stared at her in confusion. "Okay. You know where the front door is."

She shot me a sidelong glance. "Do you think it's that simple?"

I sat with her question. Nothing was ever that simple, that I knew. It was never as simple as just leaving a situation. "Of course not."

"When I started at the brothel, Miria gave me an advance to pay for my room here. I was so desperate to find employment, I didn't even think about the implications of it. I signed the contract to pay her back before I could leave and find employment elsewhere."

70

"Okay," I answered, following her so far. "How much do you have left?"

"That's the thing." Her eyes darted away, and I couldn't tell for sure, but I think her lip wobbled slightly. "I'd almost paid it off until two years ago when she...found out."

About her dissent. "Did you come out and tell her the way you told me?"

"No. She asked me one day why I referred to him as Kauvras."

I couldn't help but stare at her. "That's his name."

"It is. But he's *King* Kauvras," she murmured. "Not just Kauvras. I tried to lie when she asked me about it. I told her it must've just been a slip of the tongue. She knew though. Since then, she's been tacking on fees and charging me for arbitrary things. She turned the other girls against me, and business has been a trickle. To add insult to injury, Miria has charged me more for being late on rent. And now my balance is higher than it was when I first signed the contract."

"Why the hell wouldn't she just turn you in?" This didn't make any sense. Isa had said the other girls here weren't monsters, but surely keeping a dissenter under the same roof couldn't benefit them at all.

"Because she knows I'll turn her in for dealing auraphine. I'll turn them all in for it, since they're all involved."

I sat pin straight in surprise. "She's dealing auraphine?"

"Leechthorn isn't the only drug in Taitha, Miles." She leaned back in her chair and crossed her arms over her chest. "I fall, she falls. She keeps me close for that reason. That, and she still makes a bit of money off me when I get a one-off customer."

My head spun. I had no idea these problems even existed in Taitha. I assumed everyone here supported Kauvras, with the odd dissenter here and there. I stared at the red-haired woman sitting across from me. "Why are you telling me this, Isa?"

"Because above all else, I need a friend right now. And so do you." I blinked slowly, unable to quickly conjure up a response. I didn't have to. Isa waved a hand in front of herself dismissively. "I'm sure you didn't come to hear me blather on about my misery." She gave a weak smile, but then her brows furrowed.

"Forgive me, but *why* exactly are you here? I didn't think I'd see you again after the other night."

My reasoning felt trivial, but I forced the words out as I propped myself up on my mental walls for strength. "You're right. I think I need a friend." Sympathy lined her features. Her care wasn't necessarily what I'd wanted, but it didn't feel bad to have it. "There was something I didn't tell you the other night." She leaned forward, sympathy now replaced by concern. "I was passed up for a promotion on Selection Day. My brother wasn't. That's the real reason I was alone for Domicilium."

Isa straightened, eyes narrowed skeptically. "Your brother? You told me you didn't have any siblings."

"I don't. Not really." I patted my hands on my knees. "The guy I'm here with sometimes, Bowen," I started, nodding my head toward the door, "he and I grew up together on Merchant Street. So we're not related, but we're brothers."

"I was about to smack you for lying to me."

"And they say soldiers are the violent ones."

"That idiot is your *brother?*" She let out a dry laugh. "I overhear the other girls talking about how he can never keep it up."

I closed my eyes, wincing a bit. "Wish I didn't know that."

She gave an apologetic shrug. "So he was promoted," she prodded.

"Lieutenant Leo Bowen." It tasted like acid in the back of my throat, and no matter how hard I tried to swallow it down, it remained. My eyes trailed up to the painted ceiling, Baroque vines and roses twisting in an elegant wreath.

She crossed her arms over her chest. "It bothers you."

Isa said she was good at reading people, and she was. I flexed my jaw. I felt like I'd already said too much. It just felt so...*good* to talk to someone in this way. But another part of me knew that by speaking these things aloud, it was confirming their existence, and that made me more than uncomfortable.

I took a deep breath. "Yes. It bothers me because I work just as hard as he does, if not harder." My finger and thumb pinched the bridge of my nose, the frustration eating at me. "Between the two of us, he was always the one at the forefront. He started the fights and I backed him up. He caused the trouble and I took the punishment. It's just..."

"It's hard to see someone find success when you know deep down they don't deserve it." Isa's words came from a place of understanding. "I'm surrounded by it. But what goes around comes around. Sometimes the only thing you can do is sit back and wait."

Damn, was Isa smart. A hell of a lot smarter than me. I sat forward, craving some warmth, something positive to change the subject. "I met a girl today."

She raised a brow as one side of her mouth quirked up. "Is this what we're going to do? Talk about girls?"

I couldn't hold back the smile. There was something really comforting about this conversation. It felt normal. It felt like *friendship*. Even though our friendship was bound by blackmail and a lack of physical interest in one another. "Do you want to hear about her or not?"

"Of course I do."

◆ ◆ ◆

I was a fucking *idiot* for listening to Isa. She told me to go back to the market today to find the woman with the ocean-blue eyes. She convinced me that missing training and scrubbing a few dozen toilets would be worth it if I got to see her again. I hadn't told Isa that I'd arrived at that same conclusion the moment those blue eyes turned away from me for the first time.

Three days in a row, I milled around the market in the sunlight of the early day, missing my morning training session then paying dearly for it during the afternoon session. Fuck a perfect attendance record. I hadn't been promoted anyway. Vorkalth was all too happy to punish me. Bowen, my only potential reprieve, was at the Port of Cabillia. So for the foreseeable future, it was sore thighs from extra laps and a whole lot of dry heaving as I cleaned the barrack latrines.

As I slipped out of the barrack on the fourth morning, I told myself it would be the last day. After this, I'd give it up. There were two and a half loaves of bread going stale in a bag under my bunk and a growing collection of honey apples beside them that would soon turn to mush.

I stepped into the dusty market air in pursuit of the ocean.

Chapter 6
Cielle

The healer had been staring at Cenric's ankles for more than a few minutes now, humming in thought every so often. He'd even flipped through more than one of the books on the shelf at the back of the room, looking for some tiny piece of knowledge that could point him in the right direction. "I'm sorry to say I'm just not sure. I—"

"Haven't seen anything like it?" Cenric cut in. Discouragement hung thick in the air as his eyes landed on the ground.

I shot him a look for interrupting, but could I really blame the kid? Hope had grown quietly in my chest since Nieve had made this appointment a few days ago, but my heart sank the moment the healer's eyes landed on Cenric's legs. I could tell right then and there that he would not be the person to give us answers. He'd been kind, with gentle hands and an air about him that exuded calm. But even that couldn't take the sting out of yet another disappointment.

The healer gave a sympathetic smile. "Have you visited any of the metalsmiths in town? Some of the best in the world are right here in Taitha. I'm sure they could fashion some corrective leg braces."

A deep sigh escaped through my nose. "We were planning to try all the healers first. See if there was anything we could do to..." I brought my hands together, pursing my lips as I tried to find the right words.

"Actually fix me," Cenric said flatly.

"Hey," I said, nudging his arm. "You're not broken. You don't need fixing."

His only response was silence as he turned away from me. I tried my best to keep my heart from shattering right then and there. The healer's eyes were filled with compassion as he looked at me and offered a smile. "Keep trying. It may take a favor from the Saint of Miracles herself, but there's someone out there who can help you."

"Is there anything you can do for the pain in the meantime?" I asked, trying not to let Cenric hear the desperation I felt.

The healer walked across the room to a bureau packed with bottles of all shapes and sizes, his eyes scanning them until he found the one he'd been looking for. "You can take this as often as you need it. There is no risk of harm. Take it with food and you'll be pain-free. It will, however, make you sleepy."

I couldn't bear the look on Cenric's face. "But I don't want to sleep. I want to play."

"We'll find something, bud," I said quickly, before the healer could speak. I'm sure whatever he was going to say would've been said with good intentions, but I couldn't risk him disappointing Cenric even more. I thanked him silently as we pushed out of the doorway and into the street.

Nieve had been waiting for us, and I could tell by the look on her face that she'd been pacing. Her brows rose in silent question, but quickly fell in understanding when her gaze landed on Cenric's downcast face. For as prickly as she was, she loved Cenric.

I stopped his chair, bending down to meet his gaze. "Hey."

"I know," he answered, his eyes still trained on his lap. "I don't need the speech that everything is going to be okay."

76

Through the gloom of yet another heartbreak, an idea emerged. "I wasn't going to give you a speech. Actually, I was going to ask you, if you could have anything in the world for dinner tonight, what would it be?"

His eyes peered up at me, the blue similar to my own, but the shape all our father's. He looked just like him in miniature form. Sadness still showed in his gaze, but there was a small light that had just sparked to life, and I was going to do everything I could to keep it from being smothered again. "Anything?"

"Anything at all."

One corner of his mouth turned up just slightly. "Hmm."

"Wait!" I waved my hands in front of him dramatically. "Let me guess!"

His smile grew a bit wider. "Okay."

With my eyes squeezed shut, I made a show of thinking as hard as I could, recalling the meal that had been his favorite since he was just three. "I think you want...roasted chicken with sweet corn and cabbage."

He was close to laughing now, and I felt a small sense of relief at the sight. "How did you know?"

I threw my hands up in mock confusion. "Lucky guess!" I looked to Nieve, whose usually-stern face was beginning to show something that looked like a smile. "Nieve is going to take you home, okay? I'll go to the market and get everything I need to make dinner."

"Are you going to make it the same way Vivian does?"

I smiled. "I'm going to try my hardest." Our family had been lucky to have arguably the best chef in the Surging Isles in our employ, and she'd walked me through Cenric's favorite recipes half a dozen times before we left for Taitha. She'd side-eyed me the whole time, not daring to ask why I'd need to know a single recipe if we were planning on hiring a full staff when we arrived in Taitha. "I can't promise that it'll be exactly the same, but it'll be pretty darn close."

His eyes suddenly narrowed, brow furrowed with concern. "What about dessert?"

"Hold on." I closed my eyes again before shooting them wide and pointing my index finger in the air. "Honey apple tart?"

His face lit up, and a small part of my heart healed over. "Yay!" I ruffled his white-blond curls. "I'll see you guys soon."

◆ ◆ ◆

Chicken from the butcher. Sweet corn and cabbage from the vegetable stand. I recounted the ingredients in my head, trying to make sure I had everything I needed. Last on my list were honey apples, and I made my way to the cart that we'd become all but regulars at thanks to Cenric's love of fruit. Well, Cenric, and his birds and lizards.

A dizzying amount of children pulled at a woman's skirt. I smiled at their pleading eyes as they pointed to a cart laden with pastries. A chorus of, "Please, Mama?" swirled around her, and it didn't take long for her to break down and scoop a pile of coins from her pocket. How could such innocence exist in a city built on violence?

Something prickled over my scalp, like I had a sixth sense urging me to look around. I didn't need to do much looking, though, because I knew who it was before I even saw him. The bumbling Cabillian soldier.

For a moment, I just stood and watched as he picked up apple after apple, meticulously turning each one in his hand before placing it back in its spot. The shopkeeper was visibly aggravated. Her eyes landed on me, and for a moment her slightly squinted gaze was the only sign that she was no longer aggravated but...amused. As if something that didn't make sense had just clicked together in her mind. She looked back to the soldier, the amusement obvious on her face as she crossed her arms over her chest, almost expectantly.

The soldier had been at it for a suspicious amount of time. I cocked a brow at the shopkeeper, silently asking what the fuck this guy was doing touching every single apple on her stand. The shopkeeper only gave me a knowing smirk before nodding.

I decided to break the silence, if not for my sake, then for the poor shopkeeper's. "Following me, soldier?"

His head swung around and his dark eyes landed on me, a look of panic lacing his features. Shit... *Was* he following me?

"Following you? No, I–"

"He's bought honey apples from me four times this week," the shopkeeper cut in, her droning voice flat. "No one needs that many honey apples. Of course he's following you."

Everything about him told me I should be afraid, from the way he stood straight as an arrow to the severe cut of his jawline. He was dangerous, and I knew it. But those wide, ambivalent eyes and that timid ghost of a smile told me he was thinking the same thing about me.

For a moment, terror struck me as I thought that maybe he recognized me. It's not as if we were hiding our identities or family name, but I hadn't exactly brought leaflets to pin up all over Taitha.

"I'm sorry, miss." There was a distinct raspiness to his voice I hadn't noticed the other day, and his face was downturned as he moved to leave. No, he didn't know who I was, because that wouldn't have been his reaction. Right?

I reached a hand out, my fingers running over the leather on his arm before he passed me completely.

Nieve had told me that if I got to know him, I'd come to find that he was nothing but a ruthless asshole, just like the rumors implied. I could tell right here, right now, that wasn't true.

Time to prove Nieve wrong. At least, that's what I told myself in order to justify why I stopped him.

I offered a small smile. "I was hoping I'd find you here. What's your name?"

The shopkeeper's eyes remained on us as the soldier stared at me like I'd asked him how far from here to the moon. My eyes trailed to his neck, where a mangled scar marked the skin of his throat. What in the world could possibly cause a scar like that? It was a long moment before he answered. "Miles Landgrave."

The rasp of his voice sent a curious, warm shiver up my spine that I made a point not to think too hard about. *Miles Landgrave.* It nestled itself in my mind. I liked the sound of it, the way it flowed together, the way it seemed to fit him. *You know nothing about him, Cielle.*

My hand dropped from his arm. "Hello, Miles Langrave," I said, relishing the way his name sounded. "I'm Cielle Andyr." I probably shouldn't have given him my last name. A slight oversight.

Maybe a big oversight.

I tried my hardest not to flinch as I waited to see if recognition flitted across his face. But if he knew my name, he didn't show it. Just like the day I first saw him, though, he seemed to be concentrating on my face, assessing what he saw before him. "Hello, Cielle." His voice had slipped deeper and his tone more even, as if knowing my name gave him some sort of foothold on the situation.

"I didn't really think you were following me, you know," I said. "That is, until I found out you actually were."

He tensed slightly, nostrils flaring. Those fucking *eyes*. I bet if I stared long enough I could see galaxies swirling through them. "That's not entirely true, Miss Andyr."

I raised a brow, letting a coy smile bloom across my face. He was like Nieve — easy to rile, just with a very different response. "Isn't it, though?"

He let out a breath, shaking his head slightly as he rolled his lips together. "I just thought–"

"That you'd drag me back to your barracks and force leechthorn on me?"

His brows furrowed instantly. "What?"

I cocked my head, easily getting a read on the genuine surprise in his voice. "I've heard the rumors."

One corner of his mouth turned up. "Ah, the *rumors*. You're not from here, then."

"Smart boy."

"Where are you from?"

I hesitated, considering a lie. Something in me spoke before I could craft one that was believable. "Coldwater."

The smile suddenly disappeared from his face. His jaw tightened to a point that looked painful. "Do you support King Kauvras' mission?"

I flinched at the abrupt question and the sudden change in his expression. Maybe he did know who I was. He was a soldier, after all — a soldier of Kauvras. It was his duty to know the leaders and politics of other countries.

A non-answer, I decided, would be my best bet here. "I'm in the city, aren't I?" I mused. "Meaning I swore my support for his mission."

He leaned in slightly, the tension almost completely gone from his body. "Smart girl."

I stifled a laugh. "So tell me, Miles Landgrave," I started, "are the rumors true? Are you a violent, lawless monster of a man?"

Something flashed across his face and was gone before I had time to decipher it. "I'd like to think not, Miss Cielle."

An idea occurred to me then. A horrible idea, one rooted in nothing but the petty desire to prove Nieve wrong. An idea I absolutely had no business carrying out.

But this was my one shot at freedom before I signed it away forever the moment I set foot back in Coldwater. I chewed on my lip, deciding to take this opportunity to make a very hasty and thoughtless decision.

"Miles, how do you feel about roasted chicken and a honey apple tart?"

Chapter 7
Miles

"So...she's trying to set you up with her cousin?" Isa's face was a perfect picture of confusion. She sat across from me on her bed, a plate of stale bread and sliced, over-ripened honey apples between us.

I shrugged, just about as confused as Isa. "To be completely honest, I'm not really sure. I hope not." I thought back to the quick rundown Cielle had given me, that her cousin, Nieve, was "not the nicest" — her words, not mine — and she'd love it if I could "knock her down a peg." If it had been anyone else saying those words, I probably would've run in the other direction. But it was *her*. She could've told me to run backwards down the Iron Rise and I would've asked if she preferred I do it on my hands instead.

I really, *really* hoped she wasn't trying to set me up with this cousin.

"You're telling me she wants to prove her cousin wrong so badly that she's going to invite a strange, *armed* man into her home?"

"Hmm." I scratched the back of my head. "I guess so."

Her lip twitched in sarcastic disgust. "So you're a pawn in a weird little game she's playing."

"I seem to be, don't I?"

"That doesn't make you uncomfortable?"

I raised my palms in front of me. "If this is what it takes to see her again."

Isa laid back on her bed. "I wouldn't invite you in."

"Not unless I paid you, right?"

She rolled over to punch my arm. "Sure." She sighed, plucking a chunk of bread from the plate and wincing a tad as she chewed it. "So dinner tonight at the pretty girl's house?" she asked, waggling her eyebrows.

"When did I say she was pretty?"

Isa's eyes rolled to the back of her head. "The moment you told me you met a girl at the market, your face lit up."

I scoffed. "Please."

"What did her cousin look like?"

I opened my mouth to answer, but blew air through my cheeks instead. "Couldn't tell you."

Isa gasped playfully, her hand landing on her chest. "You have a crush," she crooned in a singsongy voice.

"Can I pay you more to leave me alone?" I quipped.

"You have a cru-ush," she taunted, making a mock kissing face. "What kind of flowers are you going to bring her?"

I side-eyed her. "Am I supposed to bring flowers?"

"Are you kidding me? Of course you're supposed to bring flowers."

Isa's tone made it sound crucial. My experience with women existed within the walls of a few brothels in town and questionable advice from Bowen. I supposed I could use all the help I could get. "Okay, I can manage flowers. What kind?"

"Everyone loves roses," she said with a shrug. "Roses are a safe bet. Not red ones, though. Too serious."

I raised my eyebrows, unaware that a flower could be serious at all. "Is there a rulebook somewhere?"

"This is shit you should already know, Miles." She grabbed a wedge of honey apple, inspecting where the flesh had begun to brown. "And you're going to wear your uniform, obviously."

"I am?"

Isa's palm slapped over her eyes. "Women love a man in uniform. That's a universal rule." I added that to my mental rulebook. "What's her name?"

I ran my tongue behind my teeth to try to keep myself some smiling like a giddy fucking child. "Cielle Andyr."

The piece of honey apple dropped to the bedspread and Isa shot upright. "*Cielle Andyr?* As in the daughter of King Bastian and Queen Anja Andyr?"

Um. My eyes widened, and I suddenly felt very, very, *very* stupid. "No."

"She from Coldwater?"

"No." I shook my head furiously as if that could somehow change the truth. Isa saw right through it. "Yes."

Her jaw popped to the side as she smiled and let out a huff of a laugh. "Well, *Sir*," she said, feigning dramatic emphasis on the title, "it would seem that tonight, you'll be dining with the royal family of the Surging Isles."

◆ ◆ ◆

It was impossible. Why the hell would the daughter of a foreign king be casually shopping in a market square in Taitha? She wouldn't be. Cielle had been holding a basket and wearing a cloak, just like every other market patron. If she were any kind of royalty, she'd have servants to do her shopping for her. And *why* would a Princess of the Surging Isles be in Taitha in the first place? If her father were here, we'd know about it, because that would mean we were at war. The house — which I found myself pacing outside of — was on the nicer side of town, but this was nowhere near the nicest home in Taitha. Nothing I'd think a *princess* would even glance at.

All that aside, I'd never even heard of her. In the furthest corner of my mind hidden away, there was maybe a whisper of a memory of the Andyr surname.

Isa was batshit. That was the answer to this whole thing.

I would know the name of another country's princess. I knew the names of plenty of foreign royals. There was... Well, Eddena's King had a daughter named... No, he had a son. Nesan's King and Queen had one son and four daughters, named... Shit. The newly appointed King Belin of Widoras was a mystery. The Invisible King. I had no idea if he had any children. Which meant...

Fuck. I couldn't name a single princess from another country. But I decided to double down on the notion that Isa had absolutely no idea what she was talking about. That was the easiest explanation to all of this.

All the while, a heavy truth hung over my head. If Cielle *was* the daughter of the King and Queen of the Surging Isles, then Kauvras' mission wasn't one she'd support. Being from Coldwater was enough to tell me where her loyalties laid.

So why the hell would she invite me for dinner?

The questions somersaulted in my head, each conclusion I drew leading to ten more, and not a single one of them was anywhere near plausible. I continued pacing at the bottom of the porch, where a wooden board had been laid over the stairs to make what seemed to be some kind of ramp. How the fuck was I supposed to act here? The bouquet of roses Isa had told me to bring suddenly felt childish, and I had to keep myself from grinding and shredding the stems in my grip.

The door swung open suddenly and I straightened to see...a little boy in a wheelchair. Okay, that explained the ramp. He peered down at me from the porch with eyes a color similar to Cielle's, though a bit more gray. I could smell something cooking inside, the scent wafting out the door and instantly making my mouth water. Maybe they had a chef.

"My cousin Nieve is wondering if you're walking around in our garden because you inhaled too much leechthorn," the boy said.

"Oh, for fuck's sake!" someone shouted from inside the house. I didn't think that was Cielle's voice. That must be Nieve. *The cousin.* "Do you have to repeat everything I say, you little shit?"

Nieve appeared suddenly, storming from around a corner and down the hall to the front door. Fists rested on shapely hips, aggravation burning in her wide-set, green eyes as she stared down at the boy. I thought *maybe* she'd been the one at the market with Cielle that first day, maybe I recognized the soft brown color of her hair, but I couldn't be sure. Objectively, she was very pretty. But she wasn't Cielle.

I opened my mouth, unsure of what exactly to say. "Apologies."

"You're Miles Landgrave," the boy said excitedly.

My smile was apprehensive as I nodded. "I am."

"I'm Cenric." He shot a hand out in front of him and gave me a grin that was missing more than a few teeth. I climbed the noticeably wobbly ramp and met his handshake, impressed by a grip that was surprisingly strong for a child so young. "This is our cousin, Nieve. She's not nice," he continued, as if he were simply stating what his cousin did for a living rather than pointing out a rather obvious character flaw. Cenric leaned in to me slightly. "Did you hear her swear?" He glanced over his shoulder to his visibly irritated cousin. "That means I get a silver piece."

"Might as well take my whole damn coin purse because your sister is a doe-eyed dumbass with a brain the size of a fucking pea."

Fucking Saints. Was she...talking about Cielle? Silent shock held me in place as Nieve settled to stand in the doorway beside Cenric. "Hello," she said harshly, blatantly looking me up and down with a sneer. "For the record, I don't want you here."

My brows raised, and I looked back to the street. "I can go–"

"No!" I heard from behind Nieve.

There she was, apron tied around her neck, grease smeared over the tawny fabric, blonde hair tied in a loose knot atop her head. Cielle's eyes were like a lightning strike when they landed on me. In that moment, I prayed to every fucking Saint that she wasn't trying to set me up with her cousin. "You're not going anywhere," she said easily. "Nieve will apologize."

Nieve swung to where Cielle stood behind her. I could only see Cielle's face as they had some sort of silent conversation of head bobs and brow raises.

"No need for apologies," I cut in, offering a smile. "I'm a big, bad Cabillian soldier, right?" Nieve simply rolled her green eyes and stormed back into the house.

Cenric wheeled himself back as his eyes caught on the bouquet in my hands. "Seashell! He brought your favorite flowers!"

Seashell. It was a fight to keep from smiling.

Cielle's face softened as her gaze landed on what was in my hands. A small smile pricked at her mouth, her eyes crinkling slightly. "Thank you," she said quietly, immediately bringing the bouquet of white roses to her nose before passing it to her brother. "They're lovely." *So are you,* I thought. "Please come in." She stepped aside, leading me through the wide hallway, past a small sitting room and into a large kitchen. Every surface was covered with an array of pots and pans, spilled flour, and all manner of grease and oil. "Cenric, grab a vase for me, bud?"

My first instinct was to ask if he could, but my silent question was quickly put to rest as I watched him maneuver his chair through the kitchen, opening a low cupboard to find a vase and place it on the countertop.

I realized now what the delicious smell was — the unmistakable scent of roasted chicken with rosemary. "You cooked?" I asked.

"No," Nieve called from where I realized she'd been standing over the kitchen table, gathering a number of books and piling them on a small shelf in the corner of the dining area. "She was wearing a greasy apron for the hell of it."

I raised my eyebrows at Nieve. "Do you like to read?" I asked, trying to break the tension as I nodded toward the books in her arms.

Cielle answered before her cousin could. "Nieve is Cenric's tutor while we're here in Taitha."

"We're going to learn about drivas soon!" Cenric shouted, his tiny balled fists shaking with excitement.

Nieve let out an incredulous laugh. "Yeah, we'll learn they aren't real."

"I think they're real," I answered with a shrug.

"I didn't ask what you thought, dick."

"Nieve," Cielle scolded in a singsong voice without looking up from her task. She was pouring melted butter over the roasted chicken, the skin a perfect shade of golden-brown. It seemed like she was floating as she moved through the kitchen, reaching for an open bottle of wine and pulling a goblet from a cupboard. "Be nice to our guest, please."

"Nasty Nieve," Cenric jeered.

Nieve's fists tightened. "I'll show you nasty."

"You'll want a drink for this," Cielle murmured as she pressed the goblet of wine into my hand. Her eyes met mine for only a split second, but it was enough to set a part of me on fire that definitely need not be on fire for a family dinner.

A verbal sparring match ensued as Cenric and Nieve tossed words back and forth, punctuated every few insults by Cielle saying things like *watch it* or *be nice*. I stood in the center of it all, feeling a bit invisible but not at all disappointed by it. I managed to keep my face neutral, but there was a warmth in my chest I'd never felt before. I was in the middle of a family. A normal family.

I relaxed as it sank in that this family was most definitely not royal.

"I'll roll over your toes again," Cenric sniped. He was unflappable while Nieve was becoming visibly wound up with every insult slung her way.

"I'll release Maple," Nieve shot back.

"I already released Maple to help find Twiggy," Cenric said matter-of-factly, crossing his arms.

I didn't know who Maple or Twiggy were, but Nieve had gone silent. Cielle, too. The tense silence was finally broken by Cielle's voice, low and calm. "Cenric, did Maple find Twiggy?"

"She's still looking."

Cielle's eyes closed and her lips pursed. "Okay then. Well, everyone, please be on the lookout for *two* common tree lizards that are currently loose somewhere in the house."

I blinked at her words, watching as Cielle began moving about the kitchen once again. Cenric tried to suppress a giggle and failed miserably as Nieve's face slowly contorted in disgust, and the moment was suddenly interrupted by... Was that a cricket chirping?

Cielle gave me a heartstopping smile. "Welcome to our home."

◆ ◆ ◆

Cenric stuck his fork into a piece of chicken on the serving tray and shoveled it straight into his mouth, which he did not close while he chewed. Neither Cielle nor Nieve gave him so much as a second glance as they piled food on their plates. The normalcy of it all confirmed once again that I wasn't dining with any kind of royalty, and I breathed a sigh of relief.

Cielle took a sip of wine before starting on her own plate. I had to consciously keep my attention off of her mouth. "So you're from Taitha, Miles?"

I cleared my throat. Obligatory small talk. I could do this. "Yes." I passed the tray of sweet corn to Nieve. She took it from me a bit too aggressively and made no attempt to hide a look that clearly communicated she'd rather I be dead. "Well, I'm originally from somewhere else."

"What the fuck does that mean?" Nieve snapped.

Cielle didn't flinch at Nieve's tone. Her icy blue eyes remained on me, unbothered by Nieve's outbursts. I tried to keep my tone easy so as not to draw any kind of pity in response. "I was in a house fire in my twelfth year. I lost my parents and was brought to an orphanage in Taitha by a friend of theirs. All I was told was that I was from a nearby city."

Everyone at the table stopped moving. Even Nieve paused, a brow raised in something that wasn't completely unsympathetic.

Cenric's brows furrowed. "That's sad."

I offered a simple smile and shrugged. "I don't think so. I grew up and became a soldier, which is what I always wanted." I recited it like it was the Saints' honest truth. It had been, at least until Isa questioned it.

The boy took a bite of cabbage that was far too big for his mouth, then slurred his words as he tried to speak around it. "You sheem reary nice for a sholdier."

"A lot of soldiers are really nice," I answered, pouring gravy over the chicken on my plate. "Not all of them, but many of them are."

"That's not what Father says," he quipped.

Cielle straightened in her seat. "He just means that people from the Surging Isles don't particularly care for the Cabillian military."

Nieve snorted. "Yeah, *that's* how he put it."

"Well..." Cielle started, bracing her hands on the deep red tablecloth and clearing her throat. "I may have left something out when I told you my name." My jaw ticked, a sudden panic rising in my gut. "Our parents," she pointed between herself and Cenric, "are sort of the...King and Queen of the Surging Isles. Well, not *sort of*. They *are* the King and Queen of the Surging Isles." Her tone was sheepish, as if she were admitting to eating the last slice of cake, rather than the fact that she was fucking royalty.

I was suddenly outside my body, and though I knew exactly what she meant, I needed to hear the words aloud. "And that means you're..."

She looked down, suddenly very concerned with the napkin in her lap. "Princess of the Surging Isles. As is Nieve." I looked to her cousin, who'd stuffed a large piece of bread in her mouth and gave me a sarcastic smile. "And my brother is Prince Cenric of the Surging Isles."

The implications of her words suddenly rang through me and I felt very uncomfortable in my seat. *How could I have been so stupid?* I pushed myself to stand, bending at the waist in a low bow. "Your Highness, please accept my deepest apologies."

"*Saints*, Miles. Please sit," Cielle laughed. "That is absolutely not necessary."

Nieve did nothing to hide her snickering as I awkwardly lowered myself back onto the chair. I prayed to every Saint that my face didn't show my embarrassment. "Royalty is to be respected."

"We're not royalty here," Cenric chimed, dropping a forkful of cabbage on his shirt and doing his best to scoop it back up with his fingers.

"Some of us are hardly royalty back home," Cielle added with a laugh, leaning forward to dab Cenric's shirt with a napkin. "But what he means is while we're in Taitha, we're going to try living a bit more...simply. I know this house is nothing *simple*, but if we'd had our father's way, we'd be in a gated estate." She straightened in her chair again, reaching for a cut of chicken.

I took a bite of mine and almost groaned. How the hell did this girl know how to cook like this? I assumed she had chefs. Probably did her whole life. She had no need for cooking skills. Distracted by the heavenly taste, I hadn't realized what I was saying when I spoke. "I've never..." I cut myself off before I could make a fool of myself. A *bigger* fool of myself.

"You've never heard of us?" One side of Cielle's mouth turned up in a smirk. "Then our parents got their wish. They didn't shelter us by any means, but they kept us out of the public eye for the most part. They wanted us to be able to move around the city relatively freely, so we're able to go unnoticed in most places." I couldn't imagine a world where someone wouldn't notice her looking like *that*. She placed a small bite of chicken in her mouth and chewed slowly. "Their thinking was the fewer people who knew who we were, the safer we'd be."

I tried to wrap my head around what she was saying. The rumor was that Kauvras was impotent, so he had no children of his own. But I knew if he did, they'd probably be surrounded by a dozen guards everywhere they went. Shit, the King himself was so crowded by guards any time he left the castle, I'd never actually even laid eyes on him.

My chin dipped in a slight nod, and I reached for my goblet to take a deep swig of wine. "If I may ask," I said carefully, "why the low profile here in Taitha?"

"Just because we had a low profile in Coldwater doesn't mean we were completely fucking invisible," Nieve snapped. Cenric rubbed his fingers together at Nieve in a silent gesture saying *another coin, please*. "We still had guards everywhere we went. They were just hidden. There was a list a mile long of places we were forbidden to go and a strict curfew every evening. Can you blame us for taking a chance at being completely normal for once?"

I blinked at Nieve, at the honesty of the answer. I wasn't sure what I'd been expecting, but there was something overwhelmingly human about it all. "I don't blame you in the slightest, actually." I raised my glass in her direction. "In fact, I applaud it."

"We came to Taitha to fix me and my legs," Cenric added, patting a hand against his thigh. His tone was even, but I could tell the words were worn, like he'd spoken them a thousand times.

A pang of hurt radiated through my chest. "You're not broken, though."

Cenric's smile was sudden and bright. "That's what Seashell says."

It's true, he wasn't. His legs may not work the way they're supposed to, but that didn't mean *he* was broken.

Cielle nodded. "Miles is right." She smiled at him before turning to me. "We're here to see the healers in Taitha. If that doesn't work out, then we'll move on to the metalsmiths for corrective braces."

That explained why they were here. "Some of the best healers in the world are here."

"So we've been told." Cielle said the words with a sigh. Cenric pushed his remaining cabbage around his plate for a moment, distracted by something I couldn't see. His sister's eyes were glued to his face. They had similar features, but I couldn't put my finger on what exactly was similar about them. "We still have a few more healers to try, right, Cenric?"

"Right!" he answered, perking up. "They're going to try to help me walk." I saw Nieve's face soften for a split second before tightening again.

Cielle's smile illuminated the entire room. I had to keep myself from staring at her. I shifted in my seat, trying to distract myself from the sight. "How long are you here in Taitha?" I had to change the subject before I flat out proposed marriage to the woman who sat across from me.

"Three months. We've been here a month already. Two more, and it's back to Coldwater." There was feigned excitement in her voice.

I tried to ward off the strange tightening in my chest. "Back to the royal duties, yeah?"

Nieve and Cielle exchanged a look I couldn't decipher, and Cielle gave an almost imperceptible shake of her head.

"Cielle is getting married when she gets home," Cenric chimed. "To the Prince of Zidderune."

My blood had absolutely no right to run cold the way it did when I heard those words. I had to keep my grip from tightening around my fork. Did I think I had an actual chance with her? Of course not. I was only here at this dinner to prove to Nieve that I wasn't a complete asshole.

I did my best to force a smile that looked genuine. "Congratulations." I was somehow able to muster up the word and say it in a way that didn't sound sarcastic.

Cielle looked at her plate, fiddling with a small pendant at her neck. A tiny, delicate seashell. "It's not quite official. No actual betrothal yet. But thank you." Once again, I had no right to feel the way I did. *No actual betrothal yet.* A bolt of relief shot through me. She looked up, giving me a close-lipped smile, her eyes so full of unsaid words that she didn't need to say. She didn't want to marry that man. It wasn't my desire telling me that. It was the truth, evident in those ocean eyes.

Cenric pointed his fork in his cousin's direction. "Nieve will get married someday, too."

She scoffed, almost choking on her chicken. "Yeah fuckin' right."

"Our uncle and aunt, Nieve's father and mother," Cielle began to explain, raising her brows toward Nieve, "have had some trouble securing a suitor."

"It's because I'm a bitch."

"Those weren't precisely the words he used," Cielle said, pursing her lips.

Nieve grinned. "Didn't have to. But I'm well aware of what I am." She reached for the wine bottle in the middle of the table and refilled her glass almost to the rim.

I swallowed hard, desperately trying to distract myself from the sudden cold sweat that dripped down my back. "You know what?" I started, raising my glass to Nieve. Nieve's face scrunched, as if crafting her response to what she thought would be a blow. "You keep being you, Nieve. There is someone out there who will love you not in spite of your view of the world, but because of it."

The table went quiet. Nieve's brows rose in surprise. The expression looked foreign on her face. I knew it wasn't one she wore often. "Thank you," she forced out, though it was barely above a whisper.

Cielle and Cenric turned so quickly to each other that I was surprised they didn't get whiplash. They sat, one staring at the other, eyes widened and mouths hanging open. "Did she just thank him?" Cenric whispered.

Cielle's eyes landed on me and I had to catch my breath. But in the same moment she turned back to Cenric. "I think she did." For a moment, I couldn't tell whether the shock was genuine or a way to rile Nieve further. "Nieve just thanked someone."

Nieve balled her napkin up in her fist and tossed it on the table, eyes rolling so profoundly I was surprised they stayed in her head. "Yeah, yeah."

"It's a miracle!" Cielle sang, shuffling to the other side of the table and planting a kiss on Nieve's forehead. "Nasty Nieve is gone!"

Cenric cheered, throwing his napkin in the air and banging his palms against the table. Nieve, on the other hand, spewed a string of expletives that would make the most seasoned soldier cringe. I sat back and watched the spectacle of it all, smiling to myself as I pushed off the thought that decayed at the edges of this moment.

Honor was never far from my mind, and I'd already compromised it once. I was sitting at a table with the royal family of the Surging Isles. Which meant...

I was sitting at a table of dissenters.

94

Chapter 8

Miles

I felt a bit like I was spinning out of control. Cielle had revealed nothing of the beliefs she and her family held about Kauvras. I didn't know why she'd told me their identities in the first place. She hadn't asked me to keep their secret. She'd simply fed me dinner, thanked me for coming and for somehow coaxing a *thank you* from Nieve, then sent me on my way.

But I didn't miss the way her eyes stayed on me for an extra moment as she and Cenric waved goodbye from the porch.

Fuck.

Sweat beaded and rolled down my back and chest as I ran. I knew this trail like the back of my hand, and the number of times I'd run it since I was a child had to be in the thousands. The fields of leechthorn glowed silver under a sky that was just beginning to lighten, and I knew they'd be cast in gold the moment the sun broke over the horizon. I watched my footing carefully, avoiding the stones in the path that had been the culprit of many twisted ankles over the years.

This early morning run had done the exact opposite of what I'd hoped it would. A clear brain was what I'd come searching for, but all the cool air had done was make it foggier. Heavier. Denser. My teeth gritted as I pushed, the final incline testing my lungs as it had done since I first ran this trail.

I'd been trying to escape something then, too. Mostly Bowen. But I was also trying to escape the fact that there was a life I'd lived before this one that I knew nothing about and never would. I ran to keep myself from wondering about a past I'd never be able to recall.

My breaths sawed in and out of my mouth as I sprinted, slowing to a stop at the small ledge that overlooked a Taitha that would soon rise for another day. There was something about being so high over the rest of the world, looking out from a vantage point no one else had. It set something within me at peace, some unknown part of me that was too deep to dig for, but I could tell was there.

I checked on my mental walls and ensured they were solid and stable before I added a few more bricks.

Fact: Isa was a dissenter. Fact: Cielle and her family were dissenters. They hadn't told me as much, but they didn't have to. Fact: I was forgoing my honor to keep them all alive. Fact: I...didn't feel guilty about it.

But then I started to feel guilty about *not* feeling guilty. I was going against everything I'd ever known in order to keep their secrets. And for what?

I decided not to add that last brick to my wall and instead let it fall to the ground and crumble. I leaned forward, hands on my knees as I caught my breath, staring out over the only city I'd ever known. The city that housed the king I thought I was proud to serve.

No. I stopped the thought. Even if I didn't agree with everything Kauvras was doing, I still swore an oath. That, above all else, was the most important thing. Honor.

Eyes closed, my hands scratched the back of my head as I let out a frustrated grunt. Maybe if I stayed out here long enough, I'd work up the nerve to honor my oath and turn them all in.

Maybe if I stayed out here long enough, I'd work up the nerve to do my fucking job.

Footsteps sounded from down the trail, snapping me from my internal conflict and sending a strange shot of panic through me. That was definitely the sound of human footsteps, not an animal trodding through the forest. No one should be out here. In the years I'd been running this trail, I'd never run into a single person. Not even Bowen knew it existed.

I crouched against the tree line, reaching for the dagger in my boot as I craned my neck to see down the tree-covered pathway. A figure appeared, still shadowed in the low light of dawn, their gait unhurried as they made their way up the trail. My eyes squinted as I listened and heard...humming. That was humming. It was a distinctive tune I'd never heard before, something resembling a lament in its sound. The person held some kind of glass container in one hand, the other hand extended for balance as they traversed the stony trail. When the figure finally moved into the light, I straightened in surprise.

"Cielle?"

The gasp she drew seemed to echo over the leechthorn fields as her hand flew to her chest. "*Saints,*" she hissed. "What the hell are you doing here?"

My brows rose, and all I could do was blink in shock. "I could ask you the same question." Her eyes suddenly trailed down my body, as if she hadn't noticed I was without a shirt until this moment. They continued until they landed on the dagger still clutched in my grip. I bent down to tuck it back in my boot, grunting a mostly unintelligible apology. Then her blue eyes were on my face, chin slightly raised as if it were a fight to keep them there. I tried not to smirk. "I'm on a run."

"I'm..." Her voice trailed off as she stared down at the glass jar in her hand before looking back to me. The smile on her face was almost as bright as the sun that had just crested the horizon, the world suddenly painted in shades of gold. "It's going to sound stupid."

"Try me, Princess."

She made a breathy noise as her tongue trailed over her teeth. "Cenric wakes up in the middle of the night, *every single night,* to feed a few of his lizards and snakes. And since he spilled his jar of crickets, he claims they *aren't happy*. He wheeled into my room an hour ago and woke me up, begging me to catch some more."

"So you're being a good big sister by coming out here and catching bugs for your little brother?"

She crossed her arms, the glass jar clutched firmly in one hand. "I'm out here because it may be the only opportunity to get some peace and quiet from the crickets in the house that no one can seem to find."

My head cocked. "You left the sound of the crickets in your house to...come listen to the crickets outside?"

"There is something infinitely more irritating when it's coming from inside. Besides," she held up the jar, giving it a gentle shake, "I was able to catch a few. Cenric will be happy with these crickets, I'll be happy I got to be alone for an hour, and Nieve will continue to be miserable as always. A world in balance."

I rolled my lips together as a very uncomfortable truth suddenly occurred to me. "Do I need to tell you how dangerous it is to be out here alone?" It was anger that first coursed through me, sudden and unexpected, at the fact that she could've so easily been hurt out here. But I tamped it down, reminding myself I had no claim over this woman and therefore no responsibility for her safety. That was a good excuse, right?

She blew air through her lips. "No. I know. But the draw of solitude was stronger than the fear of being ripped apart by a bear."

"Fair enough. How did you even find this trail?"

"I just..." Her shoulders rose and fell as she looked around a bit wistfully. "Wandered."

We stood in silence, my breath catching in my throat as I tried not to stare too long at the woman in front of me. She seemed so carefree. She was kind and compassionate, evident in the way she cared for her family. It seemed a royal upbringing hadn't hardened her in the slightest. And did she know how beautiful she was? She had to. There was no way she could see her reflection and not recognize her beauty. She didn't belong in a city like this, a city plagued by the sins of its king.

I quickly stopped that thought in its tracks, too.

"You have a tattoo." Her words were both a question and a statement as her finger pointed to my bare shoulder.

Only the very edge of it was visible from the front, so I turned slightly to show her the rest of it. Two ships on a choppy, open ocean that covered my entire left shoulder blade. Iver Finnley, a soldier from another squad, had somehow learned how to press ink into skin and had offered tattoos to any soldier in exchange for coin. On a particularly fuzzy drunken night, Bowen convinced me a tattoo was a good idea.

"What does it mean?" she asked, turning the glass jar in her hand almost absentmindedly.

I glanced over my shoulder, even though I could only see a small part of it. I shook my head and raised a shoulder. "It just means... It's just ships."

She cocked her head. "I thought tattoos were supposed to mean something." Her tone was teasing as she gave me a taunting smile.

Bowen had ended up with a skull inked on his ass. It looked more like a rotten apple though, and I debated asking Cielle what she thought *that* meant. But I thought back to the night Finnley held the needle to my skin. I just...wanted ships. That's what came to my mind when he asked what I wanted.

I shrugged again, unsure of what else to say. "Just ships."

"You live in a landlocked city."

"That I do."

"Do you dream of the open ocean then?" she asked, cocking her head playfully.

I dream of your ocean eyes, actually. "No, Princess."

"I'm just trying to figure out what would possess you to have ships tattooed permanently on your body." Her next words were cautious, like she was dipping a toe in the water to test it. "Maybe your past life."

I was thankful my quick inhale was silent. Her words struck some part of me that had long been sleeping. I wasn't sure why ships had come to my mind and I never thought to wonder the meaning behind it. A tight smile came to my face as I raised a shoulder. "Maybe."

"And the scar?"

My mouth went dry for a reason I couldn't discern. The scar on my other shoulder was another mystery to me. "It happened...before," I said carefully, and pointed to my throat. "This one, too."

She hummed, a bit of an awkward silence descending over us. My hands clenched at my sides of their own volition at the sight of the early morning sunshine on her skin. Her eyes had gone crystalline in the light, the color I'd imagine the clearest of ocean water. Something swam in the waters though, just close enough to the surface that I could see it was there, yet too deep to make out just what it was.

"Well," she started, shifting on her feet and snapping me from my trance, "I'd better be heading back. Don't want Cenric antagonizing Nieve so early in the morning. Makes for a bad day."

I cleared my throat, digging my feet deeper in the dirt as if my stance could ground me. "Let me escort you, please."

She shook her head with a polite smile. "I'll be more than fine. You continue your run. I'm sorry to have interrupted you."

I opened my mouth to tell her this was where the trail ended and my only plan was to get back down the mountain to make it to training on time. But if I insisted on walking with her, I'd look desperate, and that was not something I wanted. Fucking Saints. How the fuck could I manage to make myself look the least pathetic? "Enjoy your day," was all I managed to choke out.

She gave a small wave and turned back down the trail, leaving me staring after her. Every one of my muscles tensed. Even though the sun had risen, the forest wasn't anywhere close to safe. The animals here were nothing compared to what lurked in the Onyx Pass, but there was still all manner of wildlife prowling the forest in search of their next meal. A fact she apparently knew and had deemed worth the risk.

I decided I'd wait until she made it back down to the base of the mountain and out of the forest. From here, I'd be able to see when she left the trail and began to walk beside the leechthorn fields and back to the city. I'd know she made it down safely. That was my rationale. I'd miss training. But I'd miss training to make sure she was safe. A good trade-off.

It was a fight to keep my mind quiet for the half-hour it took Cielle to emerge from the cover of trees, her blonde hair catching the sun as she crossed the field. The greatest danger was behind her now — at least, when it came to the monsters in the forest. The monsters in Taitha were another issue.

If I left now, I could make it to training on time. But what if I started down the trail and she was hurt as she crossed the leechthorn field? No, that wouldn't happen. What the fuck would she be hurt by? An errant rock tripping her and sending her stumbling? The horror. I paced back and forth, nervous that she'd turn around and see my bumbling ass still standing in the same spot she'd left me.

She didn't turn though, and I stared as she traversed the field without incident and was swallowed by the buildings at the edge of the city. Training had started already, and I was well and truly fucked.

Well and truly.

◆ ◆ ◆

"You're distracted."

I didn't nod in agreement even though Bowen was right. I just raised my sword again, ready to work through the next sequence of moves. Training had ended hours ago, but Bowen told me he wanted to practice his swordwork. I knew it was only a matter of time before this conversation started.

"You've missed training four times in the past week," he said between panting breaths.

I chewed the inside of my cheek, parrying and missing his blow only to pivot and swing my own blade, stopping it inches before it pierced his throat. "Got you."

Bowen ignored me, instead moving into the next sequence. "Why are you missing training?"

What version of the truth should I give him?

I didn't have to worry about an explanation, because his face suddenly softened as he dropped his sword and threw an arm around me. "It's okay that you're jealous, brother," he said. He was presenting it as sympathy, but I knew better than anyone it was meant as a boast. "I know you wanted that promotion."

My brows rose, and I tried not to scoff. I wasn't jealous of him. Not in the slightest. But I decided I'd run with it. It was a lie, technically, but it would keep me from having to outwardly lie to him.

Another thing to add to my list of dishonorable acts.

"Yeah," I answered quietly. "I am jealous."

"You'll get there." His voice was maddeningly placating. I tightened my grip on the hilt of my blade, hoping he wouldn't notice my white knuckles. "Vorkalth wants you punished," he continued. "I convinced him to let me talk to you first."

My jaw clenched as I tried to control my annoyance. "Friends with Vorkalth now, are you?"

Without warning, Bowen spun and brought his sword down, but I was faster with mine. Always had been. I easily caught the blow, and though he gave me an approving nod, I could see the irritation on his face that he hadn't bested me. It'd been like that since we were kids. Good sportsmanship had never been his strong suit.

"Yeah, I'm friends with Vorkalth now." He tried to make it come across as a taunt, but there was an edge of desperation in his voice. Like he was trying to prove himself. "Does that make you angry?"

"Makes me feel bad for Vorkalth."

His face turned severe, the same expression he'd wear in the moments before he threw the first punch in a bar fight. I'd seen it plenty of times and knew it meant he wasn't fucking around. "You're on time for training from now on. Got it?"

I desperately wanted to respond with something that would piss him off, but I kept quiet. He was right. I was fucking up my chances at any kind of future promotion by letting my attention drift to anything but my duty. I blinked hard, as if I could manually shift my focus back to where it needed to be.

This was stupid. *I* was stupid, thinking I had any kind of a chance with Cielle. I was throwing away everything I'd worked for.

As if powered by a force greater than me, I backed Bowen into a corner of the training yard, taking advantage of his shitty balance to send him tripping. Satisfaction coursed through me, a reminder of the countless hours of work I'd put into perfecting my swordwork.

I made a promise to myself, then. I wouldn't see Cielle again. She'd be gone in two months, anyway. I'd focus on training, my duty, and the one thing I had above all else — my honor.

Chapter 9
Cielle

Dearest Mother and Father,

　　All is well here. I didn't invite a Cabillian soldier to our massive,
very real, very well-staffed estate last night and I don't think
he's devastatingly handsome and I definitely don't want to take
him to my bed. I definitely wasn't in a dark and dangerous forest
at a questionable hour just to get some peace and quiet, and I

definitely didn't run into said Cabillian soldier. I also didn't stare

at the sweat dripping down his chest and wish I was that sweat.

My thoughts are completely rational. I am definitely stable.

Also Cenric has been on his best behavior and Nieve is being

extremely nice to everyone.

Yours,

Cielle

P.S. Nieve did thank someone. Definitely not a Cabillian

soldier, though.

I crumpled the parchment and added it to the pile, ignoring the indiscernible shouting coming from Cenric's room down the hall. Nieve had hired another childminder, who was here to do a *trial run,* as the woman had put it. Just an hour, and I'd be right in the kitchen if anything went south. Unfortunately, it sounded like it was flying south on the back of a driva at maximum speed.

My hands scrubbed over my face as I tried everything to keep my mind on the task at hand. All I had to do was write my parents a letter. But all I could do was think about the way Miles' hand had gripped his fork last night. The way he smelled like rain and oakmoss. The way he paused, staring at me for an extra moment before he left last night.

Dearest Mother and Father,

All is well here. I invited a Cabillian soldier to our cottage last night. He is devastatingly handsome and I don't regret inviting him in. Don't worry, I'll still marry Prince Rayner when I return home. But until then, I'm going to spend a worrisome amount of time thinking about Miles Landgrave.

Yours,

Cielle

P.S. Nieve thanked someone and Cenric is a terror.

Another crumpled ball of parchment for the pile.

Marrying Prince Rayner of Zidderune would not be the worst of fates. Zidderune and the Surging Isles had a peaceful history, and my father was interested in guaranteeing that for years to come. Hence, the marriage.

I knew from a young age that my marriage would most likely be arranged. That fact had never frightened me though, because my parents' marriage had been arranged and they'd fallen deeply in love. There were far, far worse candidates than the Prince of Zidderune. The few times I'd met him, he'd been almost overly kind and very proper. And Saints, was he easy on the eyes. That didn't hurt at all. Our conversations were always pleasant enough, but he was...dry. Something was missing in our interactions that I'd always imagined my future husband and I would have. Not to mention, Zidderune was on the other side of the world, so I'd be leaving behind everything I'd ever known.

I blew air through my lips and tried to think what the hell I could write in this letter that wouldn't set alarm bells ringing. I could already picture my mother combing over every word, searching for hidden meaning indicating we were in grave danger.

Cenric's wicked laugh sounded down the hall — the kind of laugh that signaled trouble was underfoot. The childminder's shriek followed. "Put it away this instant!"

"He doesn't even bite!" Cenric yelled in return. I squinted my eyes shut, counting the childminder's footsteps through the hallway until she arrived where I sat in the kitchen, eyes wide and face red with anger.

"Your payment," I muttered, pointing to the coins I'd stacked at the edge of the table. The childminder snatched the coins before stomping out the door without a single word. I hadn't even bothered to learn her name.

Cenric wheeled into the doorway then, his facial expression neutral. A mouse sat perched on his knee, perfectly still as Cenric stroked a finger delicately over its tiny head. "That one didn't like mice, did she, Luna?"

I folded my arms on the table, dropped my head, and let out a groan. "Cenric."

He wheeled himself forward, the tiny gray mouse hopping into his cupped hand as he settled in front of me. The little thing was cute, I had to admit. But it was a fact of life that not everyone would agree with that.

"Oops," he said with a mischievous smile.

I swung my legs to face him, my hands landing on his knees delicately. His trousers were thin enough that I could feel the way his kneecaps jutted out to the sides. I knew the skin was mangled and stretched as it tried to accommodate the twisted bones beneath. "Why are we here in Taitha?" I asked quietly.

"So the healers can fix–" He cut himself off. "So the healers can help me walk."

I nodded. "In order to do that, Nieve and I will have to leave the house sometimes to go talk to the healers and schedule appointments for you, which means you need someone here to watch you."

"Yes, I know."

I straightened, rubbing the bridge of my nose. I didn't want to admit that a part of me felt like I'd bitten off more than I could chew with this trip. I didn't like the feeling of being stressed. I'd learned very quickly that my life had been very cushy back home. Something I would never take for granted again. "That means you can't keep scaring off every single childminder with your animals."

"But I don't want a childminder that doesn't like my animals." His tone was so innocent. To him, this was the most important thing in the world. Not his legs. Not learning to walk. Just his rodents, reptiles, and birds.

My chest hollowed out with a sigh. "Just try not to scare the next one off, okay? Maybe don't show them your animals. Play some games or do a puzzle instead." His brow furrowed as if I'd just told him he and his childminder should watch paint dry.

The front door swung open then and Nieve pushed through carrying an armful of books. "Was that the childminder I just saw stomping down the street?"

I stood abruptly, my chest tight with tension. "Watch him for a bit, would you?" I asked Nieve, cutting off her would-be colorful answer. "I need to run out."

◆ ◆ ◆

I didn't even know where I was going. I just knew I needed to leave the house. The stress of the last month was weighing so heavily on me that it felt like a living thing, clinging to my back. The lack of a consistent childminder, the end of the list of healers to try nearing ever closer, an impending marriage and the loss of my short-lived independence... I needed a moment.

My brain was quickly distracted as I walked up and down the streets of this side of Taitha, admiring the architecture that was so different from Coldwater's. Everything here was heavy and solid, constructed of gray stone and large logs. Even the castle was clunky, that same gray stone making up the behemoth of a structure at the center of the city.

I met the gazes of more than a few people as I walked. None of them, thankfully, showed even a hint of recognition. I wasn't sure how long it'd been, just that I noticed the sun had begun to sink toward the horizon and the houses suddenly looked less welcoming. I'd completely lost track of where I was. My first instinct was to panic, but I quelled that feeling and instead let myself enjoy it. When would I ever be lost in the streets of a foreign city again?

Music began to float down the street, some assortment of pipes and strings playing a jaunty melody. The sound beckoned me closer and I followed, down another street, around a corner and to...a pub. I blinked in surprise. Never in my life had I set foot in a pub, but before I could talk myself out of it and walk back to the cottage, I pushed through the door.

The Griffin's Back was packed to the gills, and every person seemed so incredibly different I couldn't quite get a read on the average patron. I saw who I'd always assumed would be in a pub — men with beards and mugs of ale clutched in dirty hands. But next to them was a table of women, none of them older than fifty years, all seemingly well-dressed enough to make me think they wouldn't belong in a place like this. A man in an intricately stitched surcoat spoke with another man who appeared to be a beggar, the two of them throwing their heads back in laughter.

It was a crowd of people who did not match in any way, but somehow wove together to create a beautiful tapestry.

I pulled an empty stool from the bar, folding my arms in front of me as a small, stout woman appeared on the other side of the counter. She gave me a genuine smile, showcasing her yellowed teeth and rosy cheeks. "What'll it be, darlin'?"

"Um..." *What did I want?* "Ale, please," I called over the roar of the crowd.

"What kind?"

I blinked, trying to play it cool. "The alcoholic kind?"

Her soft brown eyes crinkled and she pointed a finger in front of herself. "I know what you'll like." She poured foamy liquid from a pitcher into a mug and slid it in front of me. "Tastes the least like piss out of all the ales we 'ave here. Drink up."

I smiled in thanks, slid a coin across the counter, and raised the mug to my lips. *Oh Saints.* I cringed, trying to keep myself from spitting it right back into the mug. *This* was the one that tasted the least like piss? A shudder moved through my body, and I must not have done a good enough job at repressing it because the barkeep erupted into laughter.

Her grin was crooked as she gave me a wink. "Ye don't drink it for the taste."

"I can see why."

"Keep drinkin'." She nodded toward my mug. "You'll come to find after two or three, it's not s'bad."

I don't think there was anything I could do to make this beer *not* taste like piss, but I followed her prompt and tried another sip. This one was almost harder to force down than the first, and my throat warmed slightly as I managed to swallow.

The back of my neck prickled uncomfortably as a presence suddenly took up the stool next to me. I tensed automatically, trying to glean as much as I could in my periphery.

"Mind if I take a seat, Miss?"

I turned to see a Cabillian soldier with a small gold bar pinned at each shoulder. His black leathers were strapped to a body so impressively fit, I could see the muscles through the material. A bright white smile was etched into a chiseled face, one that looked like it belonged to a charming prince in one of the picturebooks I had as a young girl. He was the definition of perfection. Yet somehow...completely underwhelming.

I managed a tight smile. He'd done nothing to make me uncomfortable and yet, I had no desire to have any sort of conversation with him. "Not at all." *Please don't talk to me. Please don't talk to me. Please don't talk to me.*

"Haven't seen you around here."

Dammit.

I took a measured breath, trying not to seem angry that I now felt obligated to continue this exchange. "First time here." I took another sip of ale which somehow tasted a bit less like piss. I took advantage of the lack of taste by chugging down a sizable amount.

The man whistled. "A drinker. I like it."

My experience with being approached by men in pubs extended to what I'd heard my distant cousins talk about when we held gatherings with our extended family. These were cousins far enough removed from the direct royal bloodline that a trip to a pub raised no eyebrows aside from those raised at their good looks.

"Hmm," was all I could manage. I shifted in my stool, trying to angle myself away from him as the room suddenly felt ten degrees warmer. He had the looks of a Saint, and all his attention was turned on me. But I didn't want to talk. I wanted to sit here, drink my piss beer, and take a few deep breaths.

"Let me buy your next drink." His voice was dangerously smooth. I could see how another woman could fall quickly under its spell.

"Oh, um, no, thank you," I answered as pleasantly as I could. "This is my last one and then I must be on my way."

He swung his body to face me, casually propping his elbow on the bar as he stared down at me. "Or you could come with me." His accompanying smile was as dazzling as it was terrifying, and my mouth suddenly took on a sour taste that had nothing to do with the ale.

I couldn't get a read on his intentions, and that told me all I needed to know. This man was large enough that he could physically overpower me without difficulty if he didn't like my answer. "I'm actually betrothed," I said. Not the entire truth. But I couldn't say, *Well, I'll be engaged in the next three months most likely, so no.* And I was hoping maybe he'd have more respect for my fiancé than he did for me.

The man reached forward, callused hand snatching at mine like he owned it. He pulled it to his face, turning my palm over in his. "I see no ring."

I swallowed hard, pulling slightly against his grip, but he made no attempt to let me go. I desperately wanted to look over my shoulder. *Don't cause a scene. Please.* I was terrified to look around and see everyone staring. But I think what would've been even more terrifying was if no one was watching at all.

I tried again to pull away. The man's grip tightened as he yanked my hand to his mouth and planted a kiss against my knuckles. "Most women would be honored by a proposition from a man like me." His voice was even, but I could recognize an edge of irritation to it.

Panic twisted in my gut, nausea rising with the sensation. I tore my hand from his grasp, but he easily snatched it back, his grip even tighter than before. I winced at the feeling of... Saints, it felt like the bones of my hand were grinding together. Every muscle in my body tensed as he leaned in and ran his tongue over the shell of my ear.

I'd spent so much time standing in the mirror, practicing what I'd do and say in a situation like this. I thought it would be easier to speak up for myself, but all that practice failed me in this moment. The real thing was much, much more terrifying than any pretend scenario I could cook up in my head.

"You've got fire in you," he snarled antagonistically. All my survival instincts had jumped ship, leaving me completely frozen instead. "Good thing I'm not afraid of getting burned."

"Please," I mumbled, and it was more of a pathetic squeak than anything. Dammit. "Leave me be."

His breath caressed my cheek and I shuddered involuntarily, something he easily picked up on. "Looks like you don't want me to, sweetheart."

"Bowen," a voice sounded from behind me. If it had been anyone else saying it, it would've blended in with the crowd of patrons. But the low rasp had already made its way into my head, sparking my recognition immediately. Miles Landgrave stood behind me, staring straight over my head at the man. "She told you to leave her alone."

The man — Bowen — still had my hand in his, and he sucked his teeth as dropped it and sat back, his palms raised to the air. "Oh, come on. We're just having a little fun. Weren't we, sweetheart?"

I turned back to Bowen. Every quick-witted response I'd ever thought to use in a scenario such as this one had evacuated my brain, leaving a single word in their wake. "No."

He raised a brow. "What woman doesn't want to be chased?"

Miles was silent behind me and I was finally able to find my own words. "This one, actually. And every other woman, as well."

Bowen's jaw ticked, his brows furrowing for a split second before he gave a smile dripping in sarcasm. "Well then, it's a good thing Landgrave's here to save you, isn't it?" His eyes flicked to where Miles stood behind me, some kind of silent exchange happening between the men.

Miles' stance didn't relax. One hand flexed at his side. "I believe there's an officer's meeting starting soon, Bowen."

Bowen sniffed, his eyes distant for a moment before he turned them back to me. "Enjoy your evening, Miss. And Landgrave," he said, a smug look on his face as he stood mere inches away from Miles, "it's Lieutenant Bowen."

To his credit, Miles' face remained neutral, but something told me he was feeling anything but. "Yes, Lieutenant Bowen." His hand raised to his forehead in salute as Bowen gave a self-satisfied hum and pushed past him.

Miles' eyes tracked the Lieutenant as he made his way through the crowd of patrons and out the door. His shoulders were still visibly tense as he turned back to me, and I willed myself to relax. That, however, was a difficult thing to accomplish under Miles' smoldering gaze. "Like he said, enjoy your evening."

He spun on his heel. It took me a moment to realize he was leaving. "Wait."

Broad shoulders turned back to me. What was I going to do, invite him for a drink? I'd asked him to come for dinner just to piss off Nieve. He'd done it. The man owed me none of his time, and I didn't really have any business with him anymore. But damn, I wish I did.

"I..." I started, hoping I could come up with something quickly. "I wasn't expecting to see you here."

He raised a brow, and in the lantern light I was able to get a better view of the scar across his throat. I'd wanted to ask him about it at dinner, then again when I saw him on the trail, but couldn't just do it outright. The gnarled skin moved when he let out an unexpected laugh. "I wasn't expecting to see *you* here. Though you seem to have a pattern of turning up in unexpected places." He took a few cautious steps toward me. "Apologies for Bowen." He cleared his throat, his gaze faltering for a split second. "*Lieutenant* Bowen."

"He must be one of the violent, lawless brutes my father told me about."

Miles' face broke into a devastating smile. I wondered if he knew how spectacular he was to look at. "No. He's harmless." But something in the way his smile wavered made me question his response.

"Do you..." I started, readjusting my legs where they sat against the rest at the bottom of the barstool. Here goes. "Would you like to sit?"

Silence was his only response for a long moment. His face remained expressionless, the sight absolutely maddening because I could tell that just like before, there was something behind it. I swore I saw a spark of something akin to conflict flash over his features, but it was gone before I could tell for certain. Finally, he pointed a thumb over his shoulder toward the door. "Thank you for the offer, but I actually have to run."

Shit. How could I keep him here? "You just *happened* to be conveniently in the right place to save me from Lieutenant Dickwad?"

He huffed a laugh and ran his tongue over his top lip. "I *happened* to be walking by after training and caught sight of Bowen sitting at the bar with an unfortunately familiar look on his face. Thought I'd check out who was on the receiving end of it."

"Sounds a bit like you're still following me."

Miles' mouth turned up in a slight smile as he shook his head. "Not this time, Princess. Pure coincidence."

I internally cringed at the title, just like I had when I ran into him on the mountain trail. He stared intently at me, and though his eyes never left mine, I had the sneaking suspicion he'd already looked me over more than once to make sure I was, in fact, alright. "Well, I appreciate the help. But you should stay." I shrugged, trying my best not to show that his response would determine my mood for the rest of the night. "Let me buy you a drink to say thank you."

He glanced over his shoulder, emotionless except for those eyes. There was something turbulent behind them, something lurking unseen in the darkness. I'd just resigned myself to saying goodbye when he gave a quick nod. "One drink. And I'm buying."

Chapter 10
Miles

She had to be aware that every single person in this pub had their eyes on her. Some were stealing glances between sips of ale. Some were blatantly staring. Her eyes, however, were on me.

The promise I'd made myself to stay away from Cielle? That dissolved like sugar in water the moment I realized it was her suffering through Bowen's advances. Rationality was nowhere to be found and my honor was being held hostage by the anger I felt toward my brother.

"I've never been to a pub before," she said as I lowered myself to the stool beside her. "It was actually kind of fun until..."

"He really is harmless," I murmured quickly, but I don't even think *I* was convinced of that myself. I nodded to the barkeep as she placed a mug in front of me.

Cielle's body was angled just enough to face me. "You know him well?"

The sigh that left my lips was arguably involuntary. I took a gulp of ale — not the best I'd had, but far from the worst — and tried to formulate a response that wouldn't give Cielle the impression that I was anything like Leo Bowen. "He's something like a brother to me. The closest thing to family I have."

Cielle was quiet for a moment as she tapped her fingers against her mug. "Well, I know better than anyone you can't choose your family."

My chest shook with a laugh. "He and I were the only two close in age at the orphanage. All the other children were either a few years younger or a few years older. He'd been there for a while already before I arrived."

"What happened to his parents?" There was a feeling of gentleness in her voice when she spoke.

I blinked. Most people shied away from questions like this. Usually, when a person found out I was an orphan, there was an awkward, hurried apology and a not-so-discreet rush to change the subject to something more palatable. "Well," I started, "Bowen isn't technically an orphan. He was a bastard and his mother was a drunk. She dumped him there when he was eight or nine." I couldn't help but grimace when I said it.

"That's...awful. Truly, that's awful."

"It is." If there was one benefit about knowing nothing about your past, it was the fact that there was no memory of rejection to sting you. For that, I was thankful. That ghost of a memory appeared in my head, my mother's black hair shining in my mind.

"Seems like a right asshole, though." I looked down at her, unable to keep a chuckle from escaping as she pulled me from my thoughts. Her eyebrows raised, a smile forming on her lips as she shrugged. "He does. I'm sorry."

"There's no need to apologize, because you're absolutely correct, Princess." My shoulders shook for another moment before I exhaled the same sigh I'd been letting out since I was twelve. "Bowen is very good at getting what he wants."

"Is that why he's *Lieutenant* Bowen now?"

"No, he did earn that rightfully." Even if he didn't deserve the honor of the title. I reached up to scratch the back of my head, hoping she'd change the subject instead of prodding further. I shouldn't be sharing anything negative with the princess of a rival kingdom. I shouldn't be sharing anything *at all* with the princess of a rival kingdom.

Her eyes quickly darted around the pub. "It's the harmless ones you have to watch out for."

"What about your fiancé?" I blurted. *Fuck.* I didn't even feel the words come up, so there was nothing I could've done to stop them. My eyes remained on my mug, fingers splayed around it, ears ringing with embarrassment.

She was silent for so long, I was sure my question had been lost to the noise of the pub around us. I began to thank Onera that Cielle hadn't heard me, until she suddenly answered. "Not my fiancé yet. And there's nothing wrong with him." Her tone was the definition of neutral. There was no disdain or contempt in the way she said it, but there was sure as hell no love or excitement.

"That's good." I didn't know what else to say, but it was the truth. It *was* good that there was nothing wrong with him. Not good for me, but good for her.

"The Prince of Zidderune," she breathed, her eyes locked somewhere on the other side of the bar, but her mind was very clearly somewhere far away. Maybe in Zidderune with her prince. "He's very kind. I believe we'll have a very nice life together." Her tone had turned flat now, like she was reciting the words from a script she knew by heart.

I ran my tongue over my lips, trying to keep myself from saying the wrong thing. But I had a feeling anything I said in answer to her opinion would be wrong.

"One day, we'll be King and Queen of Zidderune." Her voice was quiet enough that only I heard. "Queen Cielle. If you say it quickly enough, it sounds like a disease. *Oh no,*" she said in a mock worried voice. "Poor woman. She caught the *queencielle.* She only has days to live."

I narrowed my eyes, looking down at her as she took an impressively long drink of ale. She wiped her mouth with the back of her hand and placed her empty mug on the bar. "I think it sounds nice," I offered.

She spun quickly, staring at me from under her fringe of long, dark lashes. The low light of the pub set her eyes blazing like the blue center of a fire burning too hot. "It *should* sound nice, right?" The line that formed between her brows told me she wasn't simply talking about the sound of her name. "I'll have nothing to worry about for the rest of my life aside from walking through the gardens and selecting table linens and flowers for parties. I'll move away from the ocean to his castle in Theorrid. I'll give him children and our first son will grow up to take the throne and our daughters will be married off. Just like me." She almost seemed to be out of breath. Her eyes searched mine, as if she'd find reassurance somewhere within them if she just looked hard enough. "It should sound nice, right?" she repeated, her words barely above a whisper.

At some point, the barkeep had replenished her ale, and she grabbed the mug and threw it back. Her hand trembled ever so slightly as she emptied it, my eyes wide as she slammed it down and reached up to signal the barkeep for another one.

Her eyes looked different when her gaze found me again. A bit glassy, but not because of the ale. She sat up straighter, running her hands over her lap to smooth invisible wrinkles in her skirts. Her smile was polite, as if it suddenly occurred to her that she'd been terribly rude. "Apologies. I shouldn't be talking about this. I...shouldn't even be here in this pub."

I reached out and placed a hand on her arm. I absolutely shouldn't have, but it was like I'd lost control of my movements. Against my own volition, my thumb began to trace circles over her arm. I had to physically will it to stop. *What the fuck was wrong with me?* Her eyes tracked down to the point of contact between us. Before my mind could wander anywhere else, I forced myself to drop my hand. "Don't apologize."

Her face had gone carefully blank when she looked up at me again, but her eyes were alight with the truth. Saints, the way her eyes always seemed to signal what was actually going on in her head. The real her was in there, drowning and powerless, arms waving in a desperate attempt for help. I knew this woman had to have been trained in etiquette as well as how to behave in uncomfortable situations, and she was handling it beautifully. But her eyes.

She let out an exasperated breath. "Do you ever feel like it's all been decided for you?"

I hadn't been given a mask to wear, and yet I'd been wearing one for years. The mask of the person everyone expected me to be. The same mask of the person I always thought I was. The mask of a dutiful and honorable soldier, always doing what was expected of him without hesitation or question. It was the mask I'd intended to wear for the rest of my life regardless of the one issued to me by the military.

I stared down at the beautiful woman before me. She'd unmasked herself to me. I supposed I could do a bit of the same.

"Every damn day."

Her eyes dropped to her lap, the look on her face lodging physical pain deep in my gut. "Hey," I said, desperate to say anything to take that look away. "If you had a single day to do anything you wanted, anything in the entire world, how would you spend it?"

Her lashes fluttered gently as one side of her mouth raised in a thoughtful smile. It seemed she knew I was simply trying to distract her, but she was choosing to play into my hand. I wasn't even sure where the question had come from, but I was suddenly desperate to know her answer. "I'd learn to play the harp. Well, I'd learn as much as I could in a day."

My brows rose. I wasn't sure the answer I'd been expecting, but it hadn't been that. That seemed so...achievable. "What's stopping you from doing that now?"

She shifted in her seat, the toe of her boot tapping against the leg of her barstool. "My father placed more of an emphasis on books and learning. Don't get me wrong, I don't disagree with that. I learned to play the violin, as that was deemed a *worthwhile* endeavor in his eyes. And I do love the violin, but I've always been drawn to the harp." She rapped her fingers against the bar. "'*An instrument for dreamers*', he always says." She was silent for a long moment, and I watched as the momentary excitement at the idea of learning to play the harp melted away, replaced by the coldness of reality. "And dreams only last until you wake up."

The answer resounded through me, but it was followed by a sick feeling. I couldn't keep my leg from bouncing nervously.

"You're in Taitha for another two months. That's more than enough time to pick up the basics."

Cielle straightened, her head shaking as she plastered an obviously forced smile on her face. It was a smile I could tell had been practiced a million times. "I'm here for Cenric. And to get Nieve to stop being so...*Nieve.*" I tried to think of a response, something to convince her to do this small thing for herself, but she spoke before I could. "And you? If you had one day to do anything?"

There was no need for me to think of an answer, because it was immediately on my tongue. Now I just needed to decide whether I was actually going to say the words. I reached for my ale, taking a large swig to fortify myself before placing it back on the bar with enough force that Cielle blinked in surprise. "I'd spend it in a seedy pub with the most beautiful woman I've ever met."

◆ ◆ ◆

I told Cielle I'd stay for one drink, and I honored my word. Cielle, however, made no such promise, and somewhere between her stories of growing up in the castle of Coldwater to the anxiety of finding help for her brother, Cielle got drunk.

Very drunk.

The first sign was her hands — her carefully measured movements suddenly became more clumsy after her fourth mug of ale. I didn't question her as mug after mug was set in front of her, but I offered her water at least a dozen times from the canteen at my hip. She declined each time, telling me she grew up around the sailors in Coldwater, and they'd taught her that water was for ships and whiskey was for people.

No part of me had intended to let her lose control like this until suddenly she was seven mugs deep and leaning in to tell me she was exhausted.

"I think..." she muttered, her words slurring together, "I might be-e-e...a li'l...drunk."

"Do you think so?"

"It's time...to go-o-o-o...home."

I laughed and stood, offering a hand. "I think that's probably a good idea, Princess. Think Nieve will have my balls for bringing you home so drunk?"

She took my hand, the delicate skin of her palm the complete opposite of the roughened skin of mine. "You, Sir, are fa-a-a-ar dr-druh...drunker than...I am, so probably not." I was about to correct her and tell her I was far from intoxicated, but her head fell back with a laugh that turned into a very over pronounced, very painful-sounding hiccup. "And don't you call me Princess, soldier."

"You are a princess, Princess." She found her feet, immediately swaying forward violently. I managed to grab her by the shoulders before she toppled over, trying to be as delicate as I possibly could with her. "Easy there. Don't lose your footing." There had to be some rule about touching royalty, and I'd already done it once tonight.

That, and I almost felt like she was a figment of my imagination. Like if I touched her one too many times, she'd fade away in a wisp of smoke.

"I like it," she started, hiccuping loudly and swallowing hard, "when you touch me." Her face drew into something like surprise as she covered her mouth. "Oh no-o-o-o-o. I shouldn't've said that. Shh."

Every muscle in my body froze as my chest seemed to constrict around my heart. I'd never had a reaction like this to anyone. She liked it when I touched her? *Fuck.* There was no reason I should be reacting this way.

And yet.

I gently nudged her toward the door, willing my heartrate to return to some semblance of normal. "Let's get you home, Princess."

"Yes, Sir. Take me home, soldier!" Her answer was far too loud as she swiped a hand across her forehead in mock salute. If there was anyone who wasn't staring at her before, they were now, their eyes trailing after her as we walked out into the street. She began lifting her knees clumsily in something that resembled a march. "How's my...march look, Sh-oldier? Good enough for the Cabillian m-m-military?"

Dusk had fallen, only the tops of the buildings still gilded by the sun. Cielle looked so utterly ridiculous I couldn't help but smile. "Perfect."

She threw her head back and laughed, the sound a sweet symphony of every beautiful noise in existence.

She's leaving in two months to marry a prince. She's out of your league by a longshot. She's a dissenter.

I was absolutely fucked.

We wound our way through the streets of Taitha, slowly drawing closer and closer to her cottage on Rosemary Street. I offered her water again, and this time she accepted, slugging it down before tossing my canteen — still open — back to me. She leaned in, rising to the tips of her toes as she stumbled beside me, and her whisper was anything but quiet. "I have to-o-o be sober...time the by I'm home."

Time the by? This was bad. "Not sure that's going to happen."

"I'm sober as a duck!" she declared. *Sober as a duck?* Was that a phrase they used in Coldwater? Come to think of it, I'd never seen an inebriated duck before. So, Cielle was definitely not sober as a duck.

I tried to steer her in a straight line as her steps began to pull to the right. "I'll make sure you get inside okay."

"You're sweet, y'know that?" The words ran together as she said them, a string of syllables I almost couldn't understand. "Is this how yo-o-ou entice me into letting you in my house so-o-o you can force your leechthorn on me?"

I was glad she was walking in front of me so she couldn't see me flinch. The words were quiet enough that no one passing us on the street could've heard, but I still took a quick look around to make sure. A short exhale left my nose as I fought to keep dread from rising in me.

Because at the end of the day, even though that was absolutely not my plan, her words were not far outside the realm of possibility. I always felt the reason Kauvras allowed foreigners into the city was because each one was an easy target should they show any sign of treason.

The response I managed to muster up was weak. "I'm not that much of a monster, Princess."

She suddenly turned around to look at me, her unsteady steps coming to a halt. It was all I could do not to crash into her. Though her eyes were heavy-lidded, there was something in her stare that was unmistakably sober. Her brows furrowed for a moment, almost as if she were searching my face for an answer to a question she hadn't asked. Then her eyes flickered to my mouth, and my chest tightened again. I had to pray to every damn Saint for the strength to keep my hands to my fucking self.

"I don't think you're a monster at all," she said quietly. These words were not slurred. They were clear as a blue sky, almost the same color as the eyes that had arrested every single one of my mental faculties.

We stood in the street, the people shuffling around us a mere blur as I stared down at Cielle. It was the most vulnerable I'd ever felt in my life, the most exposed. She was staring straight through me, straight through my mental walls to what was hiding behind them.

"I'm the monster they need me to be," I breathed in response.

"Monsters don't exist." Her head shook as if the answer had truly been that simple all along. "They're just weak men in disguise trying to take what little power they can." She turned on her heel, her arms shooting out beside her to keep her balance. "Come along, soldier!" Her voice betrayed nothing, as if she hadn't just completely tilted my world forever.

I stood for an extra moment, watching her blonde waves swing over her shoulders as the floodgates opened, my dread spilling out. Because monsters, I knew for a fact, were very real, though I wasn't afraid of becoming one of them. I was afraid I already was.

Kindly deliver to the Port of Coldwater

Dearest Mother and Father,

~~I got hopelessly drunk last night and may have invited the~~ ~~handsome soldier into my bed. Can't really remember, though.~~ ~~Whoops.~~

Things are going well. Cenric's appointments have proven fruitless so far, but we are still holding out hope that the answer lies somewhere in Taitha.

We hope all is well back home.

Yours,

Cielle

Chapter 11

Cielle

"Good morning, dipshit," Nieve said cheerfully as I walked into the kitchen. "You look awful."

I stumbled to the stove, bleary-eyed and exhausted, and spooned oats and fruit into a bowl. "Thanks for that."

"You're also a fucking idiot. Getting drunk with a Cabillian soldier when I had no idea where you'd run off to? Dumbass move, Cielle. Possibly your dumbest move of all."

I settled at the table across from Nieve, an array of books open before her. "Thanks for that, too." She was planning Cenric's lessons for the week, and scribbled notes adorned a sheet of parchment to her right. The sound of Cenric's wheels rolling over the floorboards in his room was a comforting sound. I took a bite of oats, trying to choke it down over the threat of nausea in my stomach as snippets of last night materialized in my head, blurry and spotty.

My palm smacked against my forehead as I pieced it all together. I'd marched through the street. Marched. And did I... Did I tell Miles I liked it when he touched me? Oh my fucking Saints. My cheeks heated with embarrassment as I prayed that part had been an ale-induced dream.

My cousin let out a mangled sigh. "But he's not...entirely unpleasant."

Nieve's eyes were on her work while I stared at her in disbelief, all traces of nausea and embarrassment suddenly gone "Was that another nicety from you? Might have to bring Miles around more often. Might even have to retire Nasty Nieve and start calling you Nice Nieve."

Her eyes rolled. "In your fucking dreams."

Nieve looked at me pointedly, a single brow raised as if she knew exactly what I was thinking. Considering we'd grown up together, I wasn't surprised she did. "Don't remember much, do you?"

I ran my hands through my hair, trying to work through the knots. "Well, I woke up alone, so I assume you scared him off."

She scoffed. "You tried to convince him to join you in bed."

I cringed, trying to recall something, anything from the end of the night. There was nothing. "So I made a fool of myself?"

"As you usually do," she sniped, a thread of nastiness in her tone, "but not any more than normal. Your soldier is just too *honorable* to come to your bed." The words were a sneer, as if it was the most negative thing she could think to say about him.

"Is it a bad thing that I proved you wrong about Cabillian soldiers?"

Her mouth turned downward as she shot me a look that told me she knew I was right and she didn't like it one bit. I, however, had to work to contain the smile that had threatened to form on my lips.

A knock sounded from the front door. Nieve didn't raise her eyes from the books in front of her. "Better go get yourself ready."

My eyes darted to the door, a shiver of anticipatory hope fluttering in my stomach. I tamped it down, because surely it couldn't be... "For?"

126

Her only answer was a hum under her breath. I shuffled to my feet and to the front door, throwing it open to see the one person I'd hoped to the Saints I would.

Miles wasn't in his leathers today. He was in brown trousers and a shirt that I could tell was meant to be loose but absolutely wasn't, his form straining against the thin, white fabric. My mouth went dry staring at him as I pulled my bottom lip between my teeth. I suddenly became highly aware of the dark circles shadowed beneath my eyes and the rat's nest I called hair.

"Morning. I told Nieve last night that I'd come to secure the ramp to the steps of your porch before my afternoon training today," he said, a small bag slung over his shoulder.

Nieve's voice sounded from the kitchen. "You almost ate shit walking up last night."

Miles shrugged. "She's not exactly wrong." He glanced over his shoulder to the plank that laid over the steps, the mid-morning light gilding his honey-brown skin. "A few nails and it should be much safer...for everyone."

My eyes closed in embarrassment, my knuckles white where I gripped the edge of the door. "Thank you." It was all I could manage to say as I tried to keep my tone from conveying the regret I felt for getting so fucking shitfaced. There was something terrifying knowing there was a portion of time I was very much involved in, but remembered nothing about. I'd completely lost control. Nieve was right. I'd been a dumbass.

"Of course, Princess," he quipped, a knowing smile on his face. He dropped his bag on the porch, its contents rustling as he pulled out a mallet and a handful of nails.

I stood awkwardly, unsure of exactly what I should be doing. "Would you like me to make you some tea?" The words were weak. *Fucking pathetic, Cielle.*

"Is that what it'll take for you to sit out here with me?"

Heat flushed through me and I had to avert my gaze. When I first met Miles, I thought he'd be fun to rile up the same way Nieve was. Watching him get flustered was a bit of a thrill. But now he'd turned it around on me, and I felt like a bumbling mess every time he looked in my direction. "I can sit out here without tea."

"Good," he said, gesturing to the bench on the porch, "because I don't particularly like tea."

I smiled, the nerves slightly dissipating as I lowered myself to the bench. "Me either."

"You feel okay this morning?" His eyes were focused on the task in front of him as he lined up a nail and started on it with the mallet.

"I think so." It wasn't the entire truth. My stomach was most definitely unsettled and the sunshine was far too bright. But most of what I felt had nothing to do with the alcohol. "You?"

His dark eyes flicked to me for a split second. "I feel great."

A fragile silence descended between us, punctuated by his mallet strikes and passersby padding across the street in front of the house. "Thank you," I blurted, "for making sure I got home last night. I'm really sorry I was so drunk."

He huffed a laugh. "Don't apologize, Princess. Happy to help." His eyes trailed up and down the wooden board, checking his work so far. "How is Cenric?"

I dropped my head back. "Still a bit of a terror. Still without a childminder."

Miles paused for a moment, reaching for another nail. "What if I can help you with that?"

One side of my mouth turned up. "Fancy yourself a bit of a childminder?"

His laugh was raspy, and his throat moved beneath the scar that marred it. "No. But I know someone who could be. Let me ask her and I'll let you know."

There was a pang of...jealousy? No. It couldn't be jealousy. But it kind of felt like it. Had I ever even been jealous before? Miles said he'd ask *her*. Who was this *her*? I blinked hard, trying to get a hold of myself, my leg beginning to bounce nervously. He reached for a nail from his bag, my eyes tracking his scarred fingers as they situated it between his teeth and then hammered another one into the board. *Good fucking Saints.*

I couldn't be thinking this. I wasn't engaged, but I was going to be. The moment I stepped off that ship onto the docks of Coldwater, I may as well be wearing a ring.

"My...friend, Isa, is looking for a job."

I feigned indifference, because finding a reliable childminder for Cenric for the next two months was one of my top priorities. Because of that, I tried not to analyze the way he called her a *friend*. "Does she have any experience with children?"

Miles kept working, but his movements seemed to tighten uncomfortably. "Not exactly. She does have experience with unruly men, though." My eyes narrowed on the man in front of me. "I met her at the Blushing Dove."

"The Blushing..." I trailed off, connecting the dots he'd left unjoined. I didn't need to guess what the Blushing Dove was.

"I hope her current...*profession* doesn't deter you. She really is great."

The laugh that escaped me was involuntary. "I wouldn't care if she was an assassin hired to kill me. If she can handle Cenric and his animals, she's hired." That was the Saints' honest truth. I did, however, have one burning question. But how the fuck was I supposed to ask this without sounding like a jealous, petty bitch? If I was being completely honest, I felt a bit like a jealous, petty bitch. My words were hesitant, and I did everything I could to try to sound more sure of myself than I was. "You met her at a brothel?"

His face suddenly shot to mine, realization marking his features. "Oh, Saints. That sounds bad." He wiped sweaty palms over his trousers as he straightened. "Isa *is* my friend. Just my friend. Nothing else."

I nodded, my cheeks reddening for some reason. It may have been a bit of humiliation that Miles was letting me into *this* part of his life. That, and a bit of jealousy I still couldn't deny.

His head dropped back, his mouth thinning to a straight line. "Fuck. This is embarrassing. I go to the Blushing Dove for companionship."

I raised an incredulous brow. "Isn't that why most men go to brothels?"

"No," he answered too quickly. "Well, yes. But Isa doesn't have any family either. So..."

Understanding washed over me. I quickly stuffed the jealousy into a tiny box in my mind and shoved it on a high shelf at the back of my brain, right next to the harp. In its place, at the front of my mind now, was something akin to heartbreak. Not so intense as heartbreak, but something that further softened the image of the so-called killer soldier in front of me.

"So Isa and Bowen are like your family."

"Kind of. But Isa and Bowen don't really know each other. I don't think they'd get along very well if they did. Isa is a recent addition to my family."

I cocked my head, surveying the man in front of me. "You're kind of a complicated person, soldier."

"What, you mean most families aren't made up of sex workers and egotistical assholes?" he asked, his shoulders relaxing slightly. I laughed, watching him return to his task, nearing the end. "He's a cool little guy, your brother. Seems very sure of himself."

"He is very sure of himself. Were you like that when you were—"

I cut myself off. Saints fucking *dammit*, Cielle. Why the fuck would I say that? *He doesn't remember his childhood.*

I looked to my lap, trying to hide my face. "I'm so sorry."

"I told you not to apologize, Princess." His smile was genuine — so genuine it almost broke my heart a bit. "Maybe I was like that when I was a child."

"Is there...anything you remember?" I pressed, nervous he would shut me down, which he had every right to do.

A sigh escaped his lips, but not one of sorrow or frustration. He thought for a moment, as if he were seeing something I couldn't. A hand coasted over the scar on his throat for a brief moment. "Sometimes I think I might remember something, or I'll hear a name that sounds almost familiar, but not enough that I can make a concrete connection."

I blinked, trying to think of something to say. "That's probably really frustrating."

"Sometimes." How could he be so easygoing and nonchalant in the face of what happened to him?

"Did you have any siblings?" I asked cautiously.

He paused his hammering for a moment, though I couldn't see the look on his face. "I don't think so." He continued his work, covering the last bit of space and gripping each side of the plank to test its stability.

"Hmm. When is your birthday, soldier?"

130

He blinked, staring up at me, a blank look over his beautifully defined features. "My birthday?"

"Your birthday." He was silent. Did... Did he not know what a birthday was? Did they not have birthdays in Taitha? "The day you were born."

"That's a good question."

Shock rang through me. "You don't know when your birthday is?"

Dark brows furrowed and his gaze suddenly seemed somewhere far away, somewhere long ago. He quickly shook his head. "I add a year to my age on the eve of each new year, so I guess if I had a birthday, that would be it."

I straightened. "That won't do. You need a birthday." Of course he did. Everyone needed a birthday. I turned to look at the door, mentally poring over my seemingly never ending to-do list. Cenric had no appointments today, only lessons with Nieve. I stood, shuffling to the front door and poking my head in to grab my cloak from the hook just inside. "You're on Cenric duty today!" I shouted to Nieve. Her stream of expletives didn't reach me before I turned back to Miles. "Today. Today is your birthday."

His face cracked into a wicked smile. "Oh, yeah?"

I nodded. "Mhm." He'd told me he was just stopping by to fix the ramp before his afternoon training session. I did my best to school my face into something resembling innocence. "And there's no training allowed on your birthday."

His face slipped into a grimace. "You know I have to train."

"No training on your birthday!" I protested, my brows raised and arms crossed. I felt a bit like a petulant little girl trying to get what I wanted, but I tried my best to look intimidating.

Miles' expression hardened and he crossed his arms, matching my stance. I was taller than most women, but he still towered over me. I didn't cower. "Cielle."

"Miles." My smile left my face, but I could feel a hint of it left that I couldn't rid myself of. A staredown ensued, one I was praying I'd win. "Mi-iles," I repeated, voice low but my tone taunting. "I'll cause a scene if you say no. Maybe get Nasty Nieve out here to belittle you."

"That's coercion."

"That's correct."

His nostrils flared. "You're impossible."

"Also correct."

His eyes glowed, the mid-morning sun making it appear as if embers floated through his irises. I felt a bit guilty at the prospect of making him miss training, but something told me he didn't want to go anyway. Maybe it was the laps he'd have to run or the orders he'd have screamed in his face. It could've been something far greater, something that sparked a tiny flicker of hope deep in an obscure pocket of my mind. One that would be dangerous to dig through.

"You win," he sighed suddenly, dropping his shoulders in an overdramatic show of defeat. "Today is my birthday."

I couldn't keep the squeal of excitement inside as I snatched his hand and glided down the ramp, admiring his handiwork as I hit the ground running. "Come on!"

"Where are we going?"

"The patisserie! It's your birthday and that means pastries for breakfast!"

Chapter 12
Miles

The sun had just slipped below the horizon, but the edges of the sky were still illuminated with the remnants of the day. Taitha's streets were dotted with torches and windows glowed from within. The city looked peaceful from all the way up here on the mountain ledge. No sign of the monsters that lurked within.

Cielle had unfolded the piece of waxed paper in her lap that held yet *another* slice of chocolate cake. She was spooning too-large chunks into her mouth as she stared out from the ledge.

My eyes were not on the city like they normally were when I came to this spot. They were trained to her mouth, glued to the way her throat worked. I swallowed hard, willing my mind to focus on anything but the way her lips ran over the tines of the fork. "I thought the agreement was *one bite for me, one bite for you?*" I asked, trying — and failing — to distract myself. She fought to keep her mouth closed around the cake as she giggled, extending the fork in my direction and offering a shrug as an apology.

I don't think I'd ever eaten so many sweets in one day, and my stomach wasn't thanking me for it. But Cielle said that birthdays meant sweets, and who was I to argue? We'd had breakfast at Emelie's Patisserie, then lunch at Angelika's Sweets Shop, then back to Emelie's for a snack when Cielle convinced me I had to try the blueberry scone I'd forgone this morning.

She swallowed the last of her cake, her voice suddenly quiet when she spoke. There was an air of hesitation there. "So you really don't remember your birthday?"

My lips pursed, Cielle and the brightening stars my only witnesses. "No."

"Maybe you don't remember the exact day, but do you remember anything about them through the years?"

I let my mind reach back into a blurry past. There was nothing but a tornado of smoke from the house fire. The smoke seemed to be more of a mist, though, and I never saw fire, only the rain I assumed had extinguished the flames. For the first time, it seemed to clear just long enough for a snippet of a memory. Between raindrops was a flash of something like the dull sheen of leather. I clung to it, desperately trying to uncover more. "I think I was given a book one year."

Cielle perked up beside me, full lips opening just a touch. "You remember?"

I concentrated, clawing at the echo of a fire-damaged, watered-down memory. Spines of books lined up on shelves. I was small, looking up at the stack that soared above me. There was a large window beside the shelf, and someone was calling out a name I couldn't quite make out. Focusing on the crowded shelves, a small bolt of joy flashed through my gut. "I think I had a lot of books."

Cielle turned her body to face me. "What kind of books?"

My eyes slammed shut as I tried to remember, but the intensity of Cielle's stare on me made my skin heat. The smoke dissipated. The memory was gone. For the first time, I felt a pang of grief. "I'm not sure. I guess they were all lost in the fire."

"You liked to read," she remarked quietly, warmth in her voice. She turned back to the city. "We can go to a bookstore. Maybe you'll see something you remember."

I shifted, the prospect of it making me a bit uncomfortable for a reason I couldn't place. "Maybe."

"Why not? Birthdays should be about the things you love." She threw her hair over her shoulder, the unruly locks cascading down her back. "I'm sorry I didn't have a real birthday present to give you."

I waited for her to laugh at her own joke, but all I heard was silence. My gaze narrowed on her. "Did you just apologize to me?"

Her mouth slanted in a half-frown as she nodded. "If I'd known it was your birthday, I would've prepared an actual gift for you."

My mouth bobbed open and shut as I blinked furiously. "You–" I cut myself off, stammering and tripping over my words.

"I could've given you a book." Her eyes were on me now, doubt etched into every feature as she shook her head. "Maybe a weapon, I don't know. Soldiers like weapons, don't they?"

Silence descended again. I could almost see her mind working as she scolded herself internally. "Today was..." I searched for words, but everything I came up with was inadequate. "You gave me the greatest gift of my life. Don't you ever apologize to me."

Her shoulders caved just slightly as she scoffed. "All I did was make up a birthday for you and force feed you sweets."

"Exactly." Cielle faced me once again, locking me in place with her gaze. "You gave me a birthday. I've never had that before."

"That's not a gift."

"It *is*." Her eyes were steady on me now, something in them I couldn't place. And it occurred to me then, this woman, who was so sure of herself that she grabbed a Cabillian soldier by the wrist and *dragged* him to a patisserie, this woman who invited an armed Cabillian soldier into her house for the sole purpose of proving a point... Maybe there was a part of her that wasn't sure of herself at all. No part of it made any sense to me, but maybe that was what I was seeing right now.

My tongue darted out over my lips as I willed myself to form words. Her eyes flickered to them for a split second. Here I went, feeling what I had no right to feel. Not when she was due to be married. I couldn't stay silent, though, the uncertainty on her face pulling the words from me. "Today was the greatest day of my life, Cielle."

Her body jolted slightly, just enough for me to notice the movement. My eyes narrowed with concern. "What?"

She was silent for a moment, her eyes trailing over the ground and back to mine. It was then I noticed we were only inches apart. At some point one of us had leaned in. Maybe it had been both of us. Heat shot through me as I breathed in her scent — vanilla and sea salt, intoxicatingly sweet.

"I..." she whispered, close enough that I could just feel her breath against my lips. "I like it when you say my name."

Fuck. The ability to form words escaped me as I grappled for something to say. I was floundering in the depths of this woman and I sure as fuck didn't know how to swim. I wasn't sure I wanted to learn, though. I'd be content to drown in her.

An unwelcome dose of reality suddenly entered my mind, as if the truth was waving a flag in an attempt to capture my attention. Training. Vorkalth. My sigh was weighted. "Today has been great. Tomorrow won't be as good, that's for sure."

Her face inched back to me carefully, ocean eyes on mine again. "It's still today for a little while longer."

She seemed to know exactly what to say to get to the deepest parts of me. But the look she was giving me went even deeper. The pouty lips turned up in a smirk, the hooded eyes, the way her tongue danced across her teeth. I had to reel in my thoughts before they darkened, because staring at Cielle... They could so easily darken.

Something sat on the tip of her tongue, I could tell. I waited, silently willing her to speak, but instead her lips met mine.

It didn't take long for my mind to catch up with my body, and my palm found her cheek, pulling her to me and closing the distance that had felt like an eternity. Her lips molded to mine, just as soft and perfect as I knew they'd be, a fire behind them that seemed to dictate everything she did. She inhaled deeply as her small hands found my chest then moved to tangle in my hair.

Need coursed through me, hot and undeniable as I deepened the kiss, angling her mouth against mine so I could take in more of her. A strained whimper left her throat and I could've imploded at the sound, her hands becoming more forceful as she

136

tried to push me to the ground. I let her, though my greater judgment was screaming at me not to take her here.

I soaked in the feeling of her as she climbed over me, straddling my hips as her hands grew more needy against my skin and her lips moved to my neck. Fucking *Saints*. I should've stopped thirty seconds ago, but my mind went blank as she nipped at the skin of my throat. All I could manage was a gasp. "Cielle."

She buckled slightly in my grip at the sound of her name. "Miles," she answered in a breathy whisper, fiending for the ties at my collar.

My hands found her wrists, the rational part of me suddenly rousing from where it'd been sleeping, just enough to stop myself. "Cielle," I repeated, more firmly this time, willing my brain to think of ice water and Vorkalth's gruesome face.

She pulled back, and though it wasn't easy to make out her face in the low light, I could feel her eyes searching mine. "I just thought..." She took a moment before scrambling off me and finding her feet, pulling her cloak around shoulders. "Saints, I'm sorry, I–"

"What did I say about apologizing?" I asked as I followed suit, quickly standing to look down at her.

She shook her head, turning away in embarrassment. "I'm sorry–"

I caught her shoulder with more force than I'd meant to and spun her back to me. It was the only point of contact between us, but it sent lightning through my entire body. "What did I say about apologizing?" I repeated, my voice a low growl. Her eyes moved back and forth between mine. "Hmm?"

The energetic, carefree woman I'd come to know began to flicker back to life, an edge of defiance accompanying her now. "You told me not to apologize to you."

"I meant it." I dropped my arm from her shoulder. Neither of us moved. I felt like I was in the training yard, sparring with an opponent, each of us daring the other to lunge first. "Do not apologize to me, especially not for *that*."

More of her spirit returned to her face, the sight settling a part of me I hadn't felt spiraling. She lifted her chin, the movement full of renewed confidence. "Been thinking about it too, then?" Her tone was teasing as she pulled her bottom lip between her teeth.

I cocked a brow as I stared her down. This was going to get dangerous very quickly. "Not at all."

"Lying is a very unbecoming trait, soldier."

Saints, she was maddening. I wanted to play this game with her, but I wasn't as sharp as she was in her responses. "I'm not lying," I started, unable to stop it. "I don't think about that at all."

She narrowed her eyes. "No?"

"No." I took a step toward her. She didn't so much as flinch. I remembered it then, the thought rolling in like a storm cloud beneath an otherwise clear sky. "Typically, I don't think about women who are engaged." With that line, I felt like I had a momentary hold on my self-control.

Her eyes darkened. "That's good, because I'm not engaged."

And there went my self-control. In that moment, it flew away like a piece of parchment in the breeze. There was nothing I could do to regain it as her tongue ran across her teeth and the edges of her mouth turned up in a wicked smile.

"So tell me, soldier, what *do* you think about?"

The tension within me was growing so taut I felt like a twig ready to snap in half. I was scrounging for any bit of sense, trying to piece together a few words, but was rendered completely speechless by the look on her face.

She reached a hand out, trailing one finger across my stomach. The muscles tensed beneath her touch as each second brought her lower and lower, ocean eyes locked on mine. "Do you think about this?"

My breath hitched in my throat as I strained against the laces of my trousers, fighting with every ounce of strength to keep my hands at my sides. "No," I lied, somehow managing to choke the words out.

Her finger ran down to my legs, circling the outline of my cock. The conscious effort it took to keep my breathing steady and my head from dropping back was almost more than I could manage. "And this?"

All I could do was hum in response. She sucked her teeth as she pulled her hand back, her eyes still on mine as she slowly ran her hands down her own thighs, and — holy shit — she was getting down on her fucking knees. My breaths were ragged at the sight of her kneeling before me, hands in her lap, eyes wide. I thought I'd been speechless in the past, but this? Fuck.

Her words were a whisper. "What about this?"

My jaw ticked as I fought to keep myself upright. Keep my hands to myself. Keep myself from fucking lunging for her. "Cielle," I whispered, desperately clawing for control.

She whimpered, her own head tipping back but her eyes never leaving mine. "Miles."

I couldn't fuck her here. Not on the fucking ground. "Cielle–"

A horn rang out, echoing out of the city and off the mountains that towered above us. A mission was returning with more Vacants. Which meant I was due back at the barracks for duty.

I couldn't help but notice the flash of disappointment in Cielle's eyes. Some part of me knew it wasn't simply because this moment was ending. It was *why* it was ending.

She took my outstretched hand and I pulled her to her feet, a coolness returning to her exterior. "You *definitely* don't think about that, do you, soldier?"

"You'll be my downfall, woman," I whispered, shaking my head, trying to tell my body to calm the fuck down.

"Maybe," she murmured almost absentmindedly as she turned back to the trail. "But I don't think you'll mind." I stood dumbfounded as I watched her walk toward the trail. "Come on, soldier. Seems like you have work to do."

Kindly deliver to the Port of Coldwater

Dearest Mother and Father,

So far, no healers have been able to help Cenric. I'm not sure if I'm growing wearier by the day or more used to the disappointment. It hasn't seemed to affect him too much. The disappointment usually slows him down for a very short amount of time before he's back to his normal self again.

~~I'm a doe-eyed dumbass, just like Nieve says. I've tangled myself up with a Cabillian soldier and he's lovely and kind and handsome and~~

We will keep working down the list of healers. Only a few left until we'll have to move on to the metalsmiths.

Yours,

Cielle

Chapter 13

Miles

Isa's hand closed around my arm with a deceptively strong grip. She pulled me through the doorway into her room, her eyes wide as the moon. "*Finally!* I've been waiting to see you for days!"

I plopped down unceremoniously on her bed. "Hello to you, too."

She handed me a goblet of wine that had been poured before I walked in, as if she had, in fact, been waiting for me. "Tell me everything!"

"First of all," I started, taking a long drink of wine, "I have a job opportunity for you."

"I'll take it."

"You don't even know what it is."

"I don't care. If it's outside the walls of this brothel, I'll take it."

I waited for her to backtrack and start asking questions, but the look on her face told me she was serious. Should I tell her the problems Cielle had encountered while trying to find a childminder? That may change her mind. On second thought, maybe it'd be entertaining to watch her figure this one out on her own. "Okay then. I'll meet you here after training."

"Now tell me everything about your date with the princess' cousin!"

Confusion entered my mind before I remembered the theory Isa had concocted. Shit, so much had happened in a matter of days. "Well," I said with a laugh that seemed to come from nowhere, "first of all, her cousin is technically a princess as well. And the date wasn't with her cousin." Isa's eyes flew wide, her hands clasped together in front of her chest in excitement. I put a palm out to stop her. "Easy, now. It really wasn't a date at all." Isa's shoulders dropped a smidge. "At least, dinner wasn't a date."

She almost quaked with excitement. "Tell me, tell me, tell me!"

I recounted the evening I spent at Cielle's house, the night at the pub, and the morning after securing the ramp to the steps of their front porch.

Isa raised a thin brow. "A bit of a handyman, are you?"

"No, but I had to find a way to see her again." Both Isa's brows raised now, concern lining her features. "It's stable, I promise. I wouldn't have done it if I didn't think I could. That little boy deserves a safe ramp."

I continued on, telling her about how Cielle gave me a birthday and the best day along with it, ending with me alone in bed with my Saints damned left hand.

A smile cast over her face, the definition of knowing. "So you're going to see her again?"

I scratched my hand over the back of my head, blowing a breath through my lips. "I shouldn't. I want to. But I shouldn't."

"She sounds pretty great."

I fell backwards onto the bed and threw my forearm over my face, squeezing my eyes shut beneath it. This feeling was foreign. I wasn't sure how to handle it. "She is great. She's more than great. She's..."

My entire body felt different, like it was suddenly alive. Like I was the moon and I'd just seen the daylight for the first time. But if I was the moon, she was the sun, forever just beyond my reach on the other side of night.

"Perfect?" Isa asked after a silence that I knew had gone on too long.

I dropped my arm to the bed beside me, my focus unintentionally zeroing in on a small crack in the painted ceiling. "I'm afraid to say yes."

"Why's that so bad?"

My throat suddenly went dry. Saying the words aloud seemed so final, like since they were still unspoken there was somehow a way to make them untrue. But they would've always been true, whether I breathed life into them or not. "She's a princess. A fucking *princess*. She's going back to Coldwater in two months to marry a prince. She's going to be a queen." I couldn't help but shake my head at the words. "And...she's a dissenter."

Isa landed a solid punch against my bicep. I furrowed my brows at the blow which was surprisingly painful. "The fuck was that for?"

"Are you stupid? Why the fuck would you even *think* that was a problem?"

She hadn't discerned exactly what the problem was, but I took a wild guess. "She's against the one thing my entire life revolves around. How is that *not* a problem?"

She looked at me like I'd just told her the sky was green. "Do you know what this is all about? Kauvras' reign? The reigns of arguably every king in the realm? It's all tiny men playing stupid fucking power games, using real people as their pawns and convincing them it's for the greater good. It's about tiny men who think they're above the rest of us just because they get to wear a ring of fucking metal on their heads." Her face had reddened, her volume growing dangerously loud. I fought the urge to shush her and glance toward the door. "That's all, Miles. All the battles, all the hatred, all the politics... Everything is fabricated by tiny fucking men."

Silence fell between us, the color of her face returning to its normal shade, her breathing slowing. Her eyes, however, stayed on me, and I felt like she was looking straight through to the truth I'd worked so hard to hide.

"It doesn't matter," she breathed. "None of it matters. And I know, deep down, you know that too."

Was she right? My stomach had managed to tie itself in knots at some point. I wanted to say I was confused, but that would've been a lie. I wasn't confused in the slightest. But I *was* conflicted. At the end of the day, all I had was my honor, and I'd already compromised it by keeping Isa's secret. I was compromising it further by keeping Cielle's.

"Landgrave!" We both jumped, eyes immediately snapping to the door at the sound of Bowen's voice. "Hurry up!"

Isa and I looked at each other, worry threading itself through her amber irises. "Did you hear him walk up?" Though her voice was barely above a whisper, the anxiety behind it was loud enough to pierce my eardrums.

I shook my head, swallowing hard. "He didn't hear anything."

"How do you know—"

"He didn't hear anything." I dipped my chin in a reassuring nod. Isa's body didn't relax as she stared at me. I repeated myself, more for my own reassurance this time. "He didn't hear anything."

Though my leathers had stayed on my body the whole time I was here, I still double checked them in the mirror when I stood. Taking care to school my face into neutrality, I swung the door open. Bowen's eyes immediately focused behind me. On Isa.

"See you after training," I said over my shoulder, my tone revealing none of the panic that had suddenly begun to crawl up my throat.

Isa's only response was a slight wave, her face completely blank as she stared back at Bowen.

◆ ◆ ◆

"What do you *mean* I'm meeting the Princess?" Isa's eyes had gone wide, her hands moving to hold her cloak over the impressive cleavage that peeked over her corset. We hadn't talked about Bowen. I doubted we would. But their encounter seemed to hang over us, never far from conscious thought.

Despite it, I couldn't help but give her a teasing smile. "Two princesses, actually. And a prince."

"When you told me you found me a job, I assumed I'd be serving ale at the barracks or something, not watching over the

Prince of the Surging Isles." She spat the words through gritted teeth.

I shrugged. "You should've asked more questions." I opened the gate to the garden in front of the cottage and lead Isa up the ramp, her steps hesitant. Her face had taken on a bit of a green hue. "Relax," I said reassuringly. But I didn't take my own advice as my fist rapped against the door. I was sweating like a fucking animal, simultaneously praying that Cielle would answer so I could see her and that she wouldn't so I didn't lose the grip I still had on my composure.

The door swung open to reveal Nieve with a familiarly sour look on her face. Her eyes traveled over me before moving to Isa, a brow raising at the woman before she crossed her arms over her chest and looked back at me. "You better have a good excuse for bringing another girl around." Isa tensed, her fist tightening where she still held her cloak over her chest.

"I do, I promise," I answered easily, offering a smile that I hoped would keep my nervousness away. "Is Cielle in?"

Nieve's eyes rolled as she walked into the house, leaving the door open in what I assumed to be a silent invitation. "Cielle! Your soldier is here! Probably going to force feed you leechthorn smoke. And he brought a...*friend.*"

"Her cousin," I said under my breath, and Isa inclined her chin in understanding.

Cielle rounded the corner into the kitchen, and though her face was forlorn and her eyes were hollow, I couldn't help but marvel at her. When those hollowed eyes landed on mine, they softened for a moment. "Miles." My name was a contented sigh on her lips, one I tried hard not to think too much about. Then she looked to Isa, her face suddenly breaking into a smile that shone brighter than the sun itself as she thrust a hand in front of her. "You must be Isa."

I could feel the tension melt away as Isa's shoulders relaxed under Cielle's stare. She took her extended hand, giving it a gentle shake. "Hello, Princess Cielle."

She shook her head, her nose wrinkling. "Just Cielle here in Taitha. Don't need Kauvras breaking down the door."

My breath caught in my throat as the two laughed at the joke that...really wasn't a joke. "Understood," Isa said graciously. "I've heard so much about you."

It felt like my ears were on fire as Cielle's eyes landed on my face, a slight smirk on her face. "Have you?"

Isa's mouth turned up in a close-lipped smile as she looked up at me mischievously. "Only good things."

"Anyway," I cut in, squaring my jaw as I tried not to grimace with embarrassment, "I thought Isa could give you some help with Cenric."

"If you'll have me with my...background," Isa said quietly. The spirit she usually spoke with was suddenly nowhere to be found.

Cielle's eyes narrowed for a moment as she realized what Isa was saying. "I don't see how that would affect your ability to wrangle an errant child." She shrugged. "But I do have some questions for you. Are you afraid of snakes?"

Isa's brows raised. "No, not at all." There was apprehension behind the words, but not the kind that denoted fear. It was more like...interest.

"Lizards?"

"Nope."

"Rodents?"

"No."

"Birds?"

"No."

"Spiders?"

"Not my favorite, but I can manage."

"Crickets?"

As if on cue, a cricket began chirping. Isa let out a laugh. "Not afraid of crickets, either."

"Good," Cielle answered with a sigh, "because there are apparently quite a lot in this house. One more question. How attached are you to your toes?"

Isa's face cocked to the side slightly. "I'd say they're more attached to me than I am to them."

Cielle's laugh sent the best kind of shiver up my spine. "Well, you may find them run over by a wheel or two during your time here."

146

Some kind of warmth expanded in my chest as I watched the two of them interact. Two people who had entered my life rather suddenly and taken up a place within me. The feeling was foreign, so comfortable it was almost uncomfortable, because along with it...came the fear of losing it. Losing them.

I shook the beginning of that dark thought away, knowing exactly where my mind would take me if I let it.

"Can I meet him?" Isa asked excitedly.

Cielle's smile faltered for a split second. "We received some bad news today." Her words were careful, and my heart lurched at their implications. "Cenric uses a wheelchair to get around," she started to Isa, "because he has some issues with his legs. That's the reason we're here in Taitha." Isa nodded in understanding as if I hadn't already told her this information. When I turned to Cielle, I knew what words would be coming next. "We visited the last of the healers today, and she wasn't able to provide any answers."

It felt a bit like the air had been squeezed from my lungs. I didn't even know Cenric that well, but I swore I could see the disappointment on his face in my mind. "I'm sorry, Cielle." My apology meant nothing, but it was all I had to offer.

Her lashes fluttered over her cheeks as she thanked me, their movement a distraction. "I was planning on making a visit to the first metalsmith today to ask about braces to help him walk. He was pretty upset earlier. He's in his room now. I was going to give him a bit of time to–"

A muffled scream split the air, followed by the unmistakable sound of a door flying open on its hinges. Then the low rumble of wheels, growing louder until Cenric rolled around the corner with a red-faced Nieve storming behind him. "You little shit! I've had it with all your fucking creatures!"

Cenric's face was red with laughter, his smile so wide I could see all the teeth he was missing. "Cha-ching! Cha-ching!" he shouted. "Keep going, Nieve! I'm going to be rich!"

"What's going on?" Cielle asked, eyes wide.

Cenric's laughter echoed through the house. "We found Twiggy and Maple!"

Isa leaned in to me, speaking out of the corner of her mouth as chaos erupted. "Twiggy and Maple?"

"I think they're lizards."

I could almost see the steam shooting from Nieve's ears. Her teeth gnashed between her jaws as veins popped from her neck. "We found Twiggy and Maple, alright. In the fucking pocket of my skirt."

Cenric howled again, slapping his knee. "It was great, Cielle! She was reading to me and Twiggy crawled out of her pocket and up her arm! And then Maple came crawling after him!"

"You insolent little shit," Nieve snapped, very clearly riled to the point of exploding.

Cielle looked to Isa, lips rolled together. "Any chance you could start today?"

◆ ◆ ◆

We walked into town side by side. I was headed for training and Cielle would make her way to the first metalsmith on her list. Her mouth had been turned up in a ghost of a contented smile since we'd left the house. She was so beyond beautiful, I had to tear my eyes away every so often to keep from tripping over my own two feet.

"I like Isa," she said suddenly, her voice a warm hum.

"Thank you for giving her a chance."

Cielle gave an airy laugh that would have stolen my breath away if I had less self-control. "Don't thank me too soon. I couldn't tell you the last time a childminder lasted more than three days with Cenric."

My shoulders rose and fell with a shrug. "I have a feeling she'll be more than fine."

A horse-drawn cart passed in front of us and I noticed Cielle craning her neck forward, trying to see something up ahead. Her gaze was fixed on a shop window, a slight puff of air leaving her when we arrived in front of it. Her shoulders relaxed, her face visibly relieved as she peered through the glass. "It's still here."

My eyes landed on the harp behind the shop window. The wood it was crafted from was heavily scratched. Some of the strings were visibly corroded. But she looked at it like it was the answer to a lifelong prayer. Though I couldn't see myself, I had a sneaking suspicion I was looking at her the same way.

Her father had called it an instrument for dreamers. Sounded like a bit of bullshit to me. "Seems you're a bit of a dreamer after all," I murmured over the din of the street.

The sigh that left her was laced with longing. "Always have been."

Kindly deliver to the Port of Coldwater

Dearest Mother and Father,

Finally, some good news to share with you. The first few metalsmiths I visited weren't hopeful when I asked them about corrective braces. I'd almost lost hope until I walked into the shop of the last one on the list. He's very optimistic about the task ahead and thinks he'll be able to fashion braces to make walking a possibility for Cenric. I'll be bringing him by in the next few days to be measured.

I still feel the lingering frustration of all the failed appointments with healers, but I suddenly find myself becoming very attached to the city of Taitha. For the first time, I think I feel a bit sad about the prospect of leaving. I will return though, as promised. ~~But I may be returning without a small piece of my heart.~~

Yours,

Cielle

Chapter 14

Cielle

Cenric's joy was infectious when I gave him the news. My heart was so full I was afraid it may burst through my chest completely. He wheeled through the house, his laughing and whooping joined by the song of the crickets. They seemed to be cheering for Cenric, too. I was sad there wasn't anything to be done in the way of treatment, but this... This was more than enough.

"I'm going to walk, Nieve!" Cenric shouted as soon as our cousin pushed through the front door. Her eyes landed on me, a look of question where there was usually disdain. "I'll get measured and have braces on my legs by next week!"

I looked up from the cutting board where I'd been chopping potatoes. I tried not to let too much hope show on my face, but I couldn't help it. "The metalsmith is optimistic. I just sent a letter to our parents with the news. They're going to be thrilled."

Nieve blinked in surprise, pausing for a moment too long before nodding apprehensively and looking at Cenric. "No more rolling over my toes, you menace."

"Now I'll be able to step on them."

"Don't you have a bird to feed or something?" she snapped, pointing her chin in the direction of the hallway.

Cenric smacked his palm against his forehead before quickly rolling around the corner. "Oh, yeah. I'm coming, Dewdrop!"

Nieve leaned against the counter, crossing her arms over her chest. Something about her expression looked even more unpleasant than normal. "This came for you today." She reached into the pocket of her cloak to hand me a letter. The wax seal bearing the crest of the Surging Isles had already been broken, and that fact sent a bolt of panic through me. Nieve knew something I didn't. The deep blue impression of a large ship should've brought me some level of comfort. It did anything but as I unfolded the parchment.

Dearest Daughter,

I know you're near the end of the list of healers and are close to moving on to the metalsmiths, but I believe we've found the remedy for what ails Cenric. I'm unable to disclose the manner, but I'm confident this is the answer.

If you have any healers left to visit, you may cancel the appointments. There is no need to visit the metalsmiths either, as Cenric will be taken care of as soon as you arrive back in the Surging Isles.

Your father and I are very proud of you for taking on this responsibility, Cielle. You are free to come home now. We're sure you're looking forward to leaving Taitha behind and returning to the safety and comfort of Coldwater. Prince Rayner is very excited to see you, too.

Give Cenric and Nieve our best.

Yours,
Mother

My fingers continued to grip the paper long after I finished reading. Something about the words unsettled me, the blood in my veins suddenly feeling too hot as it coursed through my body.

"What's the remedy?" I asked quietly, finally dropping the letter to my side.

"Do I look like I know?" Nieve answered pointedly. "Sounds questionable, though."

"Yeah."

My parents weren't rash, my mother especially. She wouldn't send a letter like this without having complete confidence in the words she wrote. What the hell could this remedy be? They'd tried everything over the years, had access to the best healers and treatments. Suddenly there was some magical cure?

Nieve reached forward, gesturing for the letter then skimming it once again. "I'll start packing."

Something reminiscent of panic sparked in my chest at her words. The feeling was hollow, and the more I thought about leaving Taitha, the deeper it grew. I straightened, trying to find the words to make the feeling stop. "Why don't you take Cenric back to Coldwater?" I blurted before I even recognized the idea had appeared in my mind.

She raised an eyebrow incredulously. "Why don't *I* take him back to Coldwater? What about you?"

"I'd...like to stay here in Taitha."

Nieve's lips pursed so tightly that the skin around her mouth went white. I was scared then, because the fact she hadn't immediately flown off the handle meant I was in danger of suffering through an outbreak of hers that would be much, much worse. She inhaled deeply, the words dangerously quiet. "You want to stay in this dirty ass city for that fucking man, don't you?"

I had nothing to lose except the only taste of independence I'd ever have in my life, and to me, that was everything. "Yes. You take Cenric back to Coldwater."

"You're taking me back to Coldwater?" We'd been so embroiled in our conversation that neither of us had heard the sound of wheels over the floorboards.

I swallowed hard, pasting a smile on my face as I turned to him. "There's been a bit of a change in plans, bud."

His brows furrowed, traces of disappointment already showing as if it had become a habit. "I'm not going to walk, am I?"

"Yes," I immediately answered, lowering to crouch in front of him. "You are going to walk. But it won't be until we're back home in the Surging Isles, so you won't be getting your braces here in Taitha."

He was so used to the hurt that he didn't even question it. He simply nodded his head, as if accepting his fate was that easy. "Okay."

"But Mother says they found the answer, and that as soon as you're back in Coldwater, you'll be able to walk." Saying it out loud sounded...odd. It just didn't make any sense that it would be so sudden and absolute, but I kept my thoughts to myself. Cenric perked up at the promise and his mouth lifted into a smile, a bittersweet sight I was terrified would end in yet another failure. I patted his knee. "You'll leave tomorrow."

His smile immediately dropped into a frown. That was...unexpected. "I don't want to go home yet."

I could almost feel the eye roll Nieve held back at the idea of staying in this city for a single moment longer. "Why not?" she asked, thankfully in a voice that didn't betray the annoyance she felt.

"I want to stay here with Miss Isa."

I blinked in surprise. "Oh, um... Okay." I turned to Nieve, her head already shaking. Cenric wanted to stay. He wanted to stay so badly that he'd put off the promise of walking for a little more time in Taitha. In that moment, I thanked the Saints for Miss Isa.

"Well if you stayed here, would you still want to have your braces made?" I asked.

He cocked his head in thought, his blonde curls bouncing with the movement. "Hmm. No. Not if I'm going to walk on my own when I get home. I can still roll over Nieve's toes until then."

"You little brat," Nieve sniped.

"It's settled then," I said cheerfully. "But we'll still have to leave as scheduled in a few weeks, okay?"

154

He nodded excitedly, immediately launching into a list of everything he learned in his book about drivas that he wanted to tell his new childminder.

"For the love of the fucking Saints," Nieve grumbled, pinching the bridge of her nose between her thumb and forefinger.

I clapped my hands together. "Go get cleaned up. Miss Isa will be here soon."

Cenric rolled around the corner, his laugh echoing through the hall. Nieve's face was crimson with rage as I shrugged, trying to look as innocently as I could. "You heard him. He wants to stay in Taitha."

"He wants to stay in Taitha," she mocked. "Give me a fucking break, Cielle. And why the fuck is Isa coming over tonight?"

"Because I made the decision that you and I were going to go out to celebrate Cenric's good news...which we can still do. It's just *different* good news."

Her face twisted into a frown. "Absolutely not."

"When else are we ever going to be able to go out to a pub?"

"Never. And I'm fine with that."

I knew there was a very real chance Nieve would not leave the house tonight just to spite me. This required me to think on my toes, and I had the perfect idea. "I'll make a bet with you."

❖ ❖ ❖

If there was one thing Nieve hated more than staying in Taitha for one more second, it was losing a bet. I hooked my elbow through her arm as we walked away from the cottage, leaving Isa at the mercy of Cenric. "You need this."

The way Nieve side-eyed me would've scared off any stranger. "You're batshit."

I'm not sure if it was a fortunate thing or an unfortunate thing, but I was beginning to think she might be right.

The Griffin's Back was not our destination tonight. I was determined to find a pub closer to home. The quicker I could get Nieve into a pub, the less time she'd have to turn around on the street and walk home.

We'd made our bet and shaken on it the same way we had since we were girls. If Nieve had a good time tonight, we could stay in Taitha. If she didn't, I'd be responsible for breaking Cenric's heart again, packing us all up, and going back to Coldwater. I was afraid that would break my heart, too.

Nieve was going to do everything she could to keep any evidence of enjoyment from peeking through her hardened exterior. I was going to do everything I could to make sure she had the time of her life. A tall order. I really had no other ideas than to bring her to a pub, even though my first experience hadn't started out in the best way. It must've been the way the night ended that gave me hope.

"Come on. Let's get shitfaced," I urged, nudging her with my shoulder.

"I can get shitfaced any time I want back home in the castle, surrounded by much nicer things and cleaner people. On good wine, too."

My head shook jerkily. "Nope. You need to get shitfaced in a pub on something that barely passes for ale."

To my surprise, she was silent, begrudgingly following along as I spotted my prize at a nearby intersection. *Rose's Respite.* I was surprised to see that Nieve's eyes were uncharacteristically bright as I urged her in the direction of the pub.

Rose's was markedly nicer than the Griffin's Back, and I breathed a sigh of relief when we pushed through the front door to see only a few people scattered throughout an interior accented with emerald and gold.

Nieve remained quiet as I pulled her to the bar, plopping down on a stool and signaling the barkeep. Two mugs of ale were pushed across the bar with a polite smile from the middle-aged man who'd poured them.

I lifted my mug to my cousin. "Cheers."

Her eyes rolled, but she touched her mug to mine and threw back a large swig. "This is fucking awful," she spat, garnering the attention of the few patrons in the pub.

I gave her a smile, the sight of seeing her do something so normal bringing me genuine joy. "I know. Isn't it great?"

◆ ◆ ◆

The words had been burning in my mouth as I sat at the bar, quietly watching Nieve. I wanted to scream that I'd told her so, but I kept quiet. She'd been tossing darts at a board with a petite, dark haired woman close to our age for an hour now. I'm not sure I'd ever heard her laugh so much.

The dark haired woman had told me her name, but I'd been so shocked by Nieve's behavior that it had gone in one ear and out the other. I declined her offer to join them for a round, afraid that if I disturbed the balance, I'd ruin what could've possibly been the first good mood she'd ever been in.

I suddenly caught the gaze of my cousin, her smiling face instantly slackening as if she'd been caught doing something she wasn't supposed to. I winked at her, which she answered with a swift middle finger and a sneer as she turned back to the board.

"I have time for one last game before my friend gets here and I'll have to leave," the dark haired woman said, plucking the darts from the target.

Nieve nodded. "Winner pays the tab."

"Then it looks like I'll be ordering the good stuff."

The two women shook hands as Nieve entered her second bet of the evening, standing at the line as their final game began. I let out a contented sigh as I finished the last of my ale. I was just buzzed enough that I made no attempt to stop my mind from wandering to a place that was equally exciting as it was terrifying. The exciting thing was that Nieve was having a great time, and she'd have no grounds to deny it. Which meant we were staying here in Taitha for another few weeks — despite my mother's request.

The terrifying thing... I really, *really* wished Miles was here. And with that, I knew I was fucked. I couldn't lie and say I hadn't thought about the prospect of meeting someone when we came to Taitha. It had been an exciting thought, the idea that I could have a final tryst with a handsome stranger before donning the crown of Zidderune.

I hadn't expected...this. I hadn't expected Miles.

The seashell on my necklace glided over the chain as I fiddled with the pendant, a deep sigh leaving me as I glanced toward the door. Maybe if I hoped hard enough, Miles would materialize right there in the doorway.

He didn't, but another man did. A soldier dressed in Cabillian black, his shorn hair the color of the richest chocolate and eyes to match. He smiled in the direction of the dark haired woman, raising a hand in greeting. That hand dropped when his eyes landed on Nieve.

"Who's your friend?" he crooned, and I internally cringed. Not at his advance, but at what would surely come from Nieve.

"Nope," the dark haired woman cut in. "Far too much woman for you."

Nieve's arms crossed as she surveyed the stranger, the man obviously unafraid of the look in her eyes. I sat as still as I could, watching as his gaze bored into her face. "You are beautiful."

"And you are a gutter rat," she quipped.

He flinched, but instead of drawing away, his face cracked into a smile. He was by no means a *gutter rat*. He was rather good looking, actually. And obviously very, very stupid. With a death wish. "Oh, you are absolutely terrifying." Nieve's nostrils flared as the man's gaze stayed locked on her. "I think I'm in love with you."

"Alright, we've got somewhere to be," the other woman laughed, slapping a hand on the man's shoulder so aggressively, I was surprised it didn't send her small frame stumbling. She reached into the pocket of her trousers and dropped a small pile of coins on the bar before offering a smile to Nieve. "Thanks for the game, and sorry about him. Say goodbye, Whit."

"You're always such a cockblock, Nell," he muttered to the woman as they made their way out of the pub.

I made a point not to comment on the way Nieve stayed eerily silent instead of ripping the man a new one. Instead I held a mug of beer in her direction and watched as she emptied it in one fell swoop. Nieve had lost the bet. Taitha was changing her after all. It sure as hell had changed me.

Chapter 15

Miles

My entire life had revolved around training. Thinking about training. Preparing for the ass kicking I'd receive at training. Thinking about the missions I'd be sent on after I completed my three years of training.

And then there was Cielle. Suddenly, my focus had changed. My duty was still at the forefront of my mind, but its light had been extinguished. What had once burned brighter than anything else could no longer burn at all. Not when she was there.

I couldn't remember the last time I'd gone twenty-four hours without seeing Cielle. I'd seen her daily for weeks at this point. But I couldn't ever escape the looming truth that our time together had an end date, and she would step off the boat in Coldwater into the arms of another man.

I hoped he appreciated her. Saints, I hoped he knew what he had, how damn lucky he was. There better not be a single day he takes her for granted.

"You don't have to go to training, you know," Cielle said quietly. We sat on her front porch, enjoying the few short hours of free time I had. Something seemed different about her today, though I couldn't figure out exactly what it was. There was just something in the way she carried herself, a low hum of ease that emanated from her. My fingers ran absentmindedly across the back of her hand as we watched the passersby in the street.

Her voice was more than quiet enough that no one would've heard her aside from me, but I still flinched at the thought of someone being privy to our conversation. "You know what happens if I miss more training? I get my ass beat, either by the amount of laps I have to run or the number of toilets I have to scrub. Maybe by Vorkalth himself."

That low hum stopped abruptly, her eyes suddenly somewhere far from here. "All for a good cause, right?"

I pursed my lips and had to keep myself from shifting uncomfortably where I sat. We'd never broached this subject. Not aloud. Not yet. Instead, it had shadowed us since the very first night, and we both knew it was there. Treason — even the mention of it — was punishable by death.

My next words were chosen very, very carefully. "For King Kauvras' cause."

Her eyes tracked a young couple that walked past the cottage, their fingers intertwined as they laughed at some secret joke. "Just come back to Coldwater with me," she murmured with a shrug. It was like she was simply suggesting we go into town for lunch, not like she was suggesting I desert my post — also punishable by death.

"It's as simple as that, huh?"

"Why can't it be?" she asked, and I knew it was a genuine question. "You can join the Surging Isles' military."

I side-eyed her. "I'm sure that would go over well."

"Do you think someone is going to come after you?"

A pit opened in my stomach, panic suddenly pooling in the chasm. "We can't have this conversation," I said quickly. I prayed that would be the end of it. The sigh she let loose sounded content, but I could tell there was much more to it. My thoughts were interrupted when the clocktower rang out. My cue to leave for training.

160

Or so I'd told her.

◆ ◆ ◆

I'd arranged it all with Isa and Nieve. I told Cielle I was going to training. In reality, I had a rare afternoon off as all military leaders had a mandatory briefing. Everything would be set up when Nieve and Cielle returned home from the market. Nieve, always very pleasant, told me she'd give me forty-five minutes to "do whatever the fuck it was." At some point in the conversation, she'd also called me a prick. But I was too busy planning in my own head to be affected by her words.

Nervousness served no purpose in this moment, yet it coursed through my body like it belonged there. Cenric sat on the settee opposite me, and had been excitedly prattling off details about a newly discovered bird for the last ten minutes. Isa sat beside him, enthusiastically asking questions that I could tell she actually wanted the answer to.

As I'd hoped, Isa and Cenric had instantly clicked. She didn't show a single sign of fear around the creatures Cenric kept. At first, her lack of reaction actually bothered him. He'd probably gotten so used to the exaggerated responses from his previous childminders that Isa must have seemed like a brick wall to him. But when he realized Isa was just as interested in animals as he was, his entire demeanor changed. He wasn't a terror at all. He was just a little boy who loved his pets.

"Seashell's going to be happy," Cenric suddenly said with a grin, apparently moving on from his avian excitement.

My hands ran over the leather stretched across my thighs as I willed my palms to stop fucking sweating. "Do you think so?"

He nodded his head emphatically. "Oh, yeah. She's been wanting one for years." A pang of hurt ran through my chest, at the fact that someone could deny anything to Cielle. I'd give her the sky if it would make her smile. "Father wanted her to learn the violin, instead."

"Why are you so nervous?" Isa asked, a single brow raised as she assessed what I was sure was a very pathetic sight.

I wouldn't have been surprised if I melted into a puddle of nerves right then and there. "I just want it to be perfect."

Cenric leaned in to Isa, his voice nowhere as quiet as he thought it was. "Why is his face so white? And why does he look like he's going to pass out?"

"Because he likes your sister."

I shot a look at Isa, who answered it with an expression that told me she was right and she had no intentions of apologizing for it.

Cenric's face twisted. "I don't think Prince Rayner will be very happy with that. Did you know he owns seven hawks?"

Isa's look morphed into an encouraging smile, which calmed the way my skin had bristled at the reminder of Cielle's intended. "Well, Cenric, in my opinion, Miles is much better than the Prince of Zidderune, and he doesn't even need *one* hawk to make it so."

Cenric answered with a toothy grin. "I think so, too."

Somewhere in the house, a cricket began chirping, sending Isa and Cenric into a fit of laughter. I couldn't tell through their hysterical giggles, but it almost sounded like they'd made up a song to the rhythm of the cricket's wings.

Suddenly I was on my feet, my body moving of its own volition when I heard the sound of a key in the lock. My heartbeat pounded in my ears as the front door swung open to reveal blue eyes that immediately found mine. She was a damn magnet to me. It took a moment for the surprise to show on her face when she realized what time it was. "What are you still doing here? Don't you have training?"

Cenric's face somehow lit up even brighter than it was before as he wheeled himself in her direction. "Seashell, look what Miles got you!"

The air left my lungs as she walked into the room. She was sunshine personified, blindingly beautiful. I watched her eyes fall on the instrument propped in the corner, and the surprise slipped away from her face. The basket she'd been holding in the crook of her elbow fell to the floor, landing upright with a dull *thud*.

"It's a little worse for wear, but I had it restrung so it should sound okay." I rubbed at my jaw as I stared, trying to bank the disappointment in my gut. A new harp would've been so much better, but with a soldier's pay it would've taken me two years. It had been tight, and it took a lot of digging and scraping to get enough together for this. I spent even more money I really didn't have on three dozen white roses that Isa and Cenric had helped me scatter around the base of the harp. Maybe a bit over the top to most, but not for her. Not for Cielle.

She took a single step toward the gift, her face still unreadable. Ocean eyes traveled up and down, lips parting as she inhaled slowly. A dainty hand reached forward as she took a few more hesitant steps. She ran her fingers up the harp's neck, over the scuffs and divots that had somehow marked the instrument throughout its unknown years of use.

She exhaled sharply. I turned to Isa, her eyes wide as she watched Cielle. I suddenly became aware of Nieve standing next to her, arms crossed and an expression of disdain twisting her face as her eyes moved from her cousin to me. The back of my neck began to burn with embarrassment. *Fuck.* She hated it.

I bit the inside of my cheek. It had been a stupid idea. I should've found a way to get her a new one. Honestly, nothing at all would have been a wiser choice. What the fuck was I doing?

She didn't turn away from the harp when she spoke again. "I love it."

I didn't relax just yet, just in case she turned around and told me she was kidding. I half expected that. "Do you? Really?"

She tore her eyes away and her gaze landed on me. Every time she looked at me, it further confirmed the Benevolent Saints were, in fact, real. "I've never seen anything so beautiful in my life."

Funny, I was thinking the same damn thing.

Her head shook slightly. "I can't accept it though."

"Why not?"

"It's too much. This must have cost…"

I shook my head. "Don't you dare even think about the cost."

"I can't accept it, Miles. I can't."

"Bullshit," I answered, only to see movement out of the corner of my eye. I turned to find Cenric with his hand outstretched. *"Nonsense,"* I corrected, digging into my pocket and placing a coin in his palm. It was a miracle I still had any left after what I'd spent, but it was one I'd gladly pay. "You're going to learn to play the harp like you've always wanted to."

Nieve scoffed from somewhere behind me. "This is nauseating," she grumbled as she headed for the front door. "I'm going on a walk to get some fresh, untainted air."

"Play something, Seashell!" Cenric shouted.

"I don't know how yet, bud," she answered, her eyes falling back to the strings, which caught the light in a way that set them shimmering. I'd never been envious of an inanimate object before, but the way she was looking at it was enough to make me feel envious of *a fucking harp.*

"Go on," I urged. "At least try it out."

She clasped her hands in front of her and began to wring them nervously. Her chin dipped in a slight nod as she lowered herself to the worn leather stool, carefully inching it closer to the harp. She held her arms in the air for a moment, her fingers hovering over the strings. "I'm not sure what to do."

My smile was encouraging. "Just see what happens."

She took a deep breath and ran one hand over the strings in a long sweep, the sound melodic and lilting as it floated through the air and settled somewhere deep within me. Her smile was timid, her eyes soft as she used her other hand to do the same thing. I may have been mistaken, but I thought I saw a sheen of tears gather in her eyes. The breath that left her body told me exactly what this meant to her.

I could see it then — a crowd gathered in front of a stage, Cielle in a flowing dress the same glimmering blue of her eyes, plucking away at the harp as people wept at its sound. Her face appeared blank, but I knew it wasn't. Because I was sitting in that crowd too, and could see the way her lips turned up just the slightest bit, the look in her eyes that told the world she was exactly where she was meant to be.

"There are also some books," I said suddenly, pointing to a small pile on the coffee table before I could lose myself in the thoughts any more than I already had. "I'm not sure how much help they'll be, but I was thinking since you already know how to read music for the violin, you could figure this out pretty easily." It was a fight to stop myself from rambling.

164

"Wow," Cenric whispered with a smile. His face turned to me and he leaned in slightly. "You did a good job, Miles. She loves it."

Warmth spread in my chest, the feeling traveling through my limbs in a way I'd never felt before. Cielle's fingers plucked over the strings again, a disbelieving laugh rising from her chest as she shook her head. "Isa," Cielle said, almost absentmindedly, her eyes still fixed on the harp in front of her. Then they turned to me, and there was an unmistakable heat burning in her gaze. "Would you mind taking Cenric to the pet shop?"

"Yes!" Cenric shouted, his tiny fists shaking in front of him with excitement.

Isa raised a brow at me, fighting to keep a knowing smile from her face. "Sure. Come on, Little Prince. Let's go."

"I'll only get one frog," he called behind him as he wheeled himself to the door. "Three tops."

"Good idea," Isa said, a hand on his shoulder as she opened the door for him. "Frogs eat crickets."

The moment the front door closed, Cielle launched herself toward me, and suddenly I knew what it felt like to truly be alive.

Chapter 16
Miles

The fervor with which her lips found mine stole the breath from my lungs. Her arms linked around my neck to pull me toward her, desperation in every move.

"Thank you," she whispered, resting her forehead against mine. My eyes landed on hers, and what I saw looking back at me...

"Why are you crying?" I asked, my palm finding her cheek and my thumb swiping across the track of the single tear that had fallen.

She swallowed hard, her throat working as she blinked furiously. "This is the kindest thing anyone has ever done for me."

"*This?*" I asked incredulously. It wasn't true. It couldn't be. "No one's ever given you a gift?"

She waved a hand in front of her, clearing her throat as she tried to collect herself. "I've received plenty of gifts, but never one so..." She turned to glance at the harp again, shaking her head. "It's perfect. You're perfect."

My mind went blank as I looked down at her. Her blue eyes were hidden from mine behind her lashes as she turned slightly, cheeks reddening. The word hung between us for a moment, and I struggled to get a grip on the fact that it was there at all. "I'm not, Cielle."

And then her eyes were on me again, and I suddenly wondered if this is what Heaven looked like. If it was, this would never get old. Her hand reached forward, the touch feather-soft as it grazed over my cheek. The look in her eyes was stripping me bare, something ablaze within them. "You are perfect, Miles."

The word was on the tip of my tongue, but it wasn't enough. *Perfect* didn't come close to describing the woman in front of me. She'd sailed far past perfect and was nothing but a tiny dot on the horizon of something far greater. I searched the depths in her eyes for the words to tell her, but how could I say that, to me, she was the sun and the entire sky? How could I put into words that my life had been muted shades of gray until she came along and showed me there had been color all along, I just hadn't found it yet? What words existed that could accurately describe the feeling of *rightness* that shot through me every time she looked my way?

I leaned forward and kissed her, trying to communicate with every movement the words I couldn't seem to conjure up. The salty tang of her tears hit my tongue as her hands ran through my hair to pull me closer to her. Suddenly she was pushing me back, the two of us stumbling through the hallway in a tangle as she drove me toward her bedroom.

"You don't..." I stuttered, panic suddenly a shock to my system as we tumbled through the doorway. How the fuck was I supposed to say this without sounding like a jackass? "I don't want you to think you have to do this because I got you a gift."

Her eyes flew so wide I was surprised they didn't fly straight from her skull. All traces of those bittersweet tears evaporated.

"You think the only reason I'm trying to undress you is because you got me a gift?"

"I just want to make sure you're doing this because you actually want to."

It was like the air in the room became charged, like the few moments before lightning struck the ground and the space between us was its point of impact. She stared at me, her eyes narrowing as her tongue ran across her lips. "What made you think I wouldn't want this?" Her expression darkened, the moon eclipsing the sun, as a hint of a wicked smile danced over her mouth. "Was it the way I kissed you on your birthday?" she asked, her palms running over my chest before pushing me back on the bed. My heart was a galloping horse in my chest, its beats so loud I swore she'd be able to hear them as she suddenly lowered herself to the floor. "Was it the way I got on my knees for you?" She pulled her bottom lip between her teeth, running her hands up my thighs, coming dangerously close to a place I'd only ever dreamed she'd be. "You liked the sight of me on my knees before you, didn't you, soldier?"

I felt like a fucking idiot. All I could do was stare as she knelt before me, eyes hooded and antagonistic.

She took a deep breath, her jaw squaring. "What have I ever done to make you think I wouldn't want you to fuck me senseless?"

Fucking *Saints*.

"If anything," she continued, standing from the floor and slowly crawling over me to hover just slightly above my hips. I was frozen in shock, as if Onera herself was staring down at me. This truly was a fucking miracle. Cielle leaned down, her lips against my ear, the hunger in her tone so evident, goosebumps rose from my skin. "I should be concerned *you* wouldn't want to."

Confusion washed through me until she pulled away and I saw the spark of mischief in her eyes. She was egging me on. Daring me. Heat replaced confusion as my arms ran down her back, lifting the hem of her shirt just enough to press my fingertips into her skin. Air rushed between her teeth at the touch, her back arching ever so slightly. "What made *you* think I wouldn't want this?" I repeated her own words back to her, pulling her head down to run my lips over her throat. "Was it how hard I was with you on top of me?" The breath rushed from her mouth now as I nipped at her collarbone. "Was it the way I would've stripped you down and taken you right there on the ledge overlooking the city? Was it the way I've thought about claiming you every single day since the day we met in the market? Making that pretty mouth call out my name?" I could feel myself teetering on the edge of losing control, and every part of me wanted to. I was starving for this woman. "What," I whispered against her skin, "have I ever done to make you think I wouldn't want to fuck you senseless?"

She was grappling for control the same as I was. "That's what you want, yeah?" she asked, pulling my bottom lip between her teeth.

"I want you." The Saints' honest truth.

"Then prove it."

My body was one step ahead of my mind as my hands found the front of her blouse and pulled, the flimsy fabric gliding as I yanked it over her head. She gasped, a shudder racking her body as she watched me, a look of amusement behind eyes that gleamed a cerulean I'd never seen before. Her corset clung tight to her chest, pushing her breasts up in a way that *almost* distracted me from her eyes.

She reached behind her back for the corset ties, but I was too impatient. The steel of my sword sang as I unsheathed it where it hung at my hip, her eyes going wide in question as she watched me. "Turn around, Cielle."

When she understood what I was doing, she didn't hesitate before turning her back to me in the ultimate sign of trust that I sure as hell didn't deserve. I threaded my blade through the laces of the corset, slicing through the cord easily and pulling the boned fabric away from her body. She shivered, turning back to me without so much as a moment's pause.

Against the muted daylight filtering in through the sheer curtains that covered the window, she was a vision silhouetted in silver. I moved to the laces of her pants, easily untying them and rolling them down her legs, her hands roving over my back as I went. I didn't want to think at this point. I just wanted her.

169

Cielle stood bare before me, her skin so smooth and inviting it took everything within me not to lunge for her. Blonde waves tumbled over her shoulders. She looked like a damn siren, designed for the sole purpose of luring me in. And I'd gladly take the bait if it meant a single moment staring into those eyes.

"You want me to prove that I want you?" I asked, my voice husky. I laid back on the bed, my head on her pillow. "Have a seat."

She blinked in confusion for a moment, looking down at the trousers that remained on my body. When her eyes found mine again, I gave her a vicious smile. "Not there. Not yet."

A smile spread across her face, but there was marked hesitation. Silence was her only response.

I couldn't keep the concern from rising in my gut. "What's wrong?"

"Nothing's wrong," she answered quickly. I almost believed it.

I propped myself up on my elbows. "We don't have to do anything you don't want to do."

"Lie back down," she said, her voice low. "I want to. I'm a bit...nervous. I haven't... *That*," she said, pointing very obviously to my face, "is new to me."

I sat up, a few wayward strands of hair falling from where I'd tied it. "We don't have to do anything you don't want to do," I repeated, each word firm and intentional.

"*Lie back down.*" I obeyed, my eyes never leaving hers. She took a fortifying breath, nodding more to herself than to me. Her steps toward me were slow, her eyes locked on mine so intensely, I don't think I could've torn my gaze away if I wanted to. Cielle climbed over me, her hands flattening against the headboard, fingers splayed as she slowly lowered herself to my mouth.

Her apprehension melted away the moment I made contact. "Oh, *Saints*," she hissed.

She tasted like spring daylight after a dark winter. The noise that came from her lips was a drug in and of itself, and I knew I could easily spend my entire life doing anything to hear it again. My arms hooked around her thighs, doing everything I could to keep her as close to me as humanly possible, but it wasn't enough. My pants strained almost painfully as I devoured her.

Cielle writhed above me, my name tumbling from her mouth amid a string of gasps and cries. Her back arched further, opening her even more to me, letting me deeper as she ground against my mouth. It was like watching a Saint come into their power — pure force and carnal energy twining together to create a pillar that held up the entire world.

The movements of her hips grew faster, the tension tightening in her body. Her hands flew from the headboard to the back of my head, nails digging into my scalp. A shudder racked her frame, her beautiful face dropping and her eyes finding mine for what was somehow a single moment and a thousand eternities.

"Miles," she gasped, and her head dropped back again, her legs beginning to shake in my arms as I ravaged her. "Miles!"

Her movements were so profound, I swore I felt her pleasure roil through me. Her muscles began to loosen atop me, quickly contracting every few seconds with the aftershocks as her breaths began to slow. I grieved the loss of her as she dropped to the bed beside me, blonde hair surrounding her as her chest rose and fell evenly. It took all my years of learning self-control not to charge her again.

"That was... Thank you," she breathed, eyes closed.

My eyes found her face and I couldn't help but smile. "Did you just *thank* me?"

"Mhm." It was little more than a moan.

I let my fingers run along her collarbone, relishing the softness of her skin as my fingers traveled between her breasts. I'd never had something so soft before. Everything in my life thus far had been hard edges. The only love I'd ever received was tough love, and the latter half of that was arguable even on its best days. I wasn't sure whether I deserved this warmth. But when her hand closed around my wrist, pressing my hand more firmly to her skin, I wasn't concerned with what I deserved anymore. I *wanted* this. Her.

She guided my touch, her eyes snapping open then going hooded again. An invitation. An animal awoke inside me, breaking free from its cage, and my words were hardly more than a growl. "You can thank me after I'm done with you."

My hands gripped her hips and I pulled her toward the edge of the bed. I reached for the ties of my pants, moving as quickly as I could. But the moment I looked to her face again, I stopped cold. The animal inside me went quiet, replaced by something else. Something ravenous in a different way.

"What?" she asked suddenly, her brows furrowing. "What's wrong?"

My head shook slightly, the movement involuntary as the weight of the moment suddenly pressed down on me. This woman, this beautiful, brilliant, kind woman...wanted me. In this moment, she wanted me. *Me.* I was the only person in the entire world seeing this right now, seeing her. How in the ever-loving fuck could I be this lucky?

"You're the most remarkable thing I've ever seen in my life," I managed to say. She looked away, a blush stealing across her cheeks. I leaned down, my palm resting against her cheek and pulling her to face me. "I mean it, Cielle."

She threw one arm around my neck, pulling me to her, our mouths crashing against each other as she reached her hand between us. I gasped when her grip closed around my length, her hand moving up and down in a way that sent my head spinning.

"You just tell me if you want to stop," I murmured as she ran the tip of my cock up and down her center. She was going to drive me mad and we'd barely even started.

"I will absolutely not be doing that, thank you," she answered with a smile, angling her hips up in invitation.

All logical thought left my body the moment I entered hers.

Chapter 17
Cielle

My vision went wobbly for a moment and I saw stars. My head was empty. It was me, Miles, and the heat that was expanding between us.

I shifted beneath him, trying to accommodate the stretch as he drove forward into me slowly, his eyes locked on mine. Seated to the hilt, he let out a mangled breath, his lips turning up in a smile that ricocheted through me. I was caught somewhere between wanting to savor this feeling and demanding he give me everything, all at once, right *fucking* now. All I could manage was to look straight at him and lose myself within the galaxies of his eyes. His gaze darkened, the look in them severe and predatory, like he was having the same internal debate I was.

He began to move, slowly but intentionally, carefully watching my face in the way he always did. I clawed at his back in time with his movements, the euphoria of this moment so all-consuming that it blotted out everything that wasn't Miles. My legs hooked around his hips, pulling him closer to me even though I knew in my heart of hearts it would never be close enough. As if he'd been waiting for the signal, his pace quickened, the feel of him inside me and on me and all around me the most overwhelmingly intoxicating sensation I'd ever known.

There was no way this was real life. Our bodies moved together like the sun rose, like something that was so natural in this world that there was no second thought to be had on its mechanics. It had always been and would forever be.

Miles pulled away wordlessly and urged me backward, guiding me to lay on the bed as he climbed in over me. His hand closed around one of my legs as he rested it against his shoulder, pushing into me once again with a groan that came from deep in his chest. I almost combusted as one hand ran up and down the leg slung over his shoulder, and the other slid from my collarbone to my stomach and landed between my thighs.

If this was what it was like to descend into madness, I'd gladly jump off the ledge. That shining peak was not too far up the mountain once again. Miles was pushing me closer, watching my face with all the calculated concentration of a soldier. His thumb began to move in different patterns, assessing the way I responded to each movement, and doubling down when I began to jerk against him.

It came out of nowhere, my eyes squeezing shut as I tipped over the edge, my hands fumbling to grab his wrists where they moved against my skin. It was a wildfire tearing through me, the destruction in its wake most welcome. And like a wildfire, what was left behind would never be the same again.

My eyes opened only to land on the sight of Miles' head thrown back, his breaths becoming more ragged as he came undone, leaning down to grasp my chin with a grip that was borderline painful in the best way. His forehead rested against mine as he groaned, our chests heaving against each other as our heads floated down from the clouds.

His fingers ran over my forehead, tucking an errant strand of hair behind my ear as the most brilliant smile I'd ever seen bloomed across his face.

"You're extraordinary," he breathed, catching my mouth in a deep kiss that sent echoes of bliss through me. I clung to him, burying my face in his neck. His scent had somehow already become a comfort to me. *He* had become a comfort to me.

This wasn't enough. It would never be enough with him, even with all the time in the world. We had a matter of *weeks,* and that had already almost been taken away from us, something I hadn't told him.

The shadows crept in then, our earlier conversation playing over in my head. I tried to push it away. I wanted the truth to be as far away from this moment as possible. That's the thing about the truth, though. You can run from it as much as you want, but it's eventually going to find you.

"Come back to Coldwater with me," I whispered against his skin.

His body tensed against me, every single muscle in his sculpted form going taut. He slowly pushed up to meet my gaze, his expression painfully blank. The silence was deafening, pushing in on my ears with what felt like physical pressure.

The breaths that left him had become measured. "It's just not that simple."

"It *is* simple, though. Here, you're a soldier. In Coldwater, you wouldn't have to be a soldier. You could be anything you want."

Miles pushed himself to sit up, offering me a hand and pulling me up with him. "Oh, yeah? What if I wanted to be a blacksmith?"

"You could be a blacksmith."

"What if I wanted to be a chef?"

"Isa told me, you know. About the steak you made when you first met her."

Genuine surprise marked his face, followed by embarrassment. "Dammit, Isa."

I playfully jabbed at his arm. "You could be a chef if you really wanted to. You'd just need a lot of training."

He went quiet for a moment, his eyes falling to the sheets. "What if I want to be a soldier?"

I shrugged, pretending I was unbothered by the conversation when in reality, a tornado was ripping through my chest. "I think I know someone who could make that happen."

"We can't have this conversation, Cielle." His voice was suddenly lower.

I pursed my lips, swallowing hard. This conversation was going to be a pushpin on our timeline. A date circled on the calendar. Our time together would be separated to before and after this very point.

My heartbeat had never returned to normal, but now it was raised and erratic for a very different reason. "I think we have to have this conversation," I said into the silence.

Miles nodded, one fist clenching and relaxing in the sheets next to him as he let out a defeated breath. "You don't support Kauvras' cause."

My ears rang as his words settled. *Kauvras.* Not *King Kauvras.* He called him Kauvras. That tiny fact was most likely insignificant, but I ran with it. It was just enough to bolster me. Because maybe there was hope of him leaving Taitha. Maybe there was hope of him leaving behind the savagery he'd be ordered to commit.

"No," I said simply. "I don't."

His eyes fell away, focusing on the headboard I leaned against. "I knew that," he murmured. "Of course I knew that. But hearing you say it is..."

I answered when his words trailed off. "Final."

"Yeah," he answered with a strained sigh. "You know what I'm supposed to do now, right?"

My chin dipped with a nod. In the grand scheme of things, I had no reason to trust this man. But I knew without a doubt that he wouldn't be the one to turn me in. It was right there, clear as day in his midnight eyes. Continued validation to bolster me. *Keep him talking. Maybe I can talk him through it.* "I had to bring Cenric here." That was the truth, and with it came raw emotion that cropped up out of nowhere, clamping around my throat. "You know that, right? I had to bring him."

His eyes softened. "I know."

"We did what we had to do to get into the city."

"I know," he repeated. The look on his face sent a pang of guilt to my chest, guilt for him. He was knowingly associating with a traitor that he was bound by duty to turn in. He was bound by law to turn me in. And Miles' honor... It was everything to him. It was all he'd ever had.

176

I swallowed hard, running my thumb over the sheets until the fabric felt scratchy against my skin. "So it's true then? The rumors about leechthorn?" I glanced up and saw his eyes closed, his mouth turned down just slightly at the corners.

"Which rumors?"

"All of them."

There was a painful pause before he finally spoke. "Yes."

"So you'll go to cities on Kauvras' orders and force leechthorn on their people?"

"Yes."

"Then bring them back here and store them in a barrack so Kauvras can build his army?"

When he finally opened his eyes, the pain that roiled behind them almost took my breath away. "Yes."

I inhaled deeply, trying to cling to the tiny seed of hope that was still sitting in my chest. He was questioning himself, I could see it. No part of me wanted him to endure the turmoil I knew was throwing him around like a rowboat in the middle of the ocean. Saints, I'd do anything to take that pain from him. But I couldn't, and I knew the only way for him to get past that pain was for me to drag him directly through it.

"How do you do it?"

He blinked a few times. "What?"

"Do you hold them down by force?" I flinched internally at the look on his face, but I continued to stare at him. "When you give them the leechthorn, do you physically hold them to the ground if they resist?"

His eyes went dead. Miles' body was here, but his mind had gone somewhere else. Maybe he was trying to protect himself from his own words. Maybe he couldn't, and what I was seeing was the result of him being forced to face the truth.

"Yes."

"Walk me through it."

I held my breath, convinced he would shut the conversation down. But he cleared his throat, squared his jaw, and looked me directly in the eye. "I haven't done it yet. But when the time comes, we'll receive orders from Kauvras." *Kauvras.* "We storm the city or village and focus on a central place, like a market or town square. Some people will surrender to avoid death or violence. Others will..." He pursed his lips, his hard façade threatening to falter. "They'll fight. In which case, we've been instructed to use physical restraint or force to subdue them. And we're supposed to be on the lookout for the Daughter of Katia."

I forgot about that part. Kauvras really was a madman.

Miles spoke like he was reading the words from a script. There was no feeling behind them, no hint of the remorse I knew had to be eating him up inside. It was a fight to keep my voice from shaking when I spoke again. "And then?"

He let out an uneven breath. "If they're too unruly, we've been instructed to kill them."

My stomach churned, ice freezing in my gut as I pushed forward. "Everyone in the village?"

"Yes."

"Children?"

The pause was excruciating as he worked his way toward his answer. "Yes."

I nodded. I'd already known the answer. My father had told us as much. I knew not every Cabillian soldier would be monstrous and violent, but I also knew that they were asked to commit atrocities I didn't even want to think about.

There was a disconnect in my head between Miles and the orders of his king. Pushing him to talk through everything in an attempt to persuade him to leave Taitha was painful for him, yes. I just hadn't anticipated it to be so gut-wrenching for me. My brain began to reconcile the kind, honorable man sitting before me with the image of him in a small village, bloodied sword in hand and a bag of leechthorn at his side. He was surrounded by people screaming, fighting, dying — and still he had to continue on.

But he wasn't there, yet. His sword was still clean. His soul was still clean. I reached out, my hand resting gently against his knee. "You can leave with us, Miles."

His jaw worked, and I could almost hear the sound of his teeth grinding together. "This is all I've ever had."

"But it's not all you have now."

His eyes found me, and though tears didn't flood them the way they flooded mine, there was a pain so excruciating I felt it in my bones.

"It's easy to stick to what you've always known," I said quietly, somehow able to blink the tears back as I swallowed hard. "There's comfort in routine and familiarity. I know it will be difficult to leave that all behind."

"I swore an oath to Kauvras."

"But he doesn't own you. You may have given him your word, but you don't have to give him your life. You don't have to give him your soul. That's yours." My thumb ran circles over his knee, fumbling over a tiny scar. Dark eyes stared down to where my skin met his. I was trying to find the words to get it through his head that he didn't need to stay here, honor be damned. "You owe it to yourself to do the right thing. Not for me, and not for Kauvras. For you."

Miles was silent for a long while as the battle raged in his mind. In one way, I was sorry I'd turned his entire life on its head. He'd been comfortably on this trajectory for years, and I'd crashed into him hard enough to throw him off course. But he had a chance to change direction, and I desperately wanted him to.

If not for me, then for himself.

Miles truly wasn't a monster, and I had a nagging feeling within me that even if he chose to stay and follow Kauvras' orders, he *still* wouldn't be a monster. He'd simply be another man bound by honor and duty, his name lost to history among all those who murdered and pillaged and died for the same reason. The same stupid, archaic, Saints damned reason.

The conversation was done, I could tell. There was nothing else I could do as I laid down my proverbial sword and prayed I'd won the battle.

"I know they call it Coldwater," I said suddenly, trying to inject my tone with something other than heartbreak, "but the water isn't really that cold. Not in the summer, at least. The ocean is crystal clear. It really is a beautiful place." Maybe I could entice him with that.

The smile he gave me didn't reach his eyes. "If it produced someone like you, then it must be." He pulled me to his chest, an urgency in his movements as I lay down beside him. The way our limbs tangled together was so perfect. *He* was perfect.

I was going to get him out of Taitha.

Kindly deliver to the Port of Coldwater

Dearest Mother and Father,

~~I've been given the most wonderful gift I could ever dream of.~~
~~Father, you may be disappointed, but I don't think you would be~~
~~if you knew how happy this makes me. Miles gave me a harp. A~~
~~real harp. The one I've been eyeing since we arrived in Taitha. I~~
~~think there's a chance he's made a lasting mark on my heart. No,~~
~~it's not a chance. He has made a lasting mark on my heart, and~~
~~I'm terrified.~~

Much to Nieve's dismay, we've decided to stay in Taitha until
our originally intended departure date. Cenric has a new
childminder — a woman named Isa — and he adores her. She's
truly wonderful, and she and Cenric took to each other
immediately. Miss Isa, as Cenric calls her, has no fear of creatures
of any kind, even insects. The first time Cenric tried to scare her
by sneaking a frog into her pocket, all she did was laugh. Cenric
was very much disappointed at first, but quickly came to realize

that a childminder who wasn't afraid of his animals was a very good thing.

Nieve's manners are still atrocious, though I think a man ~~or possibly a woman, but that's not my information to tell~~, may have disarmed her a bit ~~in a pub we definitely weren't patrons of~~. There may be hope for her yet, though I'm not sure I can say the same for myself ~~because I'm falling in love with a Cabillian soldier~~.

Yours,

Cielle

Chapter 18

Cielle

Nieve was at Rose's Respite. Again. She'd become a damn regular at a Taithan pub. The statement was almost too wild to believe. Though, I was thankful she was taking her bad mood somewhere that wasn't directly in my face.

Miles had left for a swordwork session with Bowen. Isa and Cenric had returned from the pet shop, and even though I was here to watch Cenric, Isa had remained. She sat on the settee, legs folded under her, listening intently as Cenric read from a book about drivas. I sat at the kitchen table, reviewing the list of healers and metalsmiths that had become irrelevant to us now. There was no use in poring over their names and notes anymore when my mother had promised the answer was back in Coldwater.

What answer could that be, though? What the hell sort of miracle had they found that they hadn't already tried?

I thought about this so I didn't think about Miles. About our conversation earlier. About the things he'd be ordered to do.

Nausea roiled in me, and it took all my energy to keep myself from falling apart.

"Have you ever seen a driva?" Isa asked, feigned wonder in her voice. I smiled at the question as I let it distract me, knowing Cenric would be happy to answer.

"Drivas aren't real, Miss Isa," he answered with a saddened smile. "Nieve taught me."

Isa furrowed her brows. "They *are* real. They just live in the Saints' realm."

Cenric's eyes narrowed. "Have you seen one?"

"No, not yet. Maybe one day we'll go on a big adventure to find one. How does that sound?"

Cenric squealed with excitement, and my heart warmed in my chest. Isa looked to me and winked, a knowing smile on her face that I mirrored. Before I looked back to the parchment in front of me, my gaze caught on the harp in the corner. It really was beautiful, and it settled something in me I hadn't known had been turbulently churning, until it stopped.

Isa glanced at the clock on the mantle, hopping to her feet suddenly. "I'm so sorry, Little Prince. I didn't realize what time it was. I have to get going."

"Why?" he asked, his voice whiny.

She had a shift at the Blushing Dove, something we of course had no intention of telling my little brother. "It's getting late, and I have to get home."

Cenric's eyes narrowed, and he leaned in. "Are you going to go hunt for a driva?"

Isa's palms turned up in mock surprise. "You're so smart, Little Prince! How did you know?"

He beamed, his eyes bright as he stared at his favorite childminder. "When I get back to Coldwater and I can walk, maybe I'll come back to Taitha and we can go driva hunting together."

"That's a great idea," Isa answered, tapping his nose with a finger and smiling back at him. "I'll see you tomorrow, okay?"

"Alright, bud," I interrupted. "Go change and get ready for dinner."

Isa waved and watched him wheel around the corner, letting out a contented sigh. "He really is lovely."

184

"He is. I'm glad you love him so much, because he really seems to love you."

Her smile was warm as I reached into my pocket for a handful of coins. I debated asking how much she'd make at the Blushing Dove tonight. I could offer to double it. Would that be insulting to her? I piled the coins in her hand, deciding it was safer not to trust my own judgment.

"Miles is a good guy," she blurted suddenly, her face slackened with something I didn't recognize. "Despite his *job*."

My first instinct was to freeze as I figured out how to respond, but I managed a close-lipped smile, trying to keep myself together and failing miserably. A long, strangled sigh left my mouth as I leaned back in my chair. "I know. That's the problem."

"Please forgive me for overstepping," she continued as she wrung her hands in front of her, "but try not to hold his honor against him."

I blinked, trying to take in the meaning of her words. "What do you mean exactly?" I asked apprehensively. "And please don't apologize for overstepping," I cut in before she could answer. "I actually...could really use a friend that isn't Nieve."

The smile on her face faltered, her mouth moving silently as if she were practicing the words before she spoke them. "I hold the same beliefs I assume you do." Each word was deliberate as she nodded, her brows raised expectantly.

Isa was a dissenter? I blinked wildly, understanding hitting me like a cannonball to the chest. Holy shit. "You're..."

"Yes. I'm a dissenter." The words were a whisper cloaked in a sigh, quiet enough that even I could barely hear them. "He knows, and he's vowed to keep the secret." Her eyes shot to the ceiling suddenly, one side of her mouth scrunching. "Well, I sort of tricked him into keeping the secret." I knew that would be a story in and of itself, one Isa didn't have time to tell me now. "His honor is of the utmost importance to him. From what he's told me, it's really all he's ever had."

I nodded. I knew that already, but the care in Isa's voice was undeniable.

"I'm telling you all this," she said carefully, sliding her fingertips across the wooden tabletop, "because I'm going to ask something of you."

A strange feeling entered my stomach at the unreadable look on her face. "Okay."

"Get him out of Taitha."

My breath hitched. Had he told her about our conversation earlier? Isa was a dissenter, yes. That was treason in and of itself. But for her to even suggest this to me... I blinked, and I was sure I looked like the doe-eyed dumbass Nieve always claimed I did. "I'll try." It was all I could muster.

"He's too good for this place. He's too good to be one of Kauvras' goons. Just... Please, get him out of Taitha."

"Okay."

"What's for dinner?" Cenric asked as he rolled out of the hallway and smiled at the sight of his childminder. "You're still here, Miss Isa?"

"Just saying goodbye," she quipped, ruffling his blonde hair. "I'll see you tomorrow."

Again, I debated asking her to stay, but kept quiet, instead walking her to the door and giving her a goodbye that didn't betray what I felt in my chest.

"I'm hu-u-u-ungry," Cenric whined, snapping me out of my thoughts. "What's for dinner?"

I straightened, dusting my hands down my sides as if the movement would cast away my unsettled feeling. "How about pork sausages?"

"Yes! But can I ask for something first?"

Like Isa, the look on Cenric's face was unreadable. "What is it? Another trip to the pet store?"

"That, too. But could you play me a song on your harp?"

I hadn't been expecting that. "I don't know how to play yet, remember?"

"Please, Seashell?"

"But I thought you were hu-u-u-ungry," I replied, mocking his whiny tone.

"I'm hungry for a good song." I blinked, raising my brows and fighting back a smile. "Can you just try?"

186

I followed him to the harp, appreciating the curve of the instrument as I neared. I couldn't believe it was mine. Lowering myself to the seat, I reminded myself my only audience was Cenric. It was okay if the song wasn't perfect.

My finger plucked a string, its frequency humming against my eardrums in the most pleasant way. Another note rang out when I plucked the string next to it, a stairway of musical notes extending before me as I worked my way down the strings and found my bearings.

"Wow," Cenric whispered.

"I haven't even played anything yet," I laughed.

"It's so pretty, Seashell."

He was right. Even just the single scale down the strings was beautiful. I chose a random string, its sound melding with the next note I played, building together into some semblance of music. After a few moments, I was able to find a rhythm, sort of like I did with the violin.

I played something that was as unorganized as it was enchanting — the latter half probably only because of the instrument I played it on. Even the notes I played on accident seemed to fit perfectly within the melody. I lost myself in it all, my eyes closing as the music took over my movements, some divine source seeming to guide my hands. I'm not even sure how long I played, but at some point, the music slowed and quieted, coming to a beautiful, final note, almost on its own.

"That was incredible."

I jumped at the voice, standing so quickly the stool clattered to the ground behind me. Miles stood beside Cenric, his hand on my little brother's shoulder as the two of them smiled.

"Miles," I whispered. Had he been here the whole time? Had I been so lost in the music that Cenric had let him in the front door without me even noticing? I ran my palm over my forehead, a bit bewildered.

Some sort of squawking screech sounded from Cenric's room, and before I knew it he was wheeling in that direction, yelling for Peapod and Button to *stop fighting.*

"Peapod and Button?" Miles asked quietly, eyes wide as he stared after Cenric.

I let out a sigh, suddenly very much back in the present moment. "I've never heard him say either of those names, which means they must be new. And I have no idea what that noise was, which means I have no idea what species they are." My arms fell to my side in defeat. "Did that sound like birds to you? Or frogs?"

"I'm not sure, but it didn't sound good. I'll see if I can get any information out of Isa," he answered, one side of his mouth turning up in a smile as he took a step toward me, reaching for my hands. "That song really was beautiful, Cielle."

I averted my gaze. If I'd known he'd been listening, I would've tried a little harder. No, if I'd known he'd been listening, I wouldn't have played at all for fear of fucking it all up.

"What's it called?"

I furrowed my brows. "The song?" He nodded expectantly. "It...doesn't have a name. I sort of just made it up as I went along."

His face remained unchanged. "No, you didn't."

"Yes, I did. Is it that hard to believe?"

"Yes," he said, "because that was by far the most beautiful music I'd ever heard in my life. You really just made that up right then and there?"

I shrugged, confused why he was so impressed by a random assortment of plucked strings. "I just played it."

He let out a laugh that was heavy with disbelief, shaking his head as he stared down at me. "Amazing, Princess. Absolutely amazing."

The smile that overtook me couldn't be denied, and I lowered my head in an attempt to hide from him. It was no use though, because he pulled me to his chest and rested his lips against the top of my head.

"I just wanted to stop by to say goodnight," he said quietly.

"You walked all the way across town after dinner at the mess hall just to say goodnight?"

"I just thought after our talk earlier today..."

The energy in the room changed suddenly, suddenly turning darker. My shoulders tensed, and he must've noticed because he pulled away awkwardly, straightening where he stood before me. I opened my mouth to speak, but all that came out was a choked breath. What could I say to him?

"Goodnight, Cielle," he said, leaning down to brush his lips against mine. My hands grasped at his elbows, and I willed them to stay there instead of roving the rest of him.

"Goodnight, Miles."

Chapter 19

Miles

I'd awoken in a cold sweat more than once tonight. Every time my eyes opened, I turned to the window in the barracks, praying I'd see daylight. Daylight meant I'd have something to do to distract myself.

The expression on Cielle's face when I told her what I'd be expected to do... It would forever be imprinted on my soul. No part of me would ever forget the sheer disappointment that rang through in her voice. She'd tried to hide it. Of course she did. But disappointment that profound cannot be hidden by even the most beautiful of masks.

I had to go back to see her last night, to stamp out the forlorn image of her in my head. And I had — I'd walked in on arguably the most remarkable thing I'd ever witnessed. She played the harp like she'd been doing it for years, like it had been crafted specifically for her. Her entire heart went into that song, evident in every note she plucked from the strings.

It sickened me that I could be a source of her greatest joy or her most gut-wrenching disappointment.

With every swing of my sword during training, with every evading maneuver I practiced, with every order Vorkalth screamed at us, the feeling grew heavier in my gut. It was a boulder poised at the top of the mountain, ready to tumble down and crush the brick walls I'd built around myself.

The squad had been at the archery range for an hour now. I'd lost count of the amount of arrows I'd sunk into the red painted circle in the middle of the target. I'd always felt like archery came naturally to me, and I was hoping I'd be able to lose myself to the steady rhythm of arrows sinking into straw. But, of course, it did nothing to quell the racing thoughts. I shook my head, willing it to go blank so I could add a few more bricks to my walls.

Fact: I took an oath. Fact: I was honorable enough to keep that oath. Fact: I didn't want to.

I snatched the last one from my brain, mentally slamming it to the ground and watching it turn to dust. My walls were built so I could protect myself, and I could tell a brick like that would be laid crooked and risk the entire wall. It would only be a matter of time before the whole thing crumbled.

Part of me was afraid it was already beginning to wobble.

"Landgrave!" I heard Bowen yell, and I could tell by the tone of his voice it wasn't the first time he'd called my name. "We going?"

My chest heaved as I reentered reality, staring at Bowen blankly before I caught up with the here and now. I looked around to see nothing but an empty archery range, no arrows flying through the air beside me. Every other station was empty. Training must've finished at some point, something that had gone unnoticed by me. "Yeah," I answered, wiping the sweat that dripped down my brow. "Yeah, sorry."

"You're on thin ice." If Bowen saw my face, there'd be no way to hide the weariness. Luckily, he didn't care enough to look. "You need to get your dick wet. That'll help your focus and get your mind off the fact you didn't get a promotion."

Holy shit. He still thought *that* was the problem. That was good, right? Jealousy was much easier to explain away than fucking treason. I kept my gaze down as we left the training yard. I didn't have the energy to muster up an actual response to Bowen. "Maybe."

"Why do you even go to the Blushing Dove?" he asked harshly. "I know you're not getting any action there."

I really wasn't in the mood to deal with him today. "Isa is my friend." The answer was flippant, but I'd managed to keep the irritation from my tone.

"Yeah, Felina is my friend, too," he said sarcastically. Bowen was always spouting bullshit. I didn't know why I expected anything else.

I couldn't help but grind my jaw as we walked through the streets of Taitha. My steps were uncharacteristically rigid, and I knew it was a matter of time before Bowen called me out. My internal conflict was overflowing and I had no way to keep it inside.

"The fuck is wrong with you?" Bowen spat.

Right on schedule.

I wanted to keep Bowen separate from Cielle. He didn't need to know anything about her. He was so harsh, every edge of him jagged. Sometimes I thought the only reason he was even in my life was because he'd used those jagged edges to affix himself to me. He'd dug them so far into my flesh that the wound had closed around them and there was no way to dig them out.

Anger flared in me at the thought of the night I found him looming over Cielle at the Griffin's Back. I had no claim over her then. Fuck, I had no claim over her now, either. I never would, because the only person who had any sort of claim over her was...her. But seeing someone like Bowen, so rotten and vile on the inside, talking to someone like Cielle... My blood boiled. The thought was acrid and sharp as it careened through my mind so quickly I had to consciously keep from acting on it.

Bowen took my silence as an invitation. "Trouble with your girl?" My eyes widened. I hadn't breathed so much as a word to him about Cielle. He took my silence as confirmation and leveled me with a smirk. "I've known you this long. You think I can't tell what's bothering you?"

"No trouble," I pushed out. "Everything is great. Just tired."
Bowen surprisingly seemed to drop it, but I could tell he felt like
he'd won a prize by guessing.

As much as I wanted to go see Cielle, I needed to see Isa just
as badly. I felt silly to admit I needed a friend in this moment.
But deep down, I knew what Isa was going to convince me to do.
Which was exactly why I wanted to see her.

◆ ◆ ◆

"You're *really* going to ask me if you should desert your post
to run away with the girl you love?"

I flinched at her words, so many things to pick apart among
them. *Desert my post.* The thought made my skin crawl. *Run away.*
From the oath I took, abandoning my honor like a fucking
coward. *The girl I love.*

Fuck.

My heart felt like it was torn in two as I looked at Isa, giving
her the dumbest fucking response I could've conjured up. "Yes."

Her face softened as she lowered herself to sit beside me. She
was silent for a moment, her eyes intent on the Cabillian crest
sewn into the leathers on my chest. "I'm not telling you this
because of my beliefs. I'm telling you this as your friend, okay?
Go," she said, her jaw square. "Go with her. It shouldn't be a
question."

I stared back at her, wanting so badly to listen and run straight
through the city to Cielle's doorstep. What stood in the way was
the stupid fucking wall I'd built around myself. I'd called it a
home, but I was afraid I'd unknowingly built a prison.

Every brick had been placed with the intention of giving
myself purpose. Giving my life the meaning I needed to keep
going. I had no real family, no home. I needed *something.* So I
clung to my honor, duty, and ability to follow orders, and I called
it a life. At the end of the day, they were the only things I was
guaranteed to have. Everyone and everything could burn to the
ground, but I'd still have my honor.

"I don't think I can do it," I finally said, and I almost didn't
even recognize the sound of my own voice. I felt like I was

outside my body, like my heart and brain were two separate entities, each screaming at the other to sit the fuck down.

Isa gave a long sigh. "Miles, I say this with love, as your friend. No one is going to come after you. No one will even notice you're gone."

My brows furrowed at the dig. "Thanks."

"You're an unranked soldier. They're not going to waste any time or resources chasing after you." The corners of her amber eyes crinkled with a smile as she leaned forward to lay a hand over mine. "Staying here is taking the easy way out. This is your chance to go."

I debated telling her Cielle had said something similar. My ears rang as I warred with myself. The internal struggle felt like it was going to rip me apart from the inside out.

"You have one life, Miles," she continued, filling the silence I'd provided. "You are here for one tiny blip in the entirety of existence, one tiny blip that belongs to you. And out of all the time that has passed and all the time yet to come, you and Cielle are here at the same time. Do you know how rare that is? Do you know how many things have to go right in the universe for that to happen? For two people so perfectly matched to exist at the same time is... It's nothing short of a miracle." As if she knew exactly what was happening in my head, Isa leaned forward and placed a hand on my shoulder. "So stop thinking about it and just *do it*."

Isa was right. No more thinking. No more reasoning. No more excuses. Honor be damned. If I left, I'd no longer have my honor. But I'd have Cielle.

Fact: I was a soldier. Fact: I was wrong to hold that above everything else. Because, fact: I was in love with Cielle.

I was going. Holy shit, I was going. But–

"Come with us," I blurted before I even considered the implications of the words.

Her face went blank. "What?"

I nodded, trying to quickly work through the logistics in my head. "Come with us to Coldwater. Cielle said they needed a childminder there, too. Cenric loves you. Cielle will be thrilled with the idea." I grabbed her arm, giving it a gentle squeeze as I stared at her. "Isa, come with us and get out of Taitha."

She ran her hand through her hair, a strangled noise coming from her throat that was somewhere between a sob and a laugh. "Okay."

"Okay?"

"Okay." The noise turned into a laugh thick with disbelief, the sound so genuine it warmed the blood in my veins. I folded her into a hug, laughing with her as her body shook against mine.

I let out a whoosh of a breath, relief pulsing through me as I pulled back. I was going to do this. *We* were going to do this. I was going to be with Cielle. "They're leaving a week from today. Keep quiet until then, okay? I don't know exactly what the plan is just yet."

She nodded quickly, her cheeks suddenly rosier, her face somehow brighter. As if on cue, I heard familiar footsteps in the hall.

"Let's go, Landgrave!" Bowen yelled, an overly aggressive fist pounding against the door and rattling it in its frame.

"One week," I whispered to Isa as I stood, "and you'll be out of here."

Her smile was infectious as she reached up to plant a kiss on my cheek. "One week."

Bowen's face was an unwelcome sight when I opened the door, but for the first time, it didn't bother me. "You look happier than you did when you walked in here," he drawled, smacking a hand on my shoulder. "Get your cock sucked by your *friend?*"

The annoyance that surged at Bowen was nothing compared to the excitement and determination I was working hard to conceal. "Nope."

"Well, something happened."

I kept my expression neutral, unsure of what to say. I decided on silence as we descended the stairs and paused at the front door. Bowen did no such thing and instead blew right past Hjalmar.

"No," the guard grumbled, a tree trunk of an arm shooting out to stop Bowen. "You know the drill. Can't leave until the girls say so."

Bowen reached up, placing a comically small hand on Hjalmar's forearm and pushing it out of his face. "Are you aware I'm a lieutenant in the Cabillian military?"

"Don't give a rat's ass who you are." He jammed a thick finger through the doorway, pointing to the top of the stairs. "You could be Kauvras for all I care. Can't leave until the girls say so."

Bowen leaned forward, craning his neck so his face was as close to Hjalmar's as he could manage. "I can leave whenever I want," he snarled, each word clipped as he tried to push past again.

It happened so fast my brain couldn't comprehend what I saw until Bowen was on the ground, his head lolling from side to side. Hjalmar had quickly returned to his normal position, arms crossed over his chest as if he hadn't just knocked half the consciousness from Bowen's skull.

My mouth dropped open and I froze, unable to reconcile what I'd just witnessed. I stood dumbfounded, locked in place as I watched the strings of consciousness reattach to Bowen and pull his mind back into his body. He managed to push himself to stand, one eye already turning a sickening purple as it swelled. "I'll give you that one for free," he taunted, his chest heaving.

Fucking idiot. What the fuck was he doing?

Hjalmar stared down his angular nose at Bowen, one brow raised. He looked unbothered. Bored, if anything, and I knew that was going to light a fire under Bowen's ass.

Shoulders squared, Bowen stood as straight as he could, and I knew what would come next. "Landgrave." It was a command. Not a request. Not a question. A clear command he'd given me dozens of times over the years. A clear command I'd always followed.

I'd backed him up in every scuffle in the orphanage, every barfight, every brawl he'd roped me into since I met him. It had always been me and Bowen against a world that kicked us while we were down. What I realized now, that I failed to realize all the times before, was that Bowen was the instigator behind every one.

"Landgrave," he repeated, his voice deeper.

No.

196

My hesitation wasn't because Hjalmar was a barrel-chested bear of a man who could kill me with one blow — I'd backed Bowen in a dozen fights against people bigger and stronger than us.

I chose not to follow his command because I was fucking done with Leo Bowen. I was done standing beside a shitty person and calling him my brother out of fear of being alone. I was *done*. I wouldn't be alone anymore. I had Cielle. And Isa and Cenric. Even Nieve.

I wasn't alone, and I never would be again.

Bowen's eyes were the only thing that betrayed his surprise as I kept my hands at my sides and stepped back, giving Hjalmar a nod so slight, I was surprised he saw it.

It took one right hook and Bowen was unconscious, slumped in a heap in the doorway. By the sound of Hjalmar's fist landing against the side of Bowen's face, I could tell he wouldn't be waking up any time soon. With one booted foot, Hjalmar kicked the limp body down the front steps, the guard's face expressionless the entire time. He quickly resumed his position once again without so much as a glance in my direction. I slipped past him, slowly descending the stairs and standing over Bowen's crumpled body.

His eye had swollen almost completely shut already, and a slow stream of blood trickled from one nostril to drip on the cobblestones. It'd be a Saints damned miracle if the bones of his face had stayed intact. A miracle, I knew, Onera hadn't granted.

Big, bad Bowen laid broken in the street. And if I left him here in the street, that would be it. Maybe I'd be able to recover from leaving him to face Hjalmar alone. But leaving him bruised, bloody, and unconscious? That was a line in the sand.

I stepped right over that line, over his body, heading for Cielle and a life in Coldwater.

197

Chapter 20

Cielle

Nieve and Cenric had gone to bed an hour ago. Now, it was just me, the crickets, and the nervous energy I'd channeled into chopping vegetables that didn't need to be chopped right now. I'd been jittery since my conversation with Miles, a ball of nerves thrashing around in my stomach at the miniscule possibility of leaving Taitha with him in tow.

Now, he stood silently in the front door, his eyes roving over my face as if he'd never seen me before. I ushered him through and pulled the apron over my head, balling it on the counter as soon as we entered the kitchen. The expression on his face was completely indecipherable. Nothing I'd ever seen on any face before. His lips were pursed, dark eyes somehow both weary and more alive than I'd ever seen them.

"Miles?" I asked quietly, extending a hand to cup his cheek.

A calloused hand reached up to grip my wrist, the touch gentle. "I'm coming with you."

My mind went quiet save for the sound of those words echoing through me. *I'm coming with you.* I froze, afraid that if I moved, the illusion would disintegrate. This couldn't be real. It couldn't be this easy. "To Coldwater?"

His chin dipped in a nod, a bit of the weariness slipping away from his eyes as he gave me a weak smile. "I'm coming with you to Coldwater."

My chest felt like it could simultaneously cave in and burst as my heart ran wild. Tears welled in my eyes, propelled forward by the sweetest relief I'd ever felt. But something was wrong. I could tell by the strange expression still on his face. It was icy water on a hot flame. "What?"

"Isa," he answered, the sound seeming to come with all the air in his lungs. "First, Isa."

I blinked, an ache panging through my chest at the thought of him having to leave her. I'd been so focused on getting him out of Taitha and away from Kauvras, I hadn't even thought of Isa.

"Could she..." he stumbled over the words, each one hesitant, "come with us?"

"Absolutely," I answered without hesitation. Of course she could. I was ashamed I hadn't thought to extend the offer before.

"I thought maybe she could be Cenric's permanent childminder."

I nodded emphatically. "Done. My parents will be thrilled I found someone willing to take the job."

Miles nodded, a flash of relief crossing his face before it fell away, replaced by something darker. He let out a shaky breath, and I took his hand and led him to the settee in the living room. "What, Miles?"

His dark eyes found mine and I recognized the look of grief on his face. "I lost Bowen."

I flinched, straightening in my seat as I searched his face. "What do you mean you lost him?"

"We were leaving the Blushing Dove and he got cocky," he murmured. I listened as he recounted everything in detail, pain evident in every word. Regret, too.

I didn't like Bowen. I'd met him just the one time and that was more than enough for me. Normally, I'd hold someone's friends against them. A person is only as good, only as honorable as the company they keep. In this case, though, it was different. They were brothers in every sense of the word but blood. So even though I didn't care for Bowen, my heart cracked for his brother who sat broken before me.

"Maybe he'll forgive you," I said, a hand on his knee.

A muscle feathered in his jaw and he swallowed hard, his throat bobbing as he shook his head. "It won't happen. He's vindictive and cruel. He doesn't forgive, and he sure as hell doesn't forget." He collapsed back against the settee, his hands hanging in his lap. "How do I grieve for someone who's still alive?"

I'd never seen Hjalmar, but from what Miles told me, Bowen may *not* be alive. I kept that to myself, though. I had nothing to compare this experience to. As far as losses went, I'd been blessed by the Benevolent Saints a dozen times over. I'd never lost anyone. Hell, I even had all my grandparents, something I tried not to take for granted.

"That's a good question," I answered, circling my fingers over his leg. Words failed me, and I knew nothing I offered in this moment would make him heal any faster.

Miles nodded, closing his hand around mine and bringing it to his mouth to plant a kiss across my knuckles. "I'm ready to leave Taitha."

It was a great effort to keep myself from squealing in excitement like a child. I couldn't believe it. He was coming with us. "I'm ready to take you to Coldwater," I whispered.

A smile pulled at his mouth out of nowhere, his eyes glinting in the low light like the night sky. It was the most beautiful sight, somehow made even more beautiful by the pain that preceded it. He was coming with us. He would be safe.

Kindly deliver to the Port of Coldwater

Dearest Mother and Father,

There's been a bit of a change in plans. We will be returning to Coldwater with two of its newest residents. Isa will be moving to Coldwater to act as Cenric's permanent childminder. She is more than capable of the job. I hope that your excitement at this prospect will soften the disappointment coming next.

I've fallen desperately in love. I understand the implications of breaking my promise to Prince Rayner and am prepared to do what is needed in order to smooth things over. Though I am hoping since we were not officially betrothed, the damage will be minimal. I look forward to introducing you to Miles Landgrave. You're going to love him.

We'll see you soon.

Yours,

Cielle

Chapter 21
Cielle

We would be departing in two days, and the plans were almost set in stone. Since Miles was deserting his post, we'd need to leave in the darkest hours of the night. He knew exactly where each guard station was and how to evade them. At that hour, they'd be lazy and dozing. We'd hired a man to discreetly escort us by horse-drawn cart through the Rhedrosian Mountains to the town of Aera. There, we'd board a ship headed upriver for the Widow's Sea.

We were going to tinker with Cenric's wheelchair to find a way to break it down and make it easier to transport. Or, we'd *planned* to tinker with his wheelchair. But Miles wasn't here yet. He and Isa were supposed to be here twenty minutes ago.

"Where the fuck are they?" Nieve asked in her familiar, harsh tone. "I *know* Cenric, cha-ching."

Cenric snickered to himself as he sat at the kitchen table drawing on a piece of parchment. A bird was perched on his shoulder — one I didn't recognize, but she sang softly as Cenric fed her seeds every so often. A cricket chirped from somewhere in the living room, the sound setting my nerves on edge.

I swallowed, pasting a look on my face that disguised the nervousness I felt. "Relax," I crooned, keeping my tone even. "He's probably just running late."

Miles didn't run late. Ever. I began to pick at my nails, swallowing back the anxiety that threatened to rise. *He was running late. Nothing else. He was simply running late.*

Nieve retreated to her room after an hour, huffing something about *inconsiderate assholes* as she climbed the stairs. The worry in my stomach had turned to full on knots, pulling tighter with each passing minute. I couldn't sit here any longer.

"Nieve?" I shouted up the stairs before heading to the front door. A muffled curse was her answer. "I need you to watch Cenric!"

Cenric perked up, seemingly unaware that so much time had passed as he scribbled away. "Where are you going, Seashell?"

"I'm going to find Miles."

◆ ◆ ◆

I originally started toward the town square to see if I could overhear any chatter about training or missions or, I don't know, *something* that would keep the soldiers tied up past training. But when I saw men clad in black leather casually walking the streets, I knew it wasn't his duty keeping Miles. My feet immediately turned toward the west side of town, the side that bordered the leechthorn fields.

In any other circumstance, I'd be humiliated and red-faced asking a stranger to point me in the direction of a brothel. Today, I didn't care, and I was breathless by the time I finally turned a corner to see the Blushing Dove at the end of the street. My anxiety had increased with every step, the feeling of foreboding growing larger and more prominent in my stomach.

As I neared, my eyes fell on the truly enormous man at the front door. Shit. Miles really hadn't been kidding when he described Hjalmar. And I was unsure how Bowen could be standing if he'd been at the other end of that gargantuan fist. The guard didn't bat an eye at the sight of a sweaty, disheveled mess of a woman stumbling up the front steps of the brothel. He simply nodded and stepped aside to let me through the door.

Inhibition left me the moment I entered. "Miles?" I yelled, my eyes scanning the dark, smoky interior.

"Excuse me," a petite older woman said in a hurried tone, her deep red hair piled into an intricate arrangement on top of her head. Thin, wine-red lips tipped into a sly smile when her eyes met mine. "Are you looking for employment, dear?"

"Miles Landgrave," I choked out. "Where is he?" She looked me up and down then, her expression turning to something akin to disappointment, her hand landing gently on my arm as if to lead me to the door and back to the street.

I steadied my feet on the floor, inclining my chin in defiance. "Where is Miles Landgrave?"

A woman appeared at the top of the stairs, one thin brow raised in a way that almost seemed antagonistic. "He's with Isalyne." The words should have calmed me, but there was something in her voice that shot down any inkling of relief.

I turned back to the woman in front of me. "Where is Isa's room?"

The older woman glanced over her shoulder, some silent exchange taking place between the two of them. A sigh left those thin lips, one hip popping out as if in boredom. She rested her pointer finger against her cheek. "They're in the town square, dear."

My first instinct was to thank her and leave, but I held her gaze for an extra moment. Her mouth had turned up at one side in a scathing smirk.

Something wasn't right.

I turned on my heel to leave, blowing past where Hjalmar stood at the front door. "Hey," he called, the low drone of his voice matching his size. "You're going to want to hurry." The man nodded in the direction of the street, his large arms crossed over his chest.

My lungs burned as I ran, and I cursed the fact that I was so fucking out of shape. I pushed my legs as hard as I could, gathering my cloak and skirts in my hands as best I could to keep from tripping. The sun that had been beating down on me was slowly being swallowed by a cloud, and I welcomed the small reprieve from the heat as I turned the last corner to the town square.

It was then that my heart dropped to my stomach and shattered, because there was a noose hanging from the gallows...

And Isa stood on the platform.

◆ ◆ ◆

Miles wasn't hard to find in the small crowd that had gathered. I crashed into him, clawing at his arms. "Miles, look at me. Miles, please. Look at me." His gaze didn't falter though, and he kept his eyes straight ahead on Isa. His face had drained of blood, his honey-brown skin now ashen under a thin layer of sweat. "Miles," I whispered, pulling at his collar. He was catatonic, his focus so intent on Isa, the world around him didn't exist.

The crowd had gone silent as the Commander's voice vibrated through the crowd. I could feel it. Deep down, I knew what he was saying, but my brain couldn't make sense of it. Why the fuck was Isa standing to be *executed*? What the fuck had happened?

But every thought went quiet and everything around me blurred into one single thought: *Get Miles out of here.*

"Kill her, Vorkalth!" someone shouted from the crowd. "Hang the treasonous bitch!"

I turned to Isa, her eyes already on me. She looked strangely calm, her copper red hair twisted into a thick braid that rested over one shoulder. She mouthed a message to me, the same one that had consumed all my thoughts. "Get Miles out."

It was an effort to blink back the tears that had sprung from my eyes. I didn't have time for my own emotions right now. I couldn't let Miles see this. For the love of the Saints, I couldn't let Miles see this if it was the last thing I did.

But he'd know. Even if I managed to drag him away, he'd know what happened. He'd be able to see it in his mind, because right now, he stared as Isa lowered her head to allow the executioner to place the noose over her neck. Silence swept over the crowd as he worked to tighten the rope. I didn't have time to question why she was letting him do it, why she wasn't thrashing against the ties that bound her hands and feet.

"Miles," I said under my breath, staring straight up at him. "Look at me, Miles."

He shook his head so slightly that if I weren't staring straight at him, I wouldn't have even noticed. My view swiveled to where Isa stood on the gallows, her eyes locked on Miles. They flicked to me again, and she nodded in the direction of the house. *Get him out.*

I widened my eyes as if to say, *I'm trying.*

"Miles," I begged. "Let's go, Miles."

"No." The word was spat through teeth gritted so tightly his jaw had to be aching. I pried his fist open to thread my fingers through his.

"Miles," I whispered.

"*Shh!*" the woman in front of me spat, quickly turning her head to glare at me. Still, Miles' eyes didn't move.

I knew it would be useless to tug on his arm, but still I tried. His chest began to quake, like he was stifling a sob that threatened to overtake his whole body. His face remained blank as he continued to stare, but the sweat on his brow began to bead and drip down his temple

The Commander — Vorkalth, the piece of shit — stood at the edge of the platform, yellowed eyes on Isa. I squeezed my fists together to tamp down the urge to climb the platform and gouge those eyes from his head. He inclined his head slightly, staring down his nose at her. "Last words?"

The street was silent. "I don't regret any of it, so I'll say it again." She leaned in as much as she could before the rope went taut. "Fuck Leo Bowen and every other soldier who supports Kauvras. Fuck your city. Fuck your country. And fuck. Your. King." Then she spat in the Commander's face, and the crowd had gone so still and silent we could hear the sound of her saliva landing between his brows.

Bowen.

All at once, the crowd erupted in thunderous outrage and Vorkalth stepped forward, shoving the executioner out of the way and grabbing the lever, heaving it to the side and watching as the floor dropped out from beneath Isa's feet.

The cheers somehow grew louder and every muscle in Miles' body went rigid, his hand gripping mine so hard I could almost feel my bones turn to dust. A mangled sob escaped his throat as Isa gasped, her face going red as her eyes found Miles' once again. And as the twitching of her body began to slow, I could see her lips turning up in a contorted smile, her eyes still on Miles until they were suddenly distant.

"Fucking *bitch!*" the Commander yelled at Isa's hanging body.

Vorkalth descended the stairs of the gallows in a huffing rage and the crowd quickly began to disperse, people carrying on with their days as if they hadn't just watched on as a life was extinguished. Miles stared as Isa's body was cut down, blinking hard at the sound it made when it crumpled on the cobblestones. He stared still as she was loaded into a wooden cart and pulled away.

His eyes were void of stars and galaxies.

◆ ◆ ◆

No one even spared us a second look as they shuffled past us. I didn't know how long it had been, but Miles still stood, staring. Staring. Just staring. I alternated between pressing my cheek to his chest and clutching his hand in mine, doing both with enough pressure to let him know I was right here. But I was so concerned with getting Miles home that the truth of the entire situation hadn't hit me until now.

Isa was dead. Bowen had turned her in. *Isa was dead because Bowen turned her in.* Something I'd never felt before sparked deep in my gut, hot and angry. I didn't think I'd ever been truly enraged before. Not until now. And even though it was completely foreign, I recognized it immediately. I made no attempt to stop its growth even as it heated my skin and pricked at the backs of my eyes. The worst part of it all was I knew it was a pebble compared to what was tearing through Miles this very second.

Isa was dead because Bowen turned her in. Within a matter of days, Miles had lost the two people who had ever given him any semblance of family.

The light of the day began to go dim and dull. Shops began to close, awnings pulled in and windows shut and locked. Shadows grew long before the darkness absorbed them altogether. Night had fallen over the city before I tried again to give Miles' hand a gentle tug, and this time, thank the Saints, he relented and followed me.

Nieve sat on the front porch, a book in her lap which she promptly slammed shut when she saw us approaching. She shot to her feet, hands on her hips, the picture of impatience. "Where the hell have you been?"

"Not now, Nieve," I murmured.

I prepared myself for a fight, but her energy immediately turned at whatever she saw on Miles' face as I dragged him past her. "Where's Isa?"

All I could do was look over my shoulder at her and shake my head. Her hand flew to her mouth, the color immediately leaving her face.

I brought him directly to my bed, pressing his shoulders just enough to urge him to sit on its edge. His face was blank as I knelt between his knees. "Miles, look at me."

Those eyes stayed somewhere far away. His bottom lip twitched as if the words he was going to say had died just before he spoke them. His chest shook as he exhaled.

"She's..." he stuttered, blinking fast. "She didn't fight." His eyes flicked down to me then, the darkness in them magnified in the low light. "Why didn't she fight? Why didn't *I* fight?"

There was no possible way I could rationalize what had just happened, but I was sure as hell not going to let him feel guilty for it. "What could you have done, Miles?"

"I could've put my sword through Vorkalth's chest."

"And you would've ended up with a sword through *your* chest, and Isa still would've..." I trailed off, unable to breathe life into the fact that the public execution had happened at all.

His chest rose and fell rapidly, the air moving in and out of his nose as he tried to keep himself from breaking. He looked to me suddenly, his thumb and forefinger gripping my chin. "You keep your mouth shut, Cielle, because I will *not* watch you hang for the same thing." The words were choked, the brutality of his tone not lost on me.

"I know," I said, my hand moving to rest on his wrist.

"No," he snapped, his tone suddenly harsher, his grip on my chin growing tighter. "You don't know. You don't know what I would've done if it were you with your neck in that rope today." There was a wildness in his eyes as he searched my face, as if looking for a way to make me understand. "I should've done the same thing today. I should've put my sword through Vorkalth's chest. Why didn't I do anything? Why did I just stand there?" His hands tore through his hair, the distress on his face more than I could handle.

"If you'd tried anything, you would've met the same fate." I'd say it a million times if that's what it took for him to believe it.

"Gladly," he answered, his hands suddenly on my cheeks, pulling me to stand. I stared down at him where he sat on the bed, my legs tucked between his, his eyes so intent on mine that I almost shied away from the intensity. "You cannot talk to anyone before you leave this city. You will not be caught as a dissenter, Cielle, because I will tear the city apart to get to you before you hang. I will tear this world apart. Do you understand me?"

I nodded, blinking quickly as I took in his words. "You don't need to tear anything apart, because we'll be safe in Coldwater soon."

He pulled me to his lips, his mouth urgent against mine as his arms closed around me. I could feel the choked sobs racking his body as he kissed me.

"Seashell?" Miles pulled away suddenly as Cenric rolled into the doorway of my bedroom, his form silhouetted by the light spilling in from the hall.

"Hey," I said as cheerfully as I could manage, trying to stand in front of Miles, a feeble attempt to cover the devastation on his face.

"Hey, bud," Miles said from behind me, his tone perfectly even, devoid of even a hint of the turmoil raging beneath his skin.

209

I stepped aside, watching as Cenric's face lit up at the sight of Miles. Then his brows furrowed as he looked between us. "Where's Miss Isa? She was supposed to come over today."

My breath hitched. Neither Miles nor I moved as Cenric's brows furrowed even deeper. Cenric's only experience with death was with his beloved pets. My father had told him that when a life ended, their souls were no longer in their bodies. Their physical forms were still here, but they were not, because they'd moved on to be with the Saints. No matter how my father tried to logicize it, Cenric was gutted every time he found one of his pets lying lifeless in their cage. How was I supposed to tell him about Isa?

"Why are you still up?" I asked, trying to sound as normal as possible.

"I stayed up because Miss Isa was supposed to come over. Where is she?"

"Miss Isa had to leave Taitha," Miles said quietly, no evidence of his own sorrow as he cut off my internal debate. "She really wanted to come say goodbye before she left, but she didn't have time. I'm sorry, Cenric."

"Oh," he said, his eyes falling to the floor. "Is she going to come back?"

I looked to Miles, his eyes still on Cenric. I was blinking furiously, trying to corral the tears before they spilled. "I don't think so, bud." I was glad Miles managed the words, because I couldn't.

"She must be going to look for drivas!" There was excitement in his tone that chipped away at my heart.

"Yeah!" Miles answered, echoing his excitement. "That's exactly where she's going."

Cenric inhaled slowly, his eyes wide in amazement at the lie Miles was telling him. "Wow. Maybe she *will* come back then, so she can tell us all about what she found."

Miles didn't answer immediately. His face was still carefully neutral. He was fighting for control of his emotions and his grip was slipping.

"Why don't you go see if Nieve has any pastries?" I asked, trying to disguise the quiver in my voice as excitement.

"Isn't it too late for pastries?"

210

I shrugged. "Special treat," I said, nodding to the door. "Midnight pastries."

He wheeled off excitedly, shouting for Nieve down the hall.

I turned to Miles. His eyes had glazed over and he was far away again. The light from the hearth danced in his gaze, like the very fire burned in his eyes. I knew in some way, it was. Something darkened over his face as he stood suddenly, his fiery stare landing on mine. "I'm going to kill Leo Bowen."

Chapter 22
Miles

There was no rage within me. No sorrow. No feelings of betrayal. There was simply determination to find Bowen and watch as the light in his smug face went dark.

That image pushed me to my feet and out the door before I even knew I was walking, down the ramp from Cielle's cottage and into the street. It was the earliest hours of the morning, something I could tell because the only people still out were a few stumbling drunks.

Bowen was on solo patrol tonight at the castle's eastern watchtower. I'd climb the stairs and corner him on the platform. He'd have nowhere to go but forward, straight to my blade.

"Miles!" The soft voice I'd come to know had taken on an edge of severity. "Stop!"

"Go home, Cielle," I barked over my shoulder.

"*Stop!* Don't be a fucking idiot!"

I turned to see her running toward me as fast as she could, chest heaving as she skidded to a halt before me. The torchlight in the street was dim, but I could see her red-rimmed eyes as her hands reached for my arms.

I easily shook out of her grip and took a step back, trying to put distance between myself and the one person who could stop me from doing what I was about to do.

"Go home, Cielle. Now."

Her eyes peered around, making sure the empty streets were, in fact, empty, before she quietly spoke. "What is the consequence for killing a fellow soldier?"

"I won't be caught. Go home, Cielle. I mean it. Do not follow me."

"Miles, just—"

"You and I come from different worlds, Cielle! You have a family who loves you, and you've never doubted it for a second. You will never, ever understand. Now *go home*."

Her arms dropped to her sides, her face slackening as she bit the inside of her cheek. I spun on my heel, grateful that no footsteps followed me. My eyes were affixed to the northeast, where I knew the watchtower would emerge on the skyline as I drew closer. An earthquake had started to rumble through my mind and I fought back a wince as the foundation of my mental walls began to crack. Bowen had been there as I built these walls brick by brick. Maybe he'd be there when they all came crumbling down.

And I knew for certain at that moment, the monster lurking behind the walls was thirsty for blood.

Glancing over my shoulder again, I was relieved when I saw no sign of Cielle. The truth I had yet to admit to myself was...there was a very real chance I would be caught. I didn't have the luxury of thinking through my actions right now. Not when I was this numb.

A piece of the numbness was chiseled away by the sharp edges of searing rage as I arrived at the base of the watchtower. With every flight of stairs I climbed, my lungs burned more and more, but it was nothing compared to what was erupting inside me.

I made no attempt to conceal my footsteps as I ascended. I prayed to the Blood Saints that fear was growing in his chest, larger and larger as I neared. I prayed that behind the smug exterior I knew I'd see when I crested the stairs, he'd be cowering in a puddle of terror. Because at the end of the day, he might be my lieutenant, but he was nothing more than a weak man hiding behind a mask.

Bowen stood relaxed against the wall as I pushed through the heavy wooden door at the top of the final flight of stairs. His bruised, swollen face was already pulled up in a shitty smirk, exactly as I'd expected, and he swung his sword in lazy circles. "Took you long enough."

I said nothing as I unsheathed my blade. The hot rage within me had bubbled over and turned to ice in my veins. Blood pounded in my head so furiously, I couldn't hear the sound of my own thoughts.

He leisurely glanced over the edge of the watchtower. The city was to our west, and to our east was nothing but rolling hills and farmland. "We're too high for anyone to hear your cries when I skewer you through the chest."

My lip curled. "This ends now. Stand the fuck up and face me."

He sniffed indifferently, finally straightening with a sigh, as if doing so were an inconvenience. One hand flexed at his side as he cracked each knuckle. "Let's end it, then."

Suddenly he was charging, a bull rushing toward me with rage unparalleled. But I'd trained with Bowen for years, and he was nothing if not predictable. I easily stepped to the side to dodge his swing and was ready when he pivoted and launched another strike. My blade met his and the sound of steel rang out high above the city. It wasn't long before I began to overpower him, but he suddenly dropped back, swerving to swing his sword again.

I dodged that one too, but only just. He must've been training harder, because that was a move I didn't recognize. The edge of his blade scraped against the stone floor of the watchtower, the sound sending a shiver up my spine as I turned to face him again. I'd never seen the motherfucker move so quickly, as if he'd been training for this very moment. But he was predictably unsteady on his feet. Balance had never been a strength of his, and it was

214

the most important element in any fight. That, I knew in my bones.

"Why the fuck did you turn her in, Bowen?" I growled as one blade ran against the other. He spun and landed a blow against my back with the broad side of his sword. The impact sent pain ricocheting through me and a strangled cry left my mouth, but I quickly righted myself just in time for his blade to land against mine once again.

"Because I knew you'd come here to try to kill me," he answered, his teeth gritted just as tightly as mine as he channeled all his strength into holding me off. "And I wanted to watch you die at the end of my blade."

I stepped back, using his lack of balance against him to send him stumbling forward. I swung wildly for his throat. He moved quickly enough to evade the killing blow, but not quickly enough to avoid a nick to the side of his neck. Blood coated his fingers as his hand traveled over the wound, carnal rage flooding his eyes at the sight, sending him sprinting toward me once again.

He overshot his swing, only managing to bring the pommel of his sword down against my elbow. My arm straightened on instinct and my blade flew from my grip, clattering across the stones behind Bowen.

A ruthless smile twisted his face, steely eyes burning with the same fury they had since we were kids. Only now, his chains had snapped. *He* had snapped. He raised his sword over his head, lunging for me, a scream erupting from his throat. I swerved out of his way, darting for my sword where it lay discarded, but his blade came down to scrape across my lower back. I could tell it wasn't anything deeper than the very surface, but my body still bowed in response, and I turned to see the sheen of his steel in the torchlight as it rapidly approached my head.

I did the only thing I could think to do and dropped to the ground, rolling out of the way of his strike. Bowen stood over me, the gleam of victory already shining in his eyes. But I knew Bowen, so I knew he kept too much of his weight on his front foot. Always had. I managed to kick one foot forward, hooking his front leg and buckling his knee, sending him teetering just long enough to stand and shuffle to retrieve my sword.

"This all started when we were boys," Bowen panted, straightening. He suddenly threw his blade to the ground, the sound ringing in my ears as he stared at me, fists clenched. "Let's finish it as men."

Bowen had always been better at hand to hand combat. I could take him with a sword any day. Fists? It wasn't so cut and dry. But I couldn't deny him. Not here. My only choice was to kill him with my bare hands.

I tossed my sword to the ground, making an effort to keep him from seeing my hesitation. A heady wave of sorrow suddenly washed over me as I looked at the deranged man in front of me.

"Why?" I asked through sawing breaths. "We've been brothers since we were twelve."

Bowen's lip curled, his face a deep shade of crimson. "You've always thought you were better than me. Ever since we were kids."

"You're fucking mad if you think that, Bowen."

My comment must've unlocked something in him because he was coming at me, fists moving faster than I'd ever seen them. He landed one, two, three blows against my cheek. But that balance — that's what was going to do him in again.

I ducked, his fist moving so quickly that I heard it fly through the air as I lunged forward, sweeping his legs out from under him. Any other time I would've stopped to appreciate the sound of his body hitting the ground, but I didn't have time. I pinned him easily, staring down at his bruised face, that wicked smile still curling his mouth in a way that made me nauseous.

"I fucked her, you know," he growled. "I fucked Isa before I turned her in. Paid her and everything, then took the money from her pockets before they strung up her body on the castle wall." Bile shot up the back of my throat. My fist was clenched so painfully tight I thought it would crumble into gravel.

"You were my *brother!*" I shouted, my voice even raspier than normal as I choked back a sob. "You were my fucking brother!"

"I wasn't your brother when I was at the end of Hjalmar's fists."

"I've backed you up in every single fight, whether it was justified or not!" I pushed out, shaking him by the collar as if it would knock some fucking sense into him. "I've always had your back, and I can't anymore. How could you blindly go along with Kauvras' bullshit?"

He was silent, his eyes narrowing on me antagonistically. "I knew it." I was breathing hard as he stared at me. "Always so fucking sensitive. I knew you were a fucking dissenter."

I cocked my fist back. Grief mixed with adrenaline in my veins, a thread of pride woven through it all. "Of course I am. Should've turned me in when you had the chance."

"And miss out on the opportunity to kill you myself? Where's the fun in that? But you know what will be even more fun?" he asked, eyes wild. "Fucking your girl. Think I'll do that after I end your pathetic life. She's a pretty one. *Cielle*." The way his tongue slithered over her name had my fist coming down on his nose before I even knew it was moving. Over and over again my clenched fist slammed into his face, pain radiating up my arm.

All at once I felt it — felt the ground beneath my mental walls begin to quake. A crack split the base in two, spiderwebbing between the bricks and sending bits of crumbled mortar skittering to the ground.

Bowen was fighting to stay conscious and somehow succeeding, even against every blow I landed. His nose had shifted to the side, blood spattering with every impact, leaving the taste of iron on my tongue.

"You were my brother," I ground out. Angry tears blurred my vision, the hollow pit of betrayal opening in my stomach. It yawned wider and wider with every swing of my fist, my mental walls growing weaker as my anger grew hotter. "My *brother!*"

I said I was going to kill him, and I meant it. Doing it with my bare hands would be that much sweeter.

"Miles!"

The voice stopped me mid-swing, a voice that was forever branded on my soul. Everything faded away other than its echo as it bounced off the stacked bricks in my brain that were just moments from falling. My head turned to see Cielle in the doorway of the tower, her face contorted with horror as she stared at me.

I looked down at the bloody mess that was Bowen's face as it dropped to the side. His eyes stayed on me, though, the blood gathering between his teeth as he smiled. I rose, Bowen's splattered blood dripping down my cheeks as I stared at her. I'd never wanted her to see me like this. She should never be subjected to something this raw and brutal.

She stepped forward, her palm reaching forward to rest on my bloodied cheek. "Miles," she whispered and shook her head. The concern on her face almost broke me.

"Go home," I growled, my breath coming in choked gasps as I fought to steady my pounding heart. "Please, Cielle, go home."

"No," Bowen's voice sounded from behind me. He pushed to his feet as he spat. His feet were unsteady beneath him as he tumbled to lean against the back wall of the watchtower, his back bowed over its edge. "She should stay. Winner can take her right here and now."

Anger boiled over in my chest and I lunged for him, but Cielle's voice rang out again. "Miles!" I stopped in my tracks, turning to look at her. She walked to stand between us, and in that moment I would've done fucking anything to get her away from him.

"You've got him that pussy whipped?" Bowen let out a snarling laugh. "You'll be a fun one to break."

My blood pumped so hard in my ears as I charged, I didn't even realize Cielle had started moving until her hands were on Bowen's chest, and she was heaving, heaving, *heaving* her full weight against the unbalanced bastard.

His head went over the railing, then his torso, then his feet.

Bowen didn't scream as he fell. I'd never heard the sound of a body hitting the dirt at a speed fast enough to kill on impact, but from this day forward, I'd live on knowing exactly what it sounded like, what it felt like to hear it. The *thump* reverberated through the otherwise quiet night air. Then the silence set in.

Leo Bowen was dead.

Chapter 23

Miles

Cielle snatched my sword off the ground, sliding it into the sheath at my hip when I didn't immediately take it from her hand. "Give me your canteen," she breathed hurriedly.

Confusion. Shock. Numbness. "My canteen? Why?"

"Give me your canteen, Miles."

I obliged, fumbling at my belt to hand her the canteen. I stared wide-eyed as she uncorked it and doused the blood-spattered stones, nodding to herself as she quickly inspected her work. "Now, come on," she said, her hand grasping mine as she pulled me toward the door.

I was completely frozen as I tried to form words. When they finally came, they were a choked whisper. "Why did you push him?"

Her brows rose as she stared at me, her hands closing over my arms. "You were going to kill him, Miles."

I didn't think I was breathing anymore. "You killed him."

"I wasn't going to let you die for that. We need to get out of here, *now*."

"Cielle," I breathed, the word shaky. "*You're* going to die for that."

She ran her tongue over her lips, pursing them as she continued to stare up at me, her words low when she spoke. "Why would *I* be executed because a soldier committed suicide while on solo patrol?"

"What are you talking–" It was like a bucket of cold water had been thrown over my head as understanding cascaded over me, my mind suddenly crystal clear. Goosebumps rose over my skin and fear exploded in my gut as I realized what she'd done, what was at stake. She'd washed away the only evidence of a struggle.

She'd staged a suicide.

Then we were moving, taking the stairs two at a time as we descended the watchtower. Our breaths came in labored huffs as we hit the bottom floor, sweat dripping from brows and temples. I craned my head through the doorway, looking and listening for any sign of activity. We couldn't see it, but I knew Bowen's body lay shattered on the other side of the watchtower, on the side that backed up to the farmlands. The streets were silent. It seemed that no one had seen or heard him fall.

Could we really have been that lucky?

I folded Cielle's delicate hand in mine and pulled her along, rushing between shadows on the street. We were silent as we worked our way through the torchlit city.

The woman who walked beside me was no longer a princess in my eyes. She was a warrior, a soldier in her own right. A soldier *doing* what was right.

A much better soldier than I could ever hope to be.

"Keep the doors locked until I come get you tomorrow," I murmured as we arrived at the gate in front of the cottage. I felt like the panic had crawled its way up my spine to wrap around my throat. She nodded, her face completely neutral. "I need to make sure we weren't seen."

I leaned down to take her lips with mine, her body immediately pressing into me in a way that had my gut clenching. I wasn't sure whether it was the adrenaline pumping through me or the warped grief that twisted in my core, but I was fighting back the urge to tell her I...

No, I couldn't tell her yet.

With a final kiss, I squeezed her hand and gently pushed her toward the cottage. She looked over her shoulder one last time, a storm rolling in over the ocean in her eyes.

◆ ◆ ◆

I'd managed to slip back into my bunk in the barracks unseen, but sleep hadn't found me. It had been hours that I'd been laying here, recounting what had happened over and over again. Another soldier had filled the bunk next to mine, the one that had been Bowen's before he was promoted to lieutenant. I stared over at the form sleeping beneath the sheets, my stomach churning.

My mind wandered to a place I never let it go — my life before. Before the fire, before the orphanage, before Bowen. It had been a house fire that changed everything, meaning we'd had a house. I had a home. Did I have my own bedroom? What would *they* have thought of this, the ones who'd given me a life I'd tied so tightly to honor? The woman with the black hair and the man I remembered nothing of. Had they loved each other? Had they loved me? Did they know, from somewhere beyond this realm, that I'd never properly grieved for them?

It had been hard enough to spend those few days grieving for Bowen while he was still alive and breathing. The cleaving of our brotherhood felt like a growth had been removed from my body — I was better for it, but the wound left behind was going to bleed for some time. The finality of his death was...

Complicated. I'd gone to the watchtower with every intention of killing Bowen. I would've, if Cielle hadn't stopped me. I would've bludgeoned the life from him with my bare hands and reveled in the silence that followed. And I would've grieved after I'd done it, for the loss of my brother and his soul. Though I should've grieved the loss of his soul long ago, because it had long been rotted.

But now... Now I felt like I was grieving for Cielle as well.

I couldn't count myself among the ranks of men who had taken another life before. Not yet. There was always something different about them, though. Those soldiers were dimmer. Rougher. Less likely to find the value in life since they'd seen how easily it could be pulled out from under someone.

Was Cielle feeling that now? The fear seeped into my bones as I thought of her lying alone in her bed right now, staring up at the ceiling, asking herself why she'd done it, if it had been worth it. If *I* had been worth it. Nausea roiled inside me, my body's response to a heaping, tangled mess of bereavement. Relief. Anger.

A horn sounded through the air. Morning had arrived. Bodies in the bunks around me began to stir, hopping to their feet and pulling on their leathers as torches were lit, illuminating the dusty interior of the barrack. Heavy footsteps suddenly sounded over the rustle of fabric. "Formation in five minutes!" It was Vorkalth's voice, and my stomach clenched as the words echoed through the soldiers around me.

◆ ◆ ◆

It took everything in me not to double over and vomit as I stood at attention. I knew not to lock my knees for too long so as not to lose consciousness, but it was the only thing I could do to keep myself upright. And honestly, being unconscious right now wouldn't be the worst thing in the world. Sweat poured down my back despite the mild air. The only thing on my mind was getting back to Cielle, packing up, and getting the fuck out of Taitha.

"At ease, gentlemen." The order did nothing to set me at ease in the slightest. It had come from a tall man with dark skin and eyes. I recognized him — Commander Olion Summercut. He was typically assigned to another squad, but I'd seen him here and there throughout my training. I'd always liked him, because even though he and Vorkalth held the same rank, it was evident that Summercut had some sort of silent superiority over Vorkalth.

Commander Summercut stood stick-straight with his hands behind his back as he assessed the men in front of him. "I regret to inform you all that Lieutenant Leo Bowen was called home by the Saints last night." Even though the Commander was maybe two dozen feet away, it sounded like his voice was muffled by a great distance. I blinked furiously as I tried to keep myself from cracking apart as he spoke. "The manner of his death is presumed to be suicide."

Even though we were at ease, the formation of soldiers stayed quiet just as we'd been trained to do. The energy, however, had noticeably shifted between us. I flexed and relaxed my knees, trying to distract myself from the confusing, gnarled mix of emotion in my gut.

"Training will resume as normal," Commander Summercut called before nodding and stepping back.

Vorkalth took his place, immediately screaming out a string of orders in a tone that contained not even an ounce of sympathy. I stared longingly at the gates of the training yard, at the only thing keeping me away from Cielle. I debated running now, but with no way to slip out without being spotted by Vorkalth, I had no choice but to jump in line beside the other soldiers. I lost myself to the rhythm of training, to the expletives shouted at us as we ran lap after lap and I swung my sword until my arms shook with exhaustion.

It was hours before we were finally released, and I left the training yard in a state of mind so strange, I couldn't quite define what I was feeling. There was the grief, of course, at the loss of my brother and how it ended. There was regret that I'd let him walk all over me since we were kids. And then there was the overwhelming relief that his death was ruled a suicide, and Cielle's actions — whether rash or planned — had worked. It had actually worked.

My brow still dripped with sweat as I turned the corner, walking as fast as I could without drawing suspicion. My heart jumped when I heard my name called from behind me, and I turned to see Commander Olion Summercut striding easily toward me. My hand crossed over my forehead in salute as I straightened.

"At ease," he said, a slight smile on his face. "Condolences for the loss of your friend."

I lowered my head, swallowing back the mix of emotions that seemed to catch in the back of my throat. "Thank you, Commander."

"You two were close. Were there any signs he was planning to take his own life?"

I opened my mouth to tell him that Bowen was far too vain for the thought to even cross his mind. But I caught myself. The lie slithered up my throat, the discomfort of the words I was about to speak almost unbearable. It went against everything in me to lie. But here I was.

"Yes, Sir," I answered quietly, moving my jaw from side to side nervously. "I'm..." I swallowed hard, my eyes tracing lines between cobblestones as grief surged in me. "I'm unsurprised by the manner of his death."

Summercut gave a terse nod. "Interesting. He seemed thrilled with his promotion the last I saw him." His tone held no signs of suspicion, only genuine concern. Guilt shredded through me, my honor nothing but a shriveled up husk of what it had been just days ago. "Well, again, you have my deepest sympathies."

"Thank you."

He remained silent, but he made no move to leave. Instead, he seemed to be assessing me where I stood. "Landgrave, you're a fine soldier."

Where the hell did that come from? I tried to keep myself from shifting uncomfortably under his gaze. "Thank you, sir."

"You're dedicated. You're at the top of your squad in every physical area of training, and until the last few months, your attendance record was outstanding. A small slip I'm willing to overlook." My eyes narrowed as his head cocked to the side slightly and a warm smile lit his face. "I have a proposition for you."

Chapter 24
Cielle

I spent most of last night in a state between sleep and the waking world, just deep enough in the former nightmares to meld with the latter. The crunch of bone. Miles' onyx eyes as his fists rained down upon Bowen's face. Anguish that would overtake him had he continued on to kill his brother with his bare hands.

Ending Bowen's life hadn't been in my plans for the night. I simply wanted to get Miles back to the cottage and try to convince him he didn't need to risk his own life by taking Bowen's. I knew Miles would crumble under the guilt, that he'd live the rest of his life feeling like a monster.

Bowen was the monster, not Miles. And I would do anything to keep him from feeling like he was the one who needed to hide behind a mask.

The bowl of cut fruit that sat in front of me had long gone soft. My eyes blurred as I stared at a knot in the wood of the tabletop. Nieve sat wordlessly across from me, a tinge of worry on her downturned features. For once, the sound of crickets chirping nearby didn't bother me. Silence was not my friend right now, because silence was where my thoughts had the space to spiral. Nieve had bribed Cenric with an obscene amount of silver to stay in his room for the morning, and I was thankful I didn't have to look him in the eyes and lie to him again.

"He was caught," I whispered. "That's why he's not back here yet. They caught him and they're going to execute him." My face scrunched as I dropped my face into my hands. "What if they already have?"

Nieve paused before she spoke. "Don't be so melodramatic, Cielle." But her hesitation to answer told me she was thinking the same thing.

My heart pounded against a ribcage that felt like it was collapsing in on itself. "Why hasn't he come back yet?"

"He's at training."

"Training doesn't last this long." I gnawed on my fingernails, my eyes fixed to the front door as my leg bounced.

"We should leave now," she finally said, suddenly straightening.

"I'm not leaving without him." The words came out harsher than I'd anticipated, so much so that Nieve winced. Tears flooded my eyes once again, just as they had countless times in the past twelve hours. The thought of leaving Miles in Taitha was enough to shatter me. The transport was arranged for tomorrow night, and that's when I'd be leaving. With Miles by my side, safe and in one piece.

An idea appeared in my head then, my mind suddenly clearing a small section of itself just enough to see it clearly. "You and Cenric should leave today."

Her palm flattened against the table. "Without you? You're joking."

"The only reason we were planning to leave under the cover of night was so Miles wouldn't be caught. You two can leave the city during the daylight without a problem." I nodded my head, more pieces of the puzzle falling together. "That way you can get to Coldwater and prepare my parents for…everything. My last letter was sent before…" I trailed off. I didn't want to finish the sentence. "They still think Isa is coming."

Nieve was still, and I couldn't deny the surprise I felt at the fact she seemed to be considering the suggestion.. "What about you and Miles?"

"We'll stick to the original plan and leave tomorrow night. It'll be safer for Cenric to travel without a deserter, anyway." I chewed a fingernail, nervously looking to the front door. "Please, Nieve. I'll feel so much better if you go now. We'll only be a day behind you."

"An extra day here in Taitha is an extra day you could be caught and arrested for not only treason, but fucking *murder*." I flinched at the word, unable to reconcile the crime with myself as the perpetrator. "That's not a fate I'd wish upon you."

"That may be the nicest thing you've ever said to me."

"Oh, shut the fuck up, Cielle."

The momentary smile the sentiment had given me quickly faded and an invisible weight crashed back down on my shoulders. Unwelcome thoughts stormed my head, far too loud and far too numerous to ignore.

Nieve let out a heavy sigh. "I'm not going to lie and say you did the right thing. But you did it for the right reasons."

My brows raised as I stared at my cousin. "I think *that* may be the nicest thing you've ever said to me."

"Desperate times," she answered, waving a hand in front of her. She pushed her chair back, straightening her skirts. "I'm going to pack."

The relief that surged through me was a respite in the midst of so much chaos. Breathing suddenly seemed a bit easier, but my throat constricted again with the fear that right now, Miles could be standing on the platform with a noose around his neck.

◆ ◆ ◆

"I love you, bud," I said, crouching in the doorway to fold my arms around Cenric.

He squeezed me as hard as he could manage. "I love you too, Seashell." My heart broke for him. He'd been promised so much when he came to Taitha. The best healers in the world. The best metalsmiths in the world. All of them useless in the face of the solution my parents had supposedly found.

"It's just one day," I said with as much of a smile as I could manage as my hand coasted over his cheek. "Miles and I will be right behind you."

"Promise?"

"Promise." I leaned in to give him another hug. "No trouble for Nieve on the trip home, okay?"

He nodded and rolled his eyes. "Okay."

I squeezed his arm. "Promise?"

"Promise, Seashell."

I turned to Nieve, her face resting in its typical sour expression. But her green eyes seemed lighter somehow. "I'll prepare your parents when we get there," she grumbled. "It's going to be hard to persuade the King and Queen of the Surging Isles to accept a Cabillian soldier into their home."

It would be hard, but it wasn't impossible. My parents loved me. And though I knew it would take some convincing, they'd come around. That, I was sure of. "You're up to the task."

"I have one condition."

My sigh was heavy. "What?"

"You tell *my* parents that I'm still a miserable shrew and I have no business accepting any marriage proposals. Ever."

My eyes rolled of their own volition. "Sure, Nieve." I pulled her into a hug, which she begrudgingly accepted. "Get home safe."

"You too," she answered, "with your big, scary Cabillian soldier in tow."

◆ ◆ ◆

The strings of the harp vibrated as I plucked away absentmindedly, its sweet sound echoing through the empty house. For the hundredth time tonight, I craned my neck around the corner, staring at the front door and willing the handle to turn. Dusk had arrived, but still, Miles had not.

My brain rattled in my head with every agonizing second that ticked by, conjuring up images of his beautiful face reddened by the rope that tightened around his neck. My nightmare come to life.

No. I was moving forward as if he was coming back. Because he *was* coming back.

Transport was arranged for the larger trunks and boxes we had. They'd arrive in Coldwater a few days after us. The transport for Cenric's animals would be here tomorrow. On the settee sat a pile of blankets I was planning to use to wrap the harp for transport. Everything was lined up. Everything was taken care of.

Everything but the one thing I needed most.

I'd packed a single bag with only the necessities. We needed to travel light if we wanted to get out of the city unseen. The house had been scrubbed from top to bottom, the boxes and trunks organized and organized again. Now it was just me, the harp, and the crickets.

I worked through a melody, trying to play by ear a song my mother sang to me as a little girl about the arrival of the Daughter of Katia. Something about the ebb and the flow of water and something else about fire.

The hinges of the front door squeaked and I scrambled to my feet, careening around the corner into the kitchen.

Miles stood in the doorway, his form silhouetted by the low torchlight of the street behind him. His steps were excruciatingly slow as the door clicked shut behind him and he came to stand in the light of the kitchen.

The smell of new leather was the first thing I noticed. New, expertly cut black leathers were strapped to his body, the material so dark it was like a piece had been shorn from the night sky. There was a small gold bar on each side of his collar, and the gleam of polished metal glimmered from the grip of the sword at his side. I immediately knew it wasn't the one that had come so close to bearing Bowen's blood just hours ago. Miles' every feature was drawn, lodging a sense of foreboding deep into my gut.

A breath ghosted over my lips as I stared into the deep, unyielding darkness of his eyes. "Miles?" He stood straighter than I'd ever seen him, the silence hanging between us like a living, breathing thing.

Confusion whirled from my chest, up my throat, and into my head as I tried to comprehend what I was seeing. Why was he wearing new leathers? Why was he carrying a new sword? Why was—

Everything in the world fell away as my eyes tracked down his arm, all the hope I'd been holding onto smashed to pieces in the dirt and ground beneath his brand new leather boots. Because in the crook of his elbow was a golden mask sculpted in the shape of a ram's head.

Chapter 25

Miles

"Where are Nieve and Cenric?" I asked quietly.

"They left for Coldwater. You and I are leaving tomorrow." There was no leniency in her tone. What she was stating was fact and that was it.

"I have to go."

Her face had gone from relief to confusion to pure, unbridled fury within a matter of seconds. Every feature was a hard line as she clenched her fists at her sides. "Where?" The word was enunciated through a tight jaw. I knew the anger in her eyes was nothing compared to what was brewing behind them. The storm was coming for me, and my words were going to catapult me straight into the wind and rain.

"Dry Gulch."

"You're coming to Coldwater." The words were borderline choked, but her blue eyes were still dry.

I tried to shake my head but was frozen by her stare. "I was promoted."

Her jaw worked, the muscles noticeable as her nostrils flared. "They gave you Bowen's position."

I was silent. There was no need to confirm what she already knew.

The last twenty-four hours had dragged me straight to Hell and let me burn in Liara's grip for an eternity before dragging me back to Cielle's doorstep. I'd been set in my decision to go to Coldwater. I had no choice but to pivot when Summercut told me I was being promoted.

I'd been holding what felt like the weight of the world for years, and I'd always managed to keep myself upright. But that had been nothing but a river stone compared to what I carried now. If I left Taitha, it was going to tumble and crush me beneath the pressure.

Because that weight was my stupid fucking honor.

I had the position I always wanted. I had men to lead now. And the responsibility was mine to bear. There was no way I could abandon the commitments I'd made. Even in the face of what Kauvras was doing. Even in the face of what he'd already done. My honor was promised to me so long as I made the decision to keep it intact. Cielle, a life in Coldwater, a life with *her* — none of that was promised to me.

"I don't understand. You're coming to Coldwater," she repeated as angry tears welled in her eyes.

"I'm going to Dry Gulch."

"To do what?"

I kept my face straight. "You know what."

Her head shook and her lip twitched almost imperceptibly. "Say it."

"You know what–"

Her palm slammed down on the countertop. "Dammit, Miles! Say it!" she shouted through the house. "Say the words!"

I broke her stare like the coward I was. "I'm going to expand Kauvras' army."

Now, her voice was an eerie calm, and the hairs on the back of my neck stood in response. "And how are you going to do that?"

I swallowed hard as I looked back to her, rolling my lips in a tight line. "You know how."

"You're okay with Kauvras' mission right? His cause? You must be if you're serving him even after he killed Isa." I flinched. Isa's name rang through me, leaving anger in its wake. "He *killed* Isa, and you're fine with it. So tell me what you'll be doing in Dry Gulch."

Almost every part of me wanted to tell her I was joking. It was a tiny kernel seeded deep in my chest that knew the truth. Her eyes bored into mine like a chisel through stone. "Cielle–"

"A little louder," she cut in, cupping a hand around her ear. "I can't hear you."

"*Cielle–*"

She threw her head back, the symphony that was her laugh coming out like every instrument was a touch off-tune, the unsettling sound hitting me straight in the gut. "You can't even admit it to yourself."

I knew my next words would be oil on a fire. "This doesn't have to be the end of us, Cielle," I said quietly. "When I get back–"

"No." Her head shook firmly, her mouth turned down in a frown of disgust. "You go with Kauvras and that's it."

Nausea roiled through me. I was a fool to think it would be even the most remote of possibilities, that she would want to be with me. I rifled through my brain to find any way to rationalize my choice, but every single thing I found was brittle and weak. "It's a necessary evil–"

"Are you *kidding* me?" she exploded, veins bulging in her neck. "A *necessary evil?*"

"Stop!" I shouted, clenching my fists at my sides. She didn't even flinch as my voice boomed through the house. "Just *stop*, Cielle. The boys who age out of the orphanage? This is what they do. They join the military. And when they join the military, they are at the mercy of whichever king sits on the throne. That's the way it is."

The stern look had returned to her face as she surveyed me. "Show me the book."

I narrowed my eyes in confusion. "What?"

"Show me the book where that rule is written." She crossed her arms, staring at me expectantly.

"You don't understand, Cielle."

"You're right," she scoffed, the smile on her face bordering on unhinged. Somehow still as beautiful as always but now reminiscent of something dangerous. The edges of a storm encroaching on a horizon at sunset. "I don't understand. Not in the slightest. I don't understand how you can go along with this and call it *honor*." She spat the word like it was poison in her mouth.

"Because I don't know how to be anyone else, okay?" With nowhere else to go, the fury was funneled into my words and they came out as a scream. *Shit.* My chest heaved as I stared at her, at her eyes that glinted in the lamplight like the sun setting over the ocean. "I was kidding myself thinking I could just leave Taitha and be someone else. This is my identity, Cielle. I was going to be a soldier, and now I am. *This* is who I am."

"No, it's not," she murmured, shaking her head. "It's not, Miles, and you know it." Anger burned behind her eyes as she stared up at me, unblinking. "This isn't who you are. You can take a stand, Miles! You can leave!" The volume of her words had risen again, so much passion behind them that it threatened to break me. "You don't have to do what he says!"

"I do have to do what he says. I can't abandon my post, and I sure as hell can't abandon my men."

Her face had flushed with anger, her hands waving as she spoke. "You're going to continue murdering people for him because he told you to?"

"I'm not murdering anyone."

"You're taking their lives away from them. That's murder." She shifted on her feet, her blue eyes on fire as she stared me down. "You leave Kauvras or I leave you. Those are your choices. You're not stupid, so I suggest you make the smart choice."

I was a tree and she was swinging an axe straight at my weakest point, hacking away at me, hoping I'd begin to lean and snap. She was doing everything she could to break me down, and I held no blame against her.

"You're going to commit murder, Miles," she continued when I didn't answer. "You're going to murder innocent people. You're going to continue following Kauvras' order to *murder* innocent people!" A short sob broke from between her lips. "*I* murdered someone last night," she spat between gritted teeth. "I know how it feels to take a life, whether it was justified or not. I decided that I would bear this stain forever so you wouldn't have to. And I'd gladly do it again if it kept your soul clean."

The words landed like a boulder between us, casting a fragile silence over the room as the echo of its thunderous impact faded away. Even the crickets that were ever-present in the cottage had gone quiet.

Isa had come into my life and was taken from me so damn easily. She was here and just like that she was ripped away. If I went to Coldwater and somehow ended up losing Cielle... I'd truly have nothing. Not even my honor. That was not a fate I wanted to gamble on.

"This is who I am," I whispered, though it was more to myself than to her.

"No it's not," she snapped.

We were going in circles and could continue for the rest of time. My argument was weak. My justification was weak. The truth was that this was exactly who I was, even if I didn't want to be.

"Who am I, then?" I asked. My voice was hard, but it covered up a truth I wasn't yet ready to face — I desperately wanted her to give me an answer, *any* answer, other than *soldier*.

Her nostrils flared as she stared up at me. "You're the only one who can answer that."

My heart stumbled over its next beat as we stood locked in place, each daring the other to be the one to break the weighted silence. When I finally spoke, I measured my words carefully. "You'll never understand that I'm doing what I have to do to survive."

"That's a lie, because you know that you'd do more than survive if you came back to Coldwater with me. That would be a *life*. Not survival." She rounded the counter and shouldered past me, headed for the front door. I felt the burning urge to reach for her, to catch her by the wrist and pull her close. "You're a coward,

Miles." Her voice had risen in volume, and panic poured into me. "Working for the man who killed Isa."

"Where are you going?"

She opened the front door wide before she turned back to me. "I'm going to turn myself in before you can. You're bound by your honor, right?"

"Lower your voice," I spat, pointing a finger to the open door behind her. She wasn't serious about turning herself in. There was no way. "If anyone hears you outside, you'll hang for treason."

She slammed the door, and I breathed a small sigh of relief. "You're so far up Kauvras' ass you'll probably be the one to turn me in."

"That's ridiculous and you know it."

"Do I, though?" She was unraveling before me, and I was the one who held the loose end of the thread. Her chest moved with restrained breaths as she took slow, predatory steps toward me. "Do I really know that? Because it seems to me you'd be fine watching me hang. You'd be the one to pull the lever." I flinched, doing nothing to hide it. Her words had wounded me and she could see that, but instead of slowing her down, my reaction seemed to bolster her. "Why *wouldn't* you want to see me hang?"

"Because I'm in love with you, Cielle!" I shouted, air rushing in to fill the space in which I'd been holding those words. A small but noticeable bit of the weight I'd been carrying seemed to float away. I hadn't realized how much of me those unspoken words had taken hostage. Admitting it to myself was one thing, but saying them aloud...

I loved her. I was in love with her.

Her mouth dropped open and silence expanded between us, the only sound in the house that of my heaving breaths. I didn't feel my voice lower to a whisper. "I'm in love with you."

It was a long moment before she finally looked away, crossing her arms over her chest. She suddenly looked so small, so fragile, so unlike the ray of energy she was.

Her desperate stare found mine again. Her shoulders sagged, and I had to fight the urge to reach forward and prop her up. "What do I have to do to make you come with me?" Those eyes I loved so much began to flood once again, the ocean-blue turning crystalline. Tears rolled down her cheeks in a slow cascade that she didn't wipe away.

"I can't," I answered flatly. "I can't desert my men."

She scoffed, some of the anger suddenly reinstating itself. "Your men. You were promoted *today*. Your men don't even know you exist yet."

She was taking low blows. They were blows she deserved to take, and I'd let her if she needed to. All I could do was try to make her see my reasoning. "Yes, Cielle. They are my men, whether they know I exist or not. Loyalty means something."

"Do you love them?"

I furrowed my brows. "What?"

"Generally you remain loyal to those you love."

She knew how to hold the knife and exactly where to cut. I'd never met someone so good at using my own words against me.

"If you love me," she started, her voice threatening to break, "you'll leave Kauvras' army. I don't care if that sounds manipulative. Maybe it is. But I cannot stand beside someone who so easily takes the lives of others."

I couldn't control the air that left my lungs. "I haven't–"

"Yet." Her nostrils flared. "You won't be able to say that after you arrive in Dry Gulch tomorrow."

The suffocating truth took hold of my senses. It hadn't yet dawned on me that tomorrow... Tomorrow was going to stain me with blood I'd never be able to wash away.

"You're going to be fine without me," I said, trying to shake the darkness from my brain.

"Of course I'll be fine," she answered. I didn't flinch, but her words gave me pause for a moment. She took a deep breath, shuddering slightly as it left her lips. "You didn't complete me," she started, blinking fast as if she were sorting through her mind to find the words. "I was complete before you. Just like you were complete before me. Then all the sudden, there you were. My perfect opposite. My perfect complement. Like two halves of the moon, both fine on their own but infinitely more beautiful together."

"You're not half of the moon. You are the sun, Cielle."

It almost seemed like she hadn't heard me. She'd folded in on herself and was somewhere deep within her own mind. Her eyes looked to the ground as she wrung her hands together. "I'll be fine without you, Miles, but it won't be a clean break. You'll take a piece of me with you."

The truth she laid bare and raw before me in this way... Some things ache so profoundly that words don't exist to describe the pain. She'd be taking all of me with her. The version of me that remained in Taitha would have his honor, yes, but nothing else.

I came so close to breaking in that moment. So fucking close to pulling her into my arms and sprinting out the door, straight to Coldwater. And I knew a part of me was always going to wish I had.

"You'll be fine," I repeated, and I knew it was more to convince myself of that fact than it was to validate her.

"I'll marry the Prince of Zidderune. And I'll be fine."

"No," I whispered, her words ripping through the last untouched piece of my heart. I hadn't realized that at some point, her fate in my eyes had changed. I'd no longer imagined her marrying some foreign prince. Of course, she wouldn't. "You're going to be a harpist, Cielle." I cringed at the thought that she hadn't been thinking the same thing, that she'd so easily resigned herself to a fate planning parties as the Queen of Zidderune.

She shook her head absentmindedly, as if trying to clear it as her throat bobbed. "No, I won't." I opened my mouth to argue, but she spoke before I could, a sob racking her entire frame. "So this is it, then."

I bit the inside of my cheek as tears pricked the backs of my eyes. I wanted to shake my head and tell her the entire thing had been a joke and we'd be leaving as scheduled. Instead, I did the only thing I could think to do, and kissed her.

Chapter 26
Cielle

I'd never again feel what I did in this moment. Of that, I was certain.

It was a wordless storm of lips and limbs as we became tangled in each other, his scent of oakmoss and rain entwining itself with every part of my being. It was impossible to be as physically close to Miles as I needed to be. I just prayed he felt the desperation in my movements as I lost myself in him. He reached down to lift me, my legs fitting so perfectly around him as he propped me on the kitchen counter, his mouth dragging from my lips to my neck.

"I'm sorry," he whispered frantically against my skin. "I love you."

"I hate you," I choked out, doing nothing to hide the falsity behind the words. I knew it. He knew it. My head tipped back, his tongue sliding over my neck as tears began to well. "I hate you, Miles."

"I know, love," he murmured. "Hate me for the rest of your life. I'll love you for the rest of mine." A shudder rippled through my body as his mouth worshiped the skin over my throat, his tongue tracing maps he'd never be able to follow after tonight.

This was it. This was the place where the path split in two, the place where the final decision would be made. I couldn't ignore that hope was a distant lighthouse, its flame barely visible in the stormy waters that battered us. It was dim, but it was there. And maybe I was stupid for squinting my eyes and turning my head, trying not to lose sight of it through the sheets of pelting rain. I kept my mind trained on it, willing it to stay lit.

His hands reached for my clothes, his movements commanding as he slipped them from my body and threw them to the floor before following with his leathers. I wanted to tell him to stand back so I could look at him one last time. I wanted to appreciate the beauty of everything he was, then slap him across the face and tell him he was being a fucking idiot. But all I could do was squeeze my eyes shut and pull him to me as the cold truth of reality wrapped its claws around my heart.

Miles' mouth skated over my collarbone as he palmed each breast, and the sensation made me melt into him. Emotion boiled inside of me. *How, Miles? How could you worship me like this then leave?* Tears followed that thought, hot and angry as they rolled down my face and Miles continued to move lower.

My vision almost went white when he finally made contact with my core, a wave of bliss roiling through me like the ocean waves that pounded the sand in Coldwater. He groaned against me, a hungry, animalistic sound. I could feel myself growing slicker beneath his tongue, his movements coaxing waves of pleasure from me that lit every one of my nerves on fire.

Heat grew within me, the flames licking up my spine so hot I wasn't sure how much longer I could keep myself from tumbling over the edge of this precipice. I was grateful the house was empty because I didn't think I could've kept myself from the fevered moans escaping my lips, echoing off the walls as I leaned back further on the countertop. Nothing in my life was ever going to compare to this feeling.

Until suddenly, in one swift movement, he stood and pushed himself inside me. There was nothing careful or soft about it. He was claiming me one last time, and all I could do was let him. Miles' palms found my cheeks, his thumbs wiping my tears away while his lips took mine.

"I hate you," I groaned, the words breaking as they left my mouth. "I hate you." The tears rolled down my cheeks to where our lips met. I wondered if he could taste the physical pain that was coursing through me, interlaced with the pure love I had for this man that had come out of nowhere and buried itself in my soul.

Because that's what it was. Love. I loved him.

"Hate me," he answered, his forehead resting against mine as he pumped in and out, his skin growing sleek with sweat. "Hate me, Cielle."

It was so gloriously infuriating the way love and hatred warred within my chest. I loved this man. *Saints*, I loved this man. I loved every scar on his knuckles and the way his eyes crinkled when he smiled. I loved the way he looked at me like I hung the moon and every star along with it. And a part of me even loved his stupid fucking dedication to his stupid fucking honor.

And I hated him for it, too, because all of it made me fall in love with him. What had life been like before him? I couldn't recall, but I was petrified I'd soon be forced to remember.

Miles loved me and I knew it. I could feel it in every movement he made against me, every strangled sound that left his throat. That's what made this so much harder than it should've been. He loved me. But in order to love me, it meant sacrificing his honor. He couldn't have both.

And the fact was, he loved his honor more.

I couldn't deny what had been tightening within me any longer, and a violent explosion of aching ecstasy crashed through me. I grappled for purchase against the hardness of his body, tearing my nails over his flesh as my heartbeat went wild in my chest.

I loved this man. I loved this man. *I loved this man.*

With both palms on my cheeks, he seized against me, his own climax roaring through him as he held his lips to mine so tightly it toed the line of pain. A floodgate broke within me and the tears flowed like a river now. Miles' forehead landed in the crook of my neck as his breaths continued sawing in and out of his lungs. I held him to me, legs hooked around him and fingertips digging furiously into the skin of his back, trying to memorize the feel of him in my arms.

How was I ever supposed to move on from this? How could I go on knowing that he was out there, and he'd chosen his duty over a life together? Over me?

I looked for the lighthouse in the distance, sending a prayer to Idros that he'd break the storm just long enough to calm the waters and guide Miles back to me.

Chapter 27

Miles

The ram's eyes were as cold and dead as I felt. They stared straight through me from where it sat on my bunk. As if it saw the real me. As if it knew how much of a piece of fucking shit I was. I'd yet to actually put the mask on, because once I did, it wouldn't matter if I physically removed it from my body. It would always be there, marking me as a loyalist to the honor I held so dearly, but a traitor to what was right. A traitor to my own heart.

It didn't feel like a life existed outside of this. A life outside this dusty city where monsters freely roamed the streets. Whether or not another life existed or not didn't matter though, because my duty was to the mask in front of me and the king that had ordered me to wear it.

My grip closed around the ram's horns, the cool metal quickly warming under my palms. The hands of exhaustion had wrapped around me hours ago, but every time I closed my eyes, I saw the hurt in hers. And it was my fault it was there.

My honor is all that is guaranteed to me. I repeated the thought to myself as if I read a book bearing only those words a hundred times on every page. If I went to Coldwater with Cielle and lost her, I'd have nothing. Not even my honor. *My honor is all that is guaranteed to me.*

Vorkalth had barely afforded me more than a sneer when he swore me in as lieutenant. It was a quiet ceremony with only Vorkalth, Summercut, and a few other officers as witnesses. I sat in briefings all day as they tried to prepare me to be on the leadership team of a mission. I listened, but I heard nothing. I knew we were going to Dry Gulch, but I had no idea of the strategy behind it. Just that Eserene was the final prize, and we'd be able to march on the walled city within a few years if all went well. And the entire time, we were supposed to be looking for the prophesied Daughter of Katia.

"Landgrave!" Vorkalth called, far louder than he needed to. "Formation is gathering in five minutes. Your ass better be out there."

The only thing bringing me any ghost of comfort was the fact that Cielle left Taitha this morning. She didn't need to wait until nightfall since I wasn't going with her. She could leave the city in the sunlight, as she should, safe from the dangers that lurked in the night. She wouldn't be here to see me march out of the city, and for that I was grateful. She was on her way home to a family that loved her. She was going to be fine.

I found my feet. It was time. An eternity passed as I fitted the mask to my face, the world suddenly darkening aside from the light that filtered in through the two slits of the ram's eyes. My own breathing echoed in my ears, reminding me this was, in fact, actually happening.

This was the choice I'd made.

◆ ◆ ◆

Saints fucking dammit, Cielle.

Panic flooded me, because even though I couldn't see her, I knew she was here. I could feel it.

244

We marched forward toward the edge of the city, a hundred soldiers separated into squads. A small crowd had gathered, just before the cobblestone road turned to dirt and the noise of the city dulled. One figure stood separate from the rest, closest to the end of the road.

My resolve dropped to teeter on the edge of the ravine in my stomach. I knew the slightest look from her, the slightest shift in my brain would push determination right over the edge and send me running. Straight to her.

With my mask on, I was just another faceless soldier. My squad was toward the back, and even though I marched in a line of officers separate from the other soldiers, I was still unidentifiable. I was a number on a list that would hopefully one day be justified in its existence. I was far from the only soldier wearing the head of a ram. Cielle would never be able to pick me apart from the men around me.

I marched with the wolves and bears, but the real monsters were those who hid behind their jaws and teeth.

It didn't matter what I told myself. I was one of them. I had the chance to strip myself of that title and I turned it down. I was one of them, and the ram's horns that curved on the sides of my head were concrete proof. There was nothing I could do or say that would separate me from the monsters I marched beside.

We drew closer to where Cielle stood. She was scanning the soldiers as they passed her, peering out from behind her lashes the way she always did. There was no familiar gleam of light in her eyes. Only anger and sorrow.

I kept my face forward but my eyes on her, every moment drawing me closer to her, closer to abandoning my honor altogether. I prayed she wouldn't spot me, because I wasn't sure what I would do if she did. Her eyes flitted from masked face to masked face. It was a methodical and thorough assessment of the gait of each soldier, the set of their shoulders, the way they carried their head. And I knew I wasn't safe from her.

And sure enough, her eyes landed on me and remained. They didn't move to the next soldier. She saw right through the mask, right through me. Her expression didn't change, but I could see her jaw move slightly as she ground her teeth together. She said nothing, but it didn't keep her voice from sounding in my head. *I hate you.*

Hate was good. It would help her forget me faster.

I wouldn't abandon honor for love. I couldn't. No part of my upbringing, no part of my training ever taught me that, but I could feel that belief in every muscle of my body. Every fiber of my being knew that duty came first. There was nothing more important than my honor.

So why the fuck did it absolutely gut me?

I checked in on what remained of my mental walls. Somehow, they'd remained standing. A number of bricks had fallen and turned to a heap of dust at the base of the structure. Cracks and divots marred the surface. A gust of wind would topple them completely. They were weak. *I* was weak.

My footsteps went from pronounced footfalls on stone to muffled thuds on dirt, but it did nothing to muffle the sound of my heartbeat raging in my ears, every other beat telling me to do one thing, then the other. *Go with her. Go with your men. Run now. Stay. You love her. Your honor is the only thing promised to you.*

This was it.

Chapter 28

Cielle

He marched right past me.

Epilogue

Present Day

Miles

It was Dry Gulch where I first drew my blade across a screaming throat. I knew in that moment, this was how my life would end. Lying in the wake of destruction I'd been a part of. I could tell my time had come before the beam of energy even hit my body. Malosym's strike may as well have been a lasso swinging high above Cyen's head, the Saint of Death sitting high atop his stallion as he galloped toward the heart that still beat within my chest.

It was bad. That I knew. Not because of the pain, but because of the lack of it. I felt nothing, though I'd heard the sound of ripping flesh and snapping ribs, smelled the burning skin before my body even made impact with the ground. I somehow managed to look down to see my torso, my armor melted away and a canyon of a wound below that stretched from my right shoulder to my left hip. I couldn't tell if it was the warped edges of the armor or the jagged tear of my skin that glowed blue, but everything seemed to hiss and crackle.

This would be it, then. I dropped my head toward the commotion I knew was going on but couldn't quite see clearly. Petra was...somewhere. Saints, what a fucking woman she was. A fucking warrior.

Cal was there suddenly — my brother, my real brother, crouched over me, his jaw tight and brows raised as he stared over my chest. Warmth heated my entire body, or maybe it was cold. I couldn't tell.

"Yeah," I choked out, answering the question he wouldn't ask. "Not making it out of this one."

"Don't say that, Tobyas," he whispered. "You have to stay. We need you."

A mass of smoke shot up behind him as some kind of explosion rang out. Cal jumped to his feet, sword in hand as the sky blackened once again. Something was happening. Where was Petra?

"Go, Cal," I whispered, and my brother looked at me, trying to split his attention between me and wherever Petra stood atop the rubble. "Go to her."

He hesitated, and that one small moment told me more than words ever could. "I love you," he said, crouching down and squeezing my arm, his mouth a hard line.

"I love you, brother," I answered, and my voice was weaker now. It was getting harder to talk. It was getting harder to breathe.

Drivas. I'd seen drivas. All of Katia's drivas, barreling through the sky, straight from the legends. Isa would've loved it. I'd be able to tell her all about it soon enough. I hoped Cenric was somewhere safe, and that he'd hear the news and think of her.

A minute went by, or maybe it was a day. My head seemed to roll of its own accord toward the peak of the rubble. I thought maybe I'd find Cal and Petra there, but I saw no one.

I was alone in the rubble then. The sound of screams filtered through the haze, but they seemed to meld and twist with the sound of my weakening heartbeat. Wisps of black smoke started to clear from the sky, the blue finding its way back where it belonged. Not the right shade of blue, though. Never the right shade of blue.

I'd always compared Cielle's eyes to the ocean, but I'd yet to live a day where the hue was exactly the same. The sky never lived up to it, either, and neither did any blue-eyed stranger I'd come across. She was singular in that way. In a lot of ways, really. At the center of my greatest joy and my greatest regret...was Cielle.

"I'm sorry," I whispered into the air, hoping that somehow the wind might carry the words to Coldwater. "I said I'd love you for the rest of my life." I couldn't tell if my vision was going wobbly because I was losing consciousness or because tears had started to form. "I honored that promise."

My eyes closed, a marked warmth moving through my chest and outward to all my limbs. The darkness was coming for me, and I could do nothing to stop it.

I suddenly felt the corners of my mouth turn up, because amid the screams and cries that echoed from the burning city below, from somewhere in the rubble, a cricket began to chirp.

Thank you for reading! Be sure to leave a review on your favorite platforms.

Reviews are incredibly helpful for authors. Thank you for taking the time to support me and my work.

ACKNOWLEDGEMENTS

To my trusty beta readers (who are technically alpha readers) this time around — Brigitte McGuirk, Taylor Moon, Vesta Nicol, Matrasa Connolly, Amber Peterson, Patsy Brown, and Dolene Hurst, WOW! It's been almost two years since we connected for TSoS, can you believe it? Thank you guys for sticking around — and to everyone else in my beta Facebook group. You are the ultimate hype team and truly the foundation of the publishing process. It's so exciting when I get to share a new announcement or update in the Facebook group, because you all have been here since the beginning.

To my second-round betas, Shelby Rossiter and Alexandra Moyer — your comments were EVERYTHING to me. Thank you for the feedback, the laughs, and the tears. I'm sorry I had to break your hearts again, but sometimes, art is pain.

To Ivy at Beautiful Book Covers — This is the third time you've taken what was in my head and put it on a book cover. You're beyond incredible and I'm so, so happy I logged on to Etsy one day and found you. Thank you for once again killin' it.

To the Bitches group chat — Jennifer Rogers, Ashley Garner, Jessica Pettry, Chelsea Hunzinger, and Maddie Neumann. Thanks for being you. I feel so lucky to be a part of this unhinged friend group. And to Cody Rogers, Alex Garner, and James Cook, not a day goes by that I'm not thankful to know you all.

An extra special thanks to Ashley Garner for being as wildly obsessed with questionable tropes as I am. You've been by my side throughout my entire writing journey and I'm so thankful for that. Thanks for keeping my impostor syndrome in check and for assuring me my outfits are Lauz enough.

To Keely Maldonado — My sunshine on so many dark days and quite literally the reason I have a happy, healthy little boy, I love you. I can't even explain how happy I am to have met you. What a ride it's been. Thanks for always cheering me up.

To Dr. Christy Moore — I'm so damn proud to call you a friend. You are a diamond in a sea of rhinestones, and seeing you bloom the past few years has been such an incredible honor. You are genuinely one of the best people I know all-around. I love you.

To DeAnna Hill — You did it, man. You freakin' did it. I'm so proud of you for following your dream. I'm so happy the bookish world brought us together, and I can't wait to see how far you go!!!

To Lauren (almost Moran) Peel — Another book published, another thank you for always serving me the tea while it's still boiling. Sometimes it's still so hot you burn your hands, and everyone knows that's a real friend move. Love you forever.

To Bianca Bongiorno — It's been how many years? Shit. We can't ever stop being friends now because we know far too much about each other. You're quite possibly my favorite person to talk to, especially on random weekdays when we're both ignoring our responsibilities. I'm so happy Ev gets to have you as his auntie. When we're together, it is forever the summer of 2018. And Jess, you better get your ass down here to Florida, too, because it's been far, far, far too long.

To Claire HARMON (do you realize the last time I did this you were still a Hawley?!) — College roommates always make the best of friends. You are the strongest, funniest, kindest person I know. If any characters in my books have any good qualities, it probably subconsciously came from you. I'm so honored to be your friend. Standing by your side this past February was one of the best days of my life. And to Rob, you dapper gentleman you, thanks for being Claire's perfect complement. I mean it when I say you two are nauseatingly perfect for each other.

To the stupid wloe group chat, Anna Guinta and Julia Kon — Another book, another acknowledgement. Another year gone without seeing each other. I think we can keep it up. The unhealthiest friendship I have. The dynamic of our group chat has evolved into something that outsiders would probably call the police about, but I wouldn't have it any other way. But, I'm happy we've started using the odd emoji here and there. There are some things that simply can only be conveyed through the cowboy emoji.

To all my friends, whether they be school friends or bookish friends or mom friends, thank you for standing by me, with me, behind me.

To my mother-in-law, Ann — Once again, another book has been published because of you. Your selflessness is what made this story possible, and there aren't words to describe how grateful I am for you. I'm so lucky that Ev gets to call you Grandma. Being your daughter-in-law is such a blessing that I will never, ever take for granted.

To my mother — The reason I'm able to create for a living. The encouragement behind every single endeavor. The Angela to my Michael. Thank you for always believing in me and making sure I believe in myself, too. Thank you for all the time you've spent in the car driving across the state just to help me with random projects. Thank you for being such an amazing Coco. Thank you for always hyping me up. And most importantly, thank you for loving me. Long live slug cake.

To my siblings, Steve, Lexi, and Paige — Still waiting on that game of bulldog, but I know it's coming. I'm so proud to call you my siblings. And always remember, stop or I'll start.

To my father — Thanks for being a great sounding board and supporting me through this journey. And thank you for putting in the effort.

To Joyce Fernandez — The reason ~~that~~ I question every comma I write and the reason I'm a better writer. Figures that the one section of TBoB you didn't edit had an error in it. Thank you for being such a great friend. It's hard to believe we haven't met in person (though, by the time this book is in your hands, that will no longer be true). Thank you for laughing with me, listening to me complain about anything and everything, giving me such amazing advice, and always, always, *always* believing in my work. I'm so proud of all you've done recently and all you're yet to do. You are a superstar, a badass, and an overall wonderful human being. Unceasingly you, Joyce (but, like, platonically).

To Steven — You're the hardest worker I know and the one person who can always make me laugh. Thank you for always convincing me to keep going every time I want to throw in the towel. You're the reason I'm able to do this. Your belief in me is the driving force behind everything I've created. I will forever be grateful that you pushed me to publish TSoS. Thank you for always having my back. I can't wait to see what the next year brings. And sorry for all the Amazon packages.

And to Everett — Our happy, silly, perfect little man. Being your mama is the greatest blessing I've ever received. You are my heart outside my body. I never knew something so small could bring so much joy into my life. I will forever be thankful that the universe gave you to me. I hope I can make you proud, and that you'll grow up to achieve your dream, too. I love love love you.

Lauren M. Leasure is the author of The Benevolence & Blood Series. She's an avid fantasy reader and a lover of all things mystical and magical.

A Maine native, she moved around quite a bit growing up but is now content to call Florida home.

When she's not writing, she's thinking about writing, baking sourdough bread, and spending time with her husband, Steven, their son, Everett, and their dogs, Sadie and Sport.

Made in the USA
Columbia, SC
09 February 2025